REACHING ROSE

by J.P. Grider

Reaching Rose

Published by
Fated Hearts Publishing
Copyright 2015

Edited by Sue Toth
Proofread by Indie Solutions by Murphy Rae

Cover Design by Niina Cord 2015

Cover Photography by Heather LaViola
at Heather Lyn Photos

Cover Models – Isabella Freda and Joey
Roccasanta

There are five words for which I hold the greatest contempt. On endless replay, a needle stuck in the same damaged groove, these words run through my mind. Each night before I fall asleep. Every morning as I wake. And every nightmarish moment in between.

Over.

And over.

And over.

Five words that scream at me in a silent room. Five words that have become my constant companion these past two months. Five words I'd never have fathomed would be my fate.

In my dreams, I am whole.

In my dreams, I am airborne. In the midst of my grand jeté.

In my dreams, no one has ripped my heart from my chest by telling me, *"You will never dance again."*

1

ROSE

THREE MONTHS EARLIER

"Pinch me," I tell Jordan. "Because I can't believe this is real."

"Oh. It's real. And it's happening." Both her hands land on my forearm. "And it's happening to us."

I toss my head back and laugh and scream at the same time. "Holy cow, Jordan. We're dancing on Broadway. *Broadway*," I exclaim in grateful disbelief.

"Broadway," she yells back at me, whirling around on her toes then gracefully transforming her joy into a perfect pirouette.

Opening day is still three weeks away, but that doesn't deter the adrenaline from rushing through my veins every time I'm up here on stage rehearsing. No. Way.

It is a literal dream come true for me to be performing in a Broadway musical. And to be working with the greatest choreographer this decade is the icing on the proverbial cake. Neil Trumondi is a genius.

"Rose," Gianna calls from behind me. "Wanna go get dinner with us?" By us, I know she means Camille, Ryan, and herself. "You too, Jordan."

I look at Jordan, who shrugs and then nods.

"Okay," I say for the both of us.

Jordan and I grab our bags from our lockers, and I swipe a makeup wipe over my face to get the sweat off. I redo my bun and wait for Jordan while she does the same.

2

I take out my phone to check my messages, and I see that Holly texted me four hours ago.

HOLLY: Hey, BFF. Where you been? Met this really cute guy at registration. He's in my psych class. I get the feeling Ben's wholesome and apple-pie-like, like you. Anyway, call me. Text me. Miss you.

When I start to type back how much I miss her too, Gianna comes in singing loudly, "Are we gonna go to dinner?" to the tune of "Do You Wanna Build a Snowman?" from *Frozen*. Not wanting to be one to make anyone wait, I slip my phone into my backpack and leave with my dancing friends to go have dinner.

***

"I'm telling you," Gianna says, inside the restaurant and sipping her diet soda slowly before she finishes her thought. "This has been the best. Week. Ever."

We all ardently agree with her. We've only been rehearsing for one solid week, but Gianna is right; this *has* been the most exciting week of any of our lives. Dancing in the background, along with one hundred or so other dancers, may dampen a more seasoned dancer's spirits, but to the five of us, who haven't even graduated college yet, it's a huge foot into the Broadway door. We are not off-Broadway background dancers. We are *Broadway*. And that is so very, very cool.

"Ready, ladies?" Sal, the waiter at Giovanni's, who is also one of our fellow dancers, asks.

"How do you do it, Sal?" Jordan asks. "How do you work fourteen-hour days and then come here and work four nights a week?"

"Got no choice. Nobody's paying my rent but me."

"You don't have a roommate, Sal?" I ask. Jordan and I share a very tiny one-room apartment. We can barely call it a studio, because it's literally one room with a small refrigerator, a microwave oven, a sink, and a toilet. We sleep on a pull-out couch, and we wash ourselves using the "kitchen" sink. Every chance we get, we shower at the dance studio. But it's all worth it to be living here in New York City for the summer and dancing on Broadway.

"I do, but it's still so goddamned expensive."

"It is," I agree. "I used up all my savings from working on my parents' farm just to stay here for the summer."

"Thank goodness your boss treats us well," Camille says to Sal, referring to the specially-priced menu Giovanni's has for Broadway interns and background dancers.

"Cheers to that," Ryan says, lifting his glass of cheap red wine.

"'Kay," Sal says, "It's time to order."

"Ravioli for me," I say, sipping my lemon water while the rest of my new friends order. And this is when I remember that I started to text Holly and never got to finish. I make a mental note to call my best friend when I get home later. It's been almost two weeks since I said goodbye to her at school. The last week and a half have been such a whirlwind that every time I've thought of giving her a call or shooting her a text, something has come up and I've had to slip my phone into my bag. *Holly is going to kill me.* But she'll forgive me. She's cool like that.

"You know," Gianna says. "If the director asks me to stay on after the summer, I am so going to take it. Fuck college. I can always go back. And hey, maybe I won't have to if this Broadway thing works out."

"Shit, me too," says Ryan. "My only reason for going

4

to college is to get more dance experience. What about you, Rose?"

"Oh...no, I have to finish college. I mean, I have to have some other type of background for when I'm too old to dance, no? I mean...we can't dance forever."

"Sure we can," Camille says.

"Rose is right," Jordan adds. "What if, God forbid, we got injured and could never dance again? We'd need something to..."

"Bite your tongue," Gianna snaps, knocking on the table to unjinx what Jordan just said.

"Rose, you're majoring in education, right?" Camille asks.

"Yeah. K through 8."

"That's cool. I guess teaching is as good a field as any if dancing doesn't work out," she says.

"Yeah. I was hoping to open a dance academy one day too."

"Oh my God, Rose, that's awesome. But...you mean after you make it big in New York, right?"

"Well, yeah, kind of. I mean, dancing's my life, but sometimes I think I'd like to do it on my terms as well. Like ten years from now, won't I be tired of fourteen-hour days? I also have dreams of getting married and having a family, and well, teaching school and owning a dance academy will allow me to do both. You know?"

I notice the smirks on Gianna, Camille, and Ryan's faces, but Jordan nods. She gets it. We've talked about this on the rare times we weren't dead tired and sleeping in our little room.

"I think that's a great idea," Jordan says, shooting me a wink from across the table.

"Why do you go to school in Jersey, Rose?" Camille asks.

"It's fairly close to home, and I need to be nearby in case my father's farm help calls out sick. Then he calls me to come up."

"And you just *go*?" Gianna asks, the disbelief and disapproval much too evident in her snide tone.

"Of course. It's a family business. I'm family," I say as a statement of fact and truth.

"What kind of farm?" Ryan asks.

"A farm farm. We raise cows and chickens and pigs. Sheep for my mother's knitting. We even have some horses."

"In Jersey?" Camille asks.

"Sure." I shrug.

Camille nods her approval. Gianna just rolls her eyes and smirks. I guess the more Gianna gets to know me, the more she realizes she doesn't like me. She must not think I'm hip enough, but I never claimed to be hip. Or fashionable. Or anything else I suppose she associates with a New York dancer. But I don't dance for the prestige. I do it because it's an extension of me. When I dance, my soul shines and my heart smiles. When I dance, the whole world disappears and I float in the darkness. Whether it's tap, jazz, ballet, or lyrical, I am immersed in nothing but the dance when I am on the dance floor. The only other thing that comes close is horseback riding. Bareback. But in the case of riding a horse, I let the horse become my soul, and *he* becomes the extension of me.

The jibber-jabbering at our table is lost on me for a bit while I sink into homesickness. I miss my family and my farm. I miss Holly and my friends at school. And though I love this experience I'm getting being here in New York City and on Broadway, I am looking forward to the fall when I'm back at school and back in the routine of my university classes, dance classes, and farm work. At this very moment in my life, I have everything I could ever ask for. I am happy.

Content. Grateful. Life couldn't get any better than it is right now. *Thank you, God*, I say in my head, as I'm usually in a constant state of prayer anyway, because God is my number one friend. I talk to Him all day long. Sometimes silently. Sometimes, when I'm alone, not so silently.

My own thoughts are broken through when Sal brings our dinners. "Thank you, Sal," I say when he puts my plate of ravioli in front of me.

"You're very welcome, Miss Rose," he says with a wink. Sal is sweet. He's one of the nicer guys I dance with.

By the time all of us are finished with our dinner, it is almost ten o'clock. That means in less than eight hours, we have to be standing on that stage to begin rehearsing all over again. Normally, ten o'clock is not such a late night, but the dance schedule is so exhausting that our feet, our legs, practically our entire bodies, are on fire. So when Jordan turns the key to walk inside, both of us head right for our pull-out couch, already pulled out from this morning, and crash almost immediately.

The alarm on my phone blares in my ear at exactly 4:45am. I hit the snooze button once, like I've been doing every morning for the past week and a half, and get up at precisely 4:54am to wash myself with barely warm sink water, pull my hair into a tight bun, and brush my teeth. Breakfast for Jordan and me is a packaged coffee cake that we keep on our counter, and a latte from the corner coffee house. There's no way we skimp on our coffee in the morning.

"Here's your vanilla latte, Rose," Charlie, the barista, says as she hands me my morning lifeline.

"Thanks, Charlie. You have a good day. See ya tomorrow?"

"No. Not tomorrow. Got the day off. But I'm here on Friday."

"Great. See you then."

"Crap, Rose," Jordan says, patting her pockets. "I forgot my phone. I'm going to run back to the room real quick. Don't wait. No need for both of us to rush."

"I can wait. I'll just..."

"No. Really. Neil will get mad if we both run in late. Just go."

"You really need your phone? You can use mine."

"My mom'll have a conniption if she texts me during lunch and I don't answer. I'll be five minutes. You go on ahead."

"'Kay. If you're sure. See ya in five."

I take my latte and sip on it as I wait for the do-not-walk signal to change.

When it does, my whole life changes with it.

When it does, I'm gently, or not so gently, shoved to the side while a group of eager wage-earners hastily crosses Broadway. Because I'm not one of the pushier types, I take my time, falling in step behind the crowd. I'm running through dance steps in my mind when I hear a loud horn. Not an unusual sound, I'm learning, for the streets of Manhattan.

It's in the next second that time seems to stand still and rush by in the same instant.

A disturbing screeching sound is the last thing I hear before I feel a crushing pain along my left side.

And then I feel nothing at all before my world goes black.

2

BEN

THREE MONTHS LATER

Next stop. Rehab.

I've spent the last week in the hospital, recovering from meniscus repair surgery, not to be confused with meniscus removal surgery, because the latter, though a much easier surgery with a much quicker recovery, would have a long-term effect on my baseball career. And we do not want to mess with my baseball career. It's been my goal since the first time my uncle put a plastic bat in my hand. I was about two years old, and the minute I swung the bat and hit the huge plastic baseball, watching it fly up high through my backyard, I knew. I knew I wanted to relive that feeling over and over.

And so here I am, recovering from knee repair surgery in order to prolong my impending baseball career. The one that hasn't officially started until I've been recruited by a Major League Baseball team. But that's beside the point, because even if I'm not recruited, my goals lie in baseball anyway - as a sports psychologist.

"Benito?" my mother says in question form in her native Italian accent.

"Yeah?" I ask, staring out the window as the trees pass us by.

"Are you nervous? You quiet."

I shrug, but keep my gaze out the side window. "Not

nervous, Ma. Just wish it was over with already. That's all." It's the truth. I want to get back on the field, where I belong. Not in some rehab center making strides just to walk normally again. But it is what it is. At least I should only be there for a few weeks. Coach doesn't want me to take any chances and advised me to stay in an overnight rehab for as long as possible, instead of an outpatient program, which would suit me much better.

"It will go by fast, Benito. You see," she says in her broken English.

"I know, Ma. I know."

"You got your books? I don't want you falling behind in the school." The school - her broken English at work.

"Don't worry, Ma. I'm not going to fall behind. And, yes, I have some books, but I have no classes to study for so they're just general stuff. Baseball and shit."

"Benito," she scolds. "You watcha your language. I don't like it."

"Sorry, Ma."

***

The rehabilitation center is huge. And it doesn't have that sterile hospital feeling. Rather, it has a mood not unlike that of Hunter Hill's rec center. The lobby is inviting, with its motivational framed posters, modern couches, and smiling admissions clerks, one male, one female. Ma and I are greeted by the female first, who introduces herself as Angela and checks me in.

"Have a seat," Angela tells me, "and Lisa will be right in to bring you to your room."

I turn to sit, but behind me, I hear my mother ask, "Lisa? Who is Lisa? She qualified to taka-care of my Benito?"

Dropping my head in mortification, I slink over to the

couch, prop up my crutches, and sit, pretending not to have anything to do with my mother, never mind that I was just at the desk with her.

"Yes, Mrs. Falco," Angela says pleasantly. "Lisa is the admissions nurse, and she is more than qualified to take care of your son." Angela looks over my mother's shoulder to wink at me.

I shake my head and laugh. Maybe Angela has experience with overbearing mothers.

"Oh. She's a nurse. That is good. Okay," my mother finishes and turns around.

"Ma? What the hell?"

"Benito. Language."

"Of course everyone here is going to be qualified. They don't hire morons, Ma." I shake my head at my well-meaning mother.

"Benito...do not you talk to me like I'm stupid."

I hang my head low again, this time out of shame. "You're right, Ma. I'm sorry." I don't mean to be impatient with my mother, but it's hard not to be embarrassed when she treats me like a ten-year-old.

Instead of taking a seat, my mother stands; too much energy in her tiny Italian body.

"Ma. Sit," I say, keeping my tone respectful and kind. "When the nurse comes to get us, we'll get up."

She shifts her head from side to side, scuffles a little with her feet, unsure whether she should stay standing or sit next to her youngest child, and then plops herself down next to me. Patting her mid-thigh, I repeat, "I am sorry, Ma. I didn't mean to talk fresh to you. Just a little nervous is all. I'm sorry."

She pats my thigh back. "It's okay, Benny. I'm nervous too. I don't like you being gone for so long."

"It won't be too long. A month tops. Coach wants me

11

a hundred percent before I come back. Besides, I heal quickly, I bet I'm back in two weeks."

"Don't rush it, Benny. Just get better."

A tall pretty woman walks toward us. "Ben Falco?" she asks, holding out her hand in greeting. "I'm Lisa." I grab one of my crutches with my right hand and pull myself up to shake her hand. By the time I get up, she's already shaken my mother's hand and turns back to shake mine. Maybe I should have just greeted her with a handshake before getting up, but the number one rule in our household is respect, and standing up to greet someone shows the other person that he or she is worth your effort. But I'm telling you...it takes a lot of effort these days to do anything having my left leg in a locked knee brace. I'm told they'll unlock it next week, but still, currently, it's a pain in the ass.

As we walk to my room, my duffel strategically hanging from my four fingers as I grip the crutch handle, Lisa points out several of the treatment rooms, which look exactly like the gym at school. The workout equipment is almost identical, save for a few of the pieces. Like the metal parallel bars meant for retraining the newly walking, an apparatus I'm sure I'll be making use of soon.

"Okay, Ben, this is your room," Lisa says of the small room that houses two twin hospital beds. "That other bed there by the window is your roommate Johnny's. He's an eighteen-year-old high school senior. Not in the greatest of situations, but I think the two of you will get along well. We do try to pair roommates of similar age when we can. To make your stay a little more pleasant."

I toss my bag on the empty bed closest to the bathroom, lay my crutches next to the bed and sit. "Thank you," I say to Lisa and look at my mom. "I guess you can go."

"Already?" My mother asks, turning to Lisa for confirmation.

With my mother's head turned away from me, I shake my head, pleading with Lisa to tell my mother she has to go.

Lisa's mouth strains not to smile conspiratorially as she says, "Well, Mrs. Falco, it'd be best to start Ben on his rehabilitation immediately, but you're welcome to visit during the week."

I sigh, because, knowing my mother, she'll be here every day now. Lisa's right hand turns up as if to say, "Hey, just doing my job."

"Okay, Benny. I guess I'll get going. Daddy and I will come back tomorrow to see you." My mother leans down to give me a kiss on the cheek.

"Ma, you can wait a week, really. It'll be okay. Just like college. Why take the ride again so soon?"

I look at my mother's pained face.

"Ma. It's just like I'm away at school. You don't get sad when I leave for school. What's up?"

"I don't like seeing you in this hospital." Both her arms are waving in the air as she speaks.

"It's not a hospital, Ma. It's like a gym. You know how much I like the gym. I'm training. I like it here already," I lie. "Please don't worry about me, Ma."

"Mrs. Falco, for many, this center is like a vacation. Ben will be very happy here, I can assure you."

Thankfully, Lisa's reassurance puts a worry-free smile on my mother's face. "Okay." She leans down and kisses me goodbye again. "Love you, Benny-boy."

"Love you too, Ma." A whole bunch.

***

After my mother leaves and Lisa goes over my itinerary for the next three days, I'm introduced to my physical therapist, Craig. A redheaded muscle-bound guy of about thirty, who demands that I sit in a wheelchair to give my good leg a rest.

"But I don't want someone rolling me around," I tell him. "I'm fine with my crutches."

"I get that, Falco, but it's important to keep up your strength for therapy. You'll have time on *both* your legs, don't you worry about that."

"If you insist," I say, none too happy.

"I insist. And I *can* call you Falco, right?"

"Yeah. Everybody does."

"Had a feeling. Anyway, since it's late in the day, we're not going to be doing too much with your leg. We like to keep therapy for earlier in the day, but I do want to show you around and introduce you to your nighttime nurse. Her name's Katrina, you can call her Kat, she's in her forties somewhere, but she's super cool. You'll like her."

"Okay."

Craig wheels me down the hall and I feel like an old man. This sucks. "Yo, you think you can show me how to work this thing on my own?" I ask him halfway down the corridor. "It can't be too hard, can it?"

Craig laughs. "No. It's not hard at all. This is one of the old-fashioned ones. We leave the state-of-the-art stuff for the people who have to sit in their chairs twenty-four hours a day. Just put your hands on this wheel and roll. Hope you're not afraid of using your arm muscles."

"Nope." I palm the huge rims to either side of me and roll myself down the hall.

"This here is where you'll hang out," he says of the large bright room filled with tables and chairs, leather couches, and several flat screen TVs hanging along the walls. "You can eat your dinner in here each night, or you can stay in your room. You can even ask Kat to have your dinner brought in here so you don't have to carry it yourself.

Or...you can just roll it down on your lap."

"Why? I'm not gonna be in this thing every day, am I?"

"No. But at night, for the first week or so, I'd like you to. We're going to be working hard. You'll be beat by the end of the day. No lie, I bet you'll be begging for this thing by tomorrow night."

"Let's hope not," I say in jest.

"Anyway, I'll introduce you to Kat when she's done with her other patient over there. You hungry, you want a snack or something?"

"Nah, I'm good."

"Well the fridge is right there." He points to the double-doored stainless steel monstrosity. "There's ice-cream, soda, fruit, whatever you want, just get it."

"So which one's Kat?" I ask, spotting several people in scrubs.

Craig juts his chin in the direction of a dark-haired woman talking to a sullen girl with long hair the color of the red clay pitching mound I can't wait to get back on. "She won't be with her patient long. The girl doesn't talk."

"At all?" I ask, whipping my head around to look up at Craig.

He shakes his head. "Not since she's been here. She came in like that."

"So she's mute?"

"Yup. Probably selective. Word around here is that she has the ability to speak; she just won't."

I take a better look at the girl, from her head to her wheelchair...which is one of those state-of-the-art chairs Craig was talking about. "And she's stuck in that chair all the time?"

The moment I ask, her nurse, *my* nurse, pulls her away from the table and turns her so she's able to look at the TV screen. I draw in an audible breath.

But the nurse quickly gets in the way of my sight of the girl.

"Here comes Kat," Craig says. "Kat, this here is one of your new patients."

"Ah. The ball player. Ben, right?"

"Yes." I look up at my nurse, this time remaining seated while I hold out my hand to greet her.

"Call him Falco," Craig instructs. "Everyone does."

Letting out a tight laugh, I tell her, "You can call me Ben as well. Either works."

"Okay. Ben it is. I'll leave Falco for Craig here."

"So, Ben, did Craig give you the low-down on the fridge and the wi-fi password and..."

I don't hear the rest of what Kat is saying. I can't. Because my mind *and* my eyes are focused on the girl who doesn't talk.

3

ROSE

He's staring at me too.

They all stare.

That's all they'll ever do.

Stare.

I'm nothing but a freak show for prying eyes.

Like I do all the time now, to avoid the stares, I find a point on a wall in the distance and slip back into a time when I was a complete person. A dancer on her way to her future.

Three months ago, my life was perfect.

"Oh my gosh, Mom, I can't believe I'm here. I can't believe I'm living in New York City on my own." I am just so darn excited to be living in Manhattan for the summer and dancing in a Broadway show. How awesome is that?

"It's a dream come true, baby. I'm so happy for you. But I'm going to miss you." My mother squeezes me outside my new apartment door. "My baby girl is growing up."

I pull away and grab the key that I picked up from the show's production assistant. Unlocking the old doorknob, my hand shakes. I've lived in a dorm before, but never something like this. Never a real apartment...in New York City._If Holly could see me now. Which reminds me, I have to call Holly soon. I promised her.

My first impression of the dark and dank stairwell is not good,

17

but when I open the door to the apartment, it is worse. Until a smiling blond girl peeks out from behind a wooden tri-fold screen. "Rose?" she exclaims, with her hands reaching out as if she wants to hug me.

"Jordan?"

She screams and runs toward me. "Are you as excited as I am?" she asks, wrapping her thin arms around my shoulders.

"Oh yes. If you're thinking, 'pinch me, I must be dreaming,' then I am as excited as you are." I pull away to look at her. Then I look around the room. "This is the whole apartment?"

She laughs. "Yup." Jordan looks at my mother, whose skin looks almost green.

"Mom. It's okay," I tell her, knowing what she must be thinking of the crummy apartment. "We're not even going to be spending much time here."

"It's true," Jordan says with a smile. "We're going to be daaannnnciiinnngg." She does two consecutive twirls when she says the word dancing. Jordan makes this apartment worth it. I can tell we are going to get along great. "Look," she says, calling me over with a finger. "Toilet." She points to a toilet behind that tri-fold screen. "That's where we pee."

My mom groans, but I chuckle. I am so excited that nothing could bring me down now.

"I'm going to run out and get you some groceries, hon. You and Jordan get acquainted." My mother kisses me on the cheek. "Just, if you leave the apartment, please text me, so I can let you know when I'm headed back with the food."

"Thanks, Mom."

"Do you need anything, Jordan?"

"No, I'm good, Mrs?"

"Duncan. But you can call me Sam."

"Thank you, Sam, but I'm good."

"Okay. Be back in a bit," my mother says, skewing her face when she touches the upstairs doorknob. "I'll get you all some anti-bacterial wipes too."

Jordan laughs. "The place is creepy, but isn't it exciting? Have you ever danced on Broadway before?"

"No. Never. I can't even believe I was asked. I'm in Heaven."

"Rose."

I'm in Heaven.

"Rose."

My apartment's slipping away.

"Rose."

I blink my eyes a few times and notice I am now in my room. The room at the rehab center.

"Rose," I hear Kat call out. "Rose, snap out of it. Come on, sweetheart."

I refocus my eyes and see Kat sitting on the edge of my bed right in front of me.

"We gotta get you ready for bed, honey. If you want my help, then we have to do it now."

I don't want her help.

And I don't want to do it myself.

I just...

Don't want to *be*...right now.

She reaches for me under the arm and helps me to my bed, where I sit. I avoid looking down, because that's when my chest hurts the most. "Come on, honey, there's nothing wrong with your arms. I know you can change your own shirt. So let's do it." She tosses my nightgown next to me on the bed.

I ignore her, like I always do. Like I ignore anyone who gives me instructions to do something. I've only been in this rehab center a week, but I know I've already disappointed everyone who's tried to help me. Just like I disappointed the whole staff at the hospital in Manhattan for the last three months. Well, in my defense, I was only conscious through one of those months. What I did prior to that I had no control over. Though, I'm not completely convinced I have all that much control right now. I mean, I feel bad that I just disregard everyone. I don't want to be disrespectful. But my brain won't let me obey. All the doctors say there is nothing wrong with my brain. There was no brain injury due to the accident, and the only reason I was unconscious for two months was because they put me in an induced coma...to help the healing process of the multitude of internal injuries I'd sustained.

But every time I intend to do something for myself, or attempt to speak, I can't. Something holds me back.

I take a deep breath, but that is all I do. So, Kat pulls up on my shirt, lifts my reluctant arms one at a time to free them from the sleeves, and tugs the shirt over my head. Then Kat proceeds to pull the nightgown over my head, not fussing with my bra at all. The morning nurse will wash me in the morning, so Kat will let her worry about that. "Do you want to sleep in your sweatpants, or do you want me to pull them off?" She asks me this every night, and every night I don't answer. I prefer my sweats on, and I think she knows that, so she keeps them on and lets the morning nurse deal with changing my pants and panties the next morning. For that process, I close my eyes and try to slip into my past again, because I just can't bring myself to look at my legs.

Not when one of them is missing below the knee.

4

BEN

"Ben Falco?"

I wake to the sound of a new voice. A female voice. Groggily, I say, "Yes?"

"Hi. I'm Lourdes, your morning nurse. But you can call me Lou."

"Lou...Right...Hi. I'm Ben, but you know that already." I shift in my bed to sit up.

She smiles, but doesn't laugh. "Okay, let's get you out of bed and ready for therapy. Do you need help showering?"

I shake my head vigorously, willing myself to wake up fully. "No. No. I'm fine by myself. Unless, you can help me wrap up my brace, maybe." I pause to stretch my arms. "The material beneath it shouldn't get wet, and well, I have done it myself, but I guess I don't do it correctly, because it still kinda gets wet."

"Sure. I can do that. I'll be right back."

I take a breath, push myself up against the headboard, and look to see if Johnny is in bed. He's not, he must be in therapy already. I wonder if Lou came in and helped him first, or if he has another nurse who comes in and helps him. I hate needing someone else's help. At least for me, though, it's temporary. That poor girl in the wheelchair yesterday will probably need someone's help for the rest of her life. She's missing a leg. She had pants on, so I couldn't tell if she was missing her whole leg or just half of it. Being that she is so thin, it was hard to see if a thigh was beneath her pants. But there was no mistaking that her leg was gone. The way her black sweats flattened as they fell down the front of the chair, and the lack of a foot on the foot rest, definitely implied she was missing a leg. I wonder if she'll ever walk again. They have prosthetics for that, don't they? I recall reading about a young baseball player who had both legs amputated. Maybe life won't be so hard for her.

But I bet she's dying inside right now.

I bet that's why she doesn't talk.

She probably sees no hope for her future.

But there is hope.

There's always hope.

Isn't there?

Lou walks back in my room carrying a huge roll of cling wrap.

"Hey," I say, "I have a roll like that back home. Used it to wrap up my brother's car on April Fools' Day."

"Nice. I'll have to remember that," the thirty-something-year-old lady says. "Was he pissed?"

"At first. It made him late for work." I chuckle, remembering his fuming face. "But he gives as good as he gets, so—" I lift a shoulder "—he got what was coming."

"Brothers. I got one of them too. How many you got?"

"One. And a sister. Both older."

"Ah. So you're the baby?"

"Eh. Guess so."

She laughs. "Okay, why don't we get you wrapped up? Craig's gonna be calling for you soon."

Lou quickly winds the clear wrap around my leg, starting at the top and ending beneath the brace at my lower shin. Then she snuggly tucks it in, finishing it off with a piece of duct tape.

"And here I thought you had some professional wrap or something," I joke.

"We do. Saran wrap and duct tape work better. You're pretty friendly for an injured teenage athlete."

"Teenage?" I feign offense. "I'm twenty-one. Legal."

She shakes her head. "Get in the shower, old man. Pull on the string if you need me."

Showering isn't too difficult for me, since there is a support bar running the entire width of the stall, so it takes five minutes and I'm done. I get dressed in my room and hobble over to the window to look outside. The guys are probably playing Fall Ball right now, and I'm jealous. I want to be out there. Soon enough. *Soon enough*, I tell myself.

"Look at you all ready," Lou says from the doorway.

I turn around and smile. "Not bad for a gimp, huh?" And then I immediately regret using that word.

"You know, kid, you're luckier than most here. You're injury's gonna heal soon. Some of these kids...not so much."

I nod. "Like that redhead," I mumble to myself.

"You've seen Rose?"

"Rose?" Is that her name? It's perfect for her.

"She's the only redhead here who's a patient. And I don't think you mean Craig?"

I shake my head. "No. I don't mean Craig. Can I ask what happened, or is that breaking some kind of confidentiality thing?"

"Well, yes, there are confidentiality rules, but I can say that losing a leg at that age is extremely difficult to deal with."

"Yeah." I have to stop feeling sorry for myself. I have to. The damage to my knee was done by falling and twisting it during a game. And it's been repaired. Poor Rose. She'll never get her leg back.

"Well, kid. You ready? Craig's waiting for you."

"Ready as I'll ever be."

***

During therapy, Craig unlocks my brace and allows

me to do some exercises, which involve bending my knee. Simple exercises that I'd have scoffed at before my injury are fucking hard. All I'm doing is lifting my leg and bringing it down. Or bending it slightly and raising it. Holy shit, what a difference a month makes. Last month I was bending my knee up to my chest every time I pitched a ball, now I can't even bend it a few inches.

"Not that easy, is it, Falco?" Craig laughs as I grunt, bringing my foot down to the floor from a sitting position.

"Holy shit," is my response.

"It'll get easier. Don't worry," he says with a wink.

I shake my head. "This is crazy, man."

After a half an hour of baby exercises that render me a weakling, Craig locks up my brace and tells me to take thirty minutes in the chair.

"I hate that chair, Craig. Can't I just sit in a regular chair?"

"You need your leg extended; the wheelchair has that option. You're not alone. Ninety percent of the people here are in one at one part of the day or the other. Grow a pair and sit in the chair."

I crutch my way over to the forsaken chair and sit my ass down. "Now what?"

"Well, since you like to do things for yourself, roll yourself over to the rec room. I'll bring you breakfast."

I nod and wheel myself out of the room, down the hall, and into the rec room, where Rose is sitting at a table alone, her breakfast tray in front of her.

"Mind if I sit?" I ask her, rolling up to her table, positioning myself directly across from her.

She lifts her eyes and looks me dead center in mine, but then casts them back on her lap.

"I'm Ben. I hear you're Rose. Pretty name."

Rose looks at me again, but quickly casts her eyes

back down.

"Whatchya reading?" I ask, noting the paperback book lying face down on the table next to her tray.

She doesn't look up this time. Okay. I'll leave her alone. Since I'm in here with nothing, waiting for Craig to come in with my breakfast, I wheel over to the bookshelf, grab a pack of cards, roll back to Rose's table, and play Solitaire the old-fashioned way. The way my father showed me.

Ten minutes later, a guy in scrubs comes walking over with a tray of food. "Are you Ben?"

I nod once. "Yup."

"This is for you. Craig said take an extra ten minutes."

"Sure. Thanks."

I continue to play Solitaire while I eat my runny scrambled eggs, fruit cup, and minuscule bagel. At least there are snacks in the fridge. This is not nearly enough food for me. I win my game of Solitaire and place the deck down on the table. "I'm getting something from the fridge," I tell Rose. "Can I get you anything?" Now I know she doesn't speak, but she doesn't know that I know, so it'd look unnatural if I just ignored her and didn't speak to her at all.

As expected, she doesn't respond with words, but I'm sure I saw the slight shake of her head telling me no, she didn't want anything. So she can and will communicate, no matter how slightly. I'll just have to be patient with her.

In the fridge, there are apples, oranges, pears, cups of pudding and Jell-O. Not quite the breakfast of champions, but the pudding will do. I grab three puddings - one chocolate, two vanilla. I take two spoons off the adjacent counter, put the stuff on my lap, and roll back to the table.

After I put the cups on the table, I push a vanilla and a chocolate cup toward Rose and place a spoon on her tray. "Your choice," I say with a wink.

Her eyebrows dip and she eyes me warily.

"Who doesn't like pudding, right?" I open up the extra vanilla and start eating. "Better hurry up, I'm almost done, and then you're not gonna have a choice. You're gonna have to go with the one *I* don't pick."

Her eyes roll, but the corner of her mouth lifts. She wants to smile. I know she does.

I stick the last spoonful in my mouth, and after I swallow, I say, "Uh oh. You ran out of time."

Teasingly, I move my hand across the table to grab one of the pudding cups, but before I do, I see her hand furtively move across the table toward the chocolate cup. Her hand stops before it reaches it, and she pulls her fingers back, balling them into a loose fist. Smiling to myself, but being sure to keep that smile hidden from my face, I push the chocolate pudding closer to her. "It's yours. I like vanilla better anyway."

Rose quickly drops her hands to her lap and her eyes follow.

She's looking down when I say, "I know it's only pudding, but what'd it ever do to you?"

Her chest jumps and her mouth pulls in, the way it would if she was holding back a laugh. I refrain from commenting, because I don't want to embarrass her, but I think I made the sweet girl chuckle. I finish my second cup of pudding, and I notice her looking at the pudding every once in a while, but I don't force it. I want to be her friend, and a friend doesn't make another friend feel uncomfortable, so I keep quiet. When Craig comes in to tell me my time is up, I say goodbye to her. But as I'm wheeling away, I turn to her and say, "Now don't disappoint that poor pudding cup. All he wants to do is make us hungry folk happy." I roll myself toward the door, and before I exit, I turn and notice her dainty hand reaching for the chocolate pudding. Yes. I made progress and it's only day one.

5

ROSE

I am so embarrassed. The cute boy who was staring at me yesterday sat at my table today.

Why?

At first, I thought it was so he could get a better look at the freak with the missing leg and a huge scar on the left side of her face. But then, he didn't seem to look at me at all. I mean, he didn't stare at me at all, and he only looked at me if he was asking me a question. A normal question. He didn't seem to even notice the huge red scar that starts at my forehead and travels down the length of my body. Not that he'd see the scar past my neck, since my clothes cover the rest of it, but I didn't see his eyes roam toward the left side of my face at all.

The pudding cup in my hand is still cold. Why did he get me a pudding? I wanted to say thank you. I did. But...I couldn't. If I talk, I will break. And I will feel the pain all over again. And then I will want to die...like I should have the day that truck hit me. When it sliced me down the left side of my body with its jagged metal undercarriage and sealed my fate by severing my left leg right beneath my knee. So I would never dance again.

I don't remember the accident, and the only thing I've been told was that the undercarriage of the truck had been rusted and falling apart, leaving a sharp, jagged, metal weapon to sufficiently slice me up like a side of beef. My body-long wound, up to and including my severed leg, got infected because the antibiotic they'd fed me wasn't enough to kill the damage the rusted metal had caused. After waking from my two-month induced coma, sometime during that week, I'd figured out that my left leg was missing. I'd screamed. I'd screamed louder than I ever thought my voice could go. And then I cried out for my mother and asked her if I'd ever be able to dance again.

"I'm so sorry, honey." She shook her head. "You will never dance again. I am so, so sorry," my mother said again, crying into my shoulder as she attempted to comfort me.

That was the first time I'd wished I were dead.

And I've been praying every night since then that the infection would come back and claim me for good. But God hasn't answered that prayer. For some reason, he wants me alive and suffering. For some reason, God hates me.

But today, when that boy – guy, rather – brought a pudding over to the table for me...little flutters came alive in my stomach. For the first time in over a month, I didn't want to die. For the first time in over a month, I didn't hate God back. For a moment there...I actually wanted to thank Him. I actually wanted to smile.

When Nina walks in, I place the unopened pudding on my tray, alongside my other uneaten breakfast items. It's still hard for me to eat anything, because eating is prolonging living, so I eat as little as I can. However, the chocolate pudding looks really good. Too late though. Nina is here and ready to get my uncooperative butt moving. Which never happens, because I just stare at my hands the whole time she attempts to get me to cooperate. It always ends up that she moves my legs with her own hands. Nina usually pulls me out of the chair and holds me up, even though I know I can stand on my good leg.

I don't want to be disobedient. Again, it goes against my nature to hurt someone's feelings, and not obeying them, or even responding to them, is the same as hurting their feelings. I know that. But as Dr. Rappaport says when he's rationalizing my behavior, "It's a normal reaction to such a life-changing event." Still...I should at least *try* to find the person I was before that delivery truck ended the life that I knew.

In the treatment room, Nina bends my good leg up to my chest and brings it back down. She does this about ten times before she reaches under my armpits and picks me up. I try not to give her too much trouble today, but the pain of knowing I can't do this myself is overwhelming, and I find myself slipping back in time again.

Four and a half months earlier, I'm on stage performing my solo at the Manhattan Dance Competition. Feeling inspired and at one with the stage, I begin dancing my solo, which includes my favorite, the fouetté, and end it with another favorite of mine, the fouetté jeté.

"Rose. Snap out of it, sweetie, c'mon." Nina's voice punctures my daydream, and just like that, I'm back here in my chair. "C'mon, Rose. I thought for once you were working with me, and then all of a sudden, you went into that place again. Stay with me, girl. I know you're in there." Nina sticks her arms underneath my armpits again, and this time, I use what little strength is left in my right leg to push up and onto the floor. "Thatta girl."

I'm standing on one leg. Nina instructs me to put my hands on the parallel bars on either side of me. For a moment I contemplate whether I really want to do that, but then some warm fuzzy feeling overcomes me and I do as she says. I put my hands on the bars, and she lets go of me.

"That's good, Rose. Now use your upper body to move forward. You'll have a prosthetic leg soon to help you along, but there will be times you'll need crutches to move. We want to keep your whole body strong."

A prosthetic leg? Crutches? See, these are the things that bring me down. Bring me back into my hole. I can't get past them and accept that this is my reality. This is when I want to curse God all over again for allowing this to happen to me. Nina keeps nudging me to move forward, but I don't. Instead, I stare ahead and try to slip back into my past, because that's where I feel safe.

6

BEN

It's been two days since the pudding incident, and I haven't seen Rose since. When I ask Lou if she knows anything, she says that she does, but she's not at liberty to share that information with me. So I ask Craig, who's not so much about the rules.

"Falco, man," he says, "you gotta promise me you won't say anything to anyone."

"Of course not," I promise. "I just want to know if something happened to her?"

He nods. "She had some kind of breakthrough."

"Breakthrough?" I interrupt. "That's good, no?"

"I don't know. Yes, I guess, but it was more like a break*down*. They put her in a private room, because her crying was disrupting her roommate. She was screaming all night."

"Why? What happened that caused that?"

Craig shakes his head. "I don't know her whole deal, but since she's been here, she's been like this zombie. Just stares at the walls. I mean, not all the time. Sometimes she's here in this world, but mostly, she's not."

"Really?"

"Yup. I told you how she doesn't speak, right? Well, that's the other part - her zombie-like state. But Nina, her therapist, thought she was getting through to her two days ago. She actually stood up on her own, which she hasn't done ever. But then, she started to turn into that zombie girl again, and then boom. I heard she started screaming. Not sure what triggered it, but I hear that even though she's been non-stop crying, her psychiatrist said it's a breakthrough. Her accident is finally sinking in. But...I don't know. She's a strange one."

Strange? I don't think so at all. I think she's just depressed. "She lost her leg, dude. I don't think I'd handle that well either."

"Yeah. Guess you're right."

"Damn right I'm right. I don't think I could handle losing one of my legs. And never be able to play ball again? No way. Her whole life changed because of this. I mean, I don't know how active she was before, but I'd guess that even going to the mall with her friends is going to be different. No?"

"No, man, you're right. I get that. I didn't mean anything by it. God, you like her or something?" Craig says with a quirk of his mouth.

"Like her? I don't know her. I just feel bad for her." Like her. How could I like someone I don't even know?

"Got it, man. You feel bad for her. Me too. Really, I do. I'm sorry I made it sound like I didn't."

I nod, silently accepting an apology that really needn't have been made.

"Let's get on with your therapy." Craig bends down and unlocks my brace. "I think we'll keep this unlocked for a few hours today. Get your knee moving a little more. Sound good?"

"Sounds great." It may not sound like a big deal, but when you can't bend your leg, you realize how necessary the knee is in getting around normally.

While Craig is guiding me through different exercises, he asks me if I've finally met my roommate Johnny.

"I did. He's cool. Happy guy, no?"

"Yeah. Very. He's so positive he'll walk again, you can't help but believe it too."

"Right? I feel guilty just being here. I mean, my injury is nothing. I could've done this from home, but my coach convinced me it'd be best for my career. I'm not like everyone else here, though. It's just..."

"Don't feel bad. You need to be here if you want it done properly. And hey, your insurance pays, so you might as well. Daily therapy is better than a couple times a week. Not everyone has permanent or severe injuries here. There are plenty of patients just recovering from surgeries. Stop knocking yourself."

He's right, but it doesn't help me feel less guilty about not being severely injured.

Craig continues running me through exercises, and when my hour is up, he lets me use crutches to walk to the rec room or the cafeteria. I choose the rec room, because I'm really hoping Rose will be in there today, and I highly doubt that she'll be in the cafeteria. I kind of doubt she'll even be out of her room, but I hope anyway. I scan the room as soon as I enter, but immediately learn she's not there. Not a redhead in sight. But I do see Johnny, so I hobble over to his table and pull out a chair. As I do, a burning pain shoots from my knee up my leg and I flinch.

"Hey, Ben," Johnny says, "you okay?"

My eyes are closed when I answer him. "Yeah." I pinch my eyes closed tighter before opening them. "Wow. Just a bad pain. I'm good." I sit down, set my crutches to the side and ask Johnny how he's doing.

"Good. Making progress in therapy, so that's always good."

"Yeah? Progress?"

"Yup." But he doesn't elaborate, and I get the feeling there was no real progress at all.

Again, my guilt kicks in, but I smile anyway. "That's awesome, Johnny. Great news."

"Yeah. So when you get that brace off?" he asks me.

"I don't know. Soon, I think." I lift my leg to show him my knee. "Got it unlocked today." But I feel like I'm bragging, so I ask about him. "So, you go to college?" I ask, not thinking if it was appropriate to ask or not. I mean, he is a quadriplegic; *can* he go to school?

But without missing a beat, Johnny says, "That's the plan. I'm a senior in high school right now. My accident happened this past spring, during my junior year. I get a lot of tutoring, so I completed my junior year. Hopefully I won't have to redo this year, since I'll be out the entire year most likely. So, in answer to your question, I don't go to college, but the plan is to go for engineering."

I raise an eyebrow. "So you're smart, I assume?"

He laughs. "Genius." Johnny takes a deep breath, as he does frequently between sentences. "Good thing my brain wasn't affected in the accident, huh?"

Nodding, I smile, not too sure what to say, so I ask, "What happened?" Hopefully it's okay to ask.

"Fell off a ladder, cleaning my mom's gutters." He shakes his head. "See what happens when you don't have a dad around. The loser left my mom and me, so I take care of everything for her." For the first time since talking to him, I see a frown on his face. But it's quickly hidden when he says, "That's why I'm going to recover. She needs me. And she needs those gutters cleaned...I fell before I even made a dent in them."

Again, I nod, but this time he leaves me speechless. Literally, I don't know what to say, and he sees me fumbling.

"Dude. It's okay. I'm gonna be fine."

He's gonna be fine. It hits me the differences between his outlook and Rose's. What is it that causes such extremes in the mind? Why do some people face trauma with such optimism and some with such pessimism? How would I react in a similar situation? Fortunately for me, it's a hypothetical situation, but for Johnny and Rose, it's their reality.

"So, what about you?" Johnny interrupts my thoughts.

"You go to college, right? I asked Lou. She said you're a big-time ball player?"

I laugh. "I play ball, yeah. Hunter Hill. Ever heard of it?"

He nods. "I have. Good school. Great engineering department."

"I've heard. I'm going for sports psychology. Love the mind. There's never a concrete answer to how it functions," I say, reminding myself that I may never know the answer to why Johnny and Rose react so differently to their respective circumstances.

"So you're pretty smart, too, I suppose."

Again, I laugh. "Not even close. But I do try hard."

He laughs with me, and then one of the aides comes in with a tray of food for each of us. "Anything you guys need besides lunch?"

"No, but thank you," I tell him.

"Yeah, thanks," Johnny says.

"No problem. It's why I'm here. Marti'll be in to help you in a second," the aide tells Johnny.

When he walks away, I ask Johnny, "Is everyone here super nice?"

"Everyone *I've* come across in the past month."

"You've been here for one month?"

"A month and a half." His frown reappears when he looks down at his food.

I feel bad for the guy. He can't even feed himself. What will happen if the future he sees is not the one intended for him? Will he succumb to depression like Rose? Or will he thrive? As optimistic as he is, something tells me anything but what he expects...will kill him.

His lunch aide, Marti, comes in to feed him, and Johnny keeps smiling through lunch, but all the while he's chatting away, I come to the conclusion that maybe his optimism is a façade that hides his true emotions. Maybe his outlook is not so different from Rose's. And maybe I'm going to have my work cut out for me when I finally become a psychologist.

After the Major Leagues.

7

ROSE

I'm not ready to get back out there, but at least the tears have stopped. Not sure what came over me, but I had a complete meltdown in front of Nina and didn't stop crying for thirty-six hours straight - give or take a few minutes. Dr. Rappaport keeps telling me that it was some kind of breakthrough, but I don't feel better, I feel worse. But it doesn't matter, because he insists I leave my private room and move back in with my roommate, Kimberlee. Which makes me feel bad for Kimberlee, because I know she is uncomfortable around me. *I'm* uncomfortable around me. Kat rolls me into my old room after dinner and Kimberlee is sitting in the corner chair, watching television. She looks at me before averting her eyes and returning her attention to the television. She's in here because she had a stroke and had to relearn how to do many mundane things, including talking, which I must say she does very well now. Kimberlee was talkative the first night I moved in, telling me all about how she is prone to seizures and that those seizures were related to her stroke. She had to relearn how to walk, and eat with a utensil, and write. Everything. But she recovered fast, and I'm sure she'll be going home soon. I wouldn't know though, because that's the last time she spoke to me. When someone doesn't respond to you at all, there is no reason to keep communicating with them. I didn't respond. She doesn't talk to me anymore.

Since I broke down and cried two and a half days ago, it's harder to keep my emotions in check. My throat is constantly hurting from holding back more tears, and my eyes burn from keeping them from falling out. But Dr. Rappaport doesn't want me to be by myself. He says that would be counterproductive and so I need to be out and attempting to socialize with the rest of the patients and staff. Socialize? I've forgotten how to do that.

The night is quiet and I fall asleep quickly, one thing that hasn't been hard for me since the accident. I love to sleep. I long for it during every waking hour. But morning comes too soon when I wake to Lou nudging me in the arm.

"Come on, love, it's time to get up." She places some wipes and a washcloth on my table tray and helps me sit up in bed. "Let's try to do this on your own today. Please?" she asks, and I feel bad that I've been so uncooperative. But today, I find myself reaching for the wipes.

I know Lou wants to scream with pleasure, because, yeah, I just attempted to do something for myself, and I don't even know why. But she refrains from singing "Hallelujah," and I'm grateful.

"Would you like me to leave you alone?"

Yes, I do, but I don't think I can stand on my own yet. Not because my good leg may not be strong enough, but because one look at my half-leg may send me straight into another breakdown and I'll fall. And if I fall, how will I get up? These are the thoughts that scare me. The normal everyday tasks I took for granted before my accident have become the exact things that scare me now.

I attempt to shake my head, so Lou knows I don't want her to leave. It's a start, right? Shaking my head, as imperceptible as it may have been.

Lou's smile brightens. "Come on, girl, let me help you up." She lifts me up, and instead of putting me in my wheelchair, she places a walker in front of me. "I think it's time now, sweetie, to use this. I know this is all new to you, but you need to help yourself. You got fitted for that prosthesis, and it's going to be here any day now. You need to be ready, and..." She pauses, because she sees me frown.

She sits me back down on the bed and sits next to me. With her hand on my left thigh, the thigh that doesn't have a whole leg attached to it, she sucks a breath in. "I know this is hard on you, honey. And I'm not your psychotherapist or psychiatrist, I'm just your nurse, but as your nurse, I'm telling you how important it is for your recovery to do things for yourself. Sitting here in this slump you've been in—" she shakes her head "—it's not going to help you move forward." She tips her head in Kimberlee's direction, even though the curtain's drawn. "Look at our friend over there...you over there, Kimberlee?"

"You bet I'm here," Kimberlee announces joyfully.

"She came in here with no idea if she'd ever be normal again, and look at her. She's ready to leave. You know why?"

She waits for a response from me, but I don't offer one.

"Because I rock," Kimberlee responds for me.

"That's right," Lou agrees, "she rocks. She knew right from the beginning that her attitude was key in recovering." Lou sighs. "I know not everyone who keeps their head up gets the results they want, but I do know that if you don't even try, there is no possible way to recover. The physical wound may heal, but your heart and mind won't, and then where will you be?" She raises her eyebrows at me in question.

I answer her with the slip of a tear that I did not want to let out. She uses her thumb to wipe it away, but more follow, and now I'm afraid that they won't stop again.

"Use those tears for good, Rosie. They mean you care. They mean you want to move forward."

Kimberlee's bed squeaks, and next thing I know, she's standing in front of me. "I know you don't like to talk," she says to me, "but talking about it, getting it out, it helps. Shit, I *couldn't* talk in the beginning, and that was rough. My brain was screaming. But once I figured it out...you couldn't shut me up." Kimberlee sways her head from side to side. "Well, *you* shut me up," she says of my refusal to respond to anything she'd said to me. "But seriously, Rose. You're only hurting yourself. I'll shut up now." Kimberlee winks and walks back behind her curtain.

"Come on," Lou says, getting up and pushing the walker back in front of me. "Let's get you cleaned up."

I use the sleeve of my robe to wipe the rest of my tears, but no more are shed. My tears don't continue, so maybe I'm breaking through after all.

***

During physical therapy, Nina can't believe her eyes. "Girl, look at you," she exclaims, singing my praise, because I'm finally walking along the parallel bars on my own. "Look at those guns. So, you do have muscle in those skinny arms of yours."

If I were talking, I'd say, "My arms ain't skinny, they're strong." Because they are strong. I've always been strong. It's one of the reasons I'm a good dancer.

Was a good dancer.

As hard as it is, I try to shake it off.

I'll never be a dancer again.

But I'm not dead, and so I guess I need to at least learn to walk.

I take a deep breath and push myself forward. After about ten minutes of "running relays" through the parallel bars, I joke to myself, my arms hurt. As strong as they used to be, I guess not using them weakened them.

"Good job, Rose." Nina literally pats me on the back.

"I'm proud of you. I know today was rough, but you made a huge stride. Please keep that in mind...please," she almost begs.

I blink my eyes, knowing that isn't the best of responses, but it's the best I can give at the moment.

"Do you think you can manage on your own in your chair?" She looks me in the eyes.

Do I want to keep depending on someone else to push me everywhere I need to go? I certainly know how to use this power wheelchair, so do I continue being an obnoxious ass and have someone push me around, or can I continue with my efforts and direct the chair myself?

I respond by pushing on the chair's joystick and rolling forward a foot.

Her grin widens as she nods. "Atta girl. C'mon, I'll walk with you to get some lunch." Which is a good idea, because I don't trust myself to move on my own once I'm by myself. "I'll get you to the rec and then I'll have someone bring in your lunch. Good?"

She looks at me for a response, but all I can manage is a blink.

"I'll take that as a yes," she says and keeps one hand on the back of my chair while I wheel myself to the rec room. It's only been three days since I sat in here, but it feels longer. And it may be egotistical of me, but I'm afraid everyone is staring at me, so I keep my eyes on the floor in front of me. "Girl, look where you're going," Nina reminds me. "You gotta look at the road ahead of you, Rose."

I look up, and the first person I see is Ben. Looking right at me. Quickly, I drop my head down again and stop wheeling myself.

"Rosie, what's going on?" Nina asks, exasperated. "C'mon, girl." She gives up on me and pushes me to an empty table. "I'll have your lunch brought to you." Nina walks away, leaving me alone and paranoid.

I'm so hyper-aware all of a sudden. It's as if that breakdown I had the other day broke my shut-off valve and turned on my emotions. I don't like it at all. Closing my eyes, I try to slink back into my daydreams and shut the room out so that I'm alone with my past. But it doesn't come. I close my eyes tighter, willing my past life, before the accident, to appear behind my eyelids, but it remains black, the sounds of the rec room breaking in too loudly for me to get there. Wetness takes the place where my dreams should be. No. I won't let them fall. Damn these tears. Why did I have to break down the other day? Why couldn't I just remain empty and emotionless? Damn that chocolate pudding. He did this to me. *He* broke through my resolve. *He* made me feel again.

8

BEN

"You're gonna sprain an eyelid or two closing them so tight. At the very least you're gonna give yourself a headache."

Her eyes pop open and she moves her joystick so she's backed away from me an inch.

"I don't have leprosy or anything like that, if that's what you're concerned about." I know she isn't concerned about that, but I wanted to try to make her laugh. I failed.

She turns her chair to the left, positioning her back to the table.

I'm about to say, "It's gonna be hard to eat with your back to the table," but I refrain, realizing she's turned her scarred side away from me. I see the aide walk in with Rose's food and signal her to bring it to the table next to where we're sitting. I move to my table, grab my tray, set it on my lap, and wheel myself to the table that Rose is facing. "Sit here with me?" I ask her, rather than tell her.

She eyes her food, but then looks back at her lap.

"Come on. Really. I don't bite." I try to keep my voice sincere; my intent really isn't to be obnoxious and annoy her.

Her lip quirks, but she doesn't move forward. Instead, she remains with her back up against the other table and stares at her hands on her lap.

I don't continue to stare at her; that would just be rude. So I return to finishing the lunch on my tray and try to come up with something I can say that would make her smile. My brain comes up empty.

"Hey, Ben." I hear his joyful voice across the room. If he could move his limbs, I'm sure his arm would be waving wildly.

"Johnny. Dude."

He maneuvers his chair by blowing into a straw-like tube and makes his way over to me. With a heavy breath, he says, "Mind if I eat here?"

"No, dude, be my guest."

"And you don't mind my being spoon-fed like a baby?"

"Cut the shit. You know I don't."

"Just thought after you saw it once, you might've, maybe, got repulsed by me."

"Right. Johnny, this is Rose," I say, nodding my head in her direction. "Rose, this is Johnny."

Rose's eyes rise, but she doesn't lift her head.

"Hey, Rose. Nice to meet you."

Johnny looks at her, waiting for a reaction, then he looks at me. "The girl who doesn't talk, right?" he whispers unsuccessfully.

I roll my eyes, but out of the corner of one, I see her grimace.

"And he's the boy who can't move," I say jokingly to Rose.

"He's got that right," Johnny says, chuckling, still waiting for a reaction from our mute friend.

"So, how's therapy going?"

"Eh. Same ol'. Someone else moving my legs for me and shit."

I just nod, because, yeah...that sucks.

"It's all part of the game, Ben. Gotta have faith, right?"

Again, I nod, but this time I try to say something encouraging. "Gotta have faith, man. You'll be fixing your mom's gutters again in no time." I just wish I could believe that for him. But he does, and maybe that's all it takes for him to actually do it.

"Damn right I'll be up there. Mom's got no one. She counts on me."

I take a bite of my sandwich, but when I look up, Johnny's got that frown again. Though he swipes it away when he sees me notice.

"Hey, Marti's here." Johnny greets his female aide, with the male name, with a smile.

"Hungry?" Marti puts his tray down and takes the seat next to him.

"You know it."

All the while Marti feeds Johnny, he keeps up conversation, and it occurs to me that maybe his act is just that. It's starting to feel forced, and I'm wondering if he really doesn't believe he'll get better. For his sake, I hope he does.

And all the while Marti is feeding Johnny and Johnny is chatting in between mouthfuls, Rose is watching. Not noticeably, but when she doesn't realize I'm looking at her, I see it. What I'm getting is that she's amazed at Johnny's ability to be happy despite his condition. I could be wrong. Chances are I am. But as I've said before, the mind intrigues me, and so does Rose.

A few moments later, Rose's therapist or nurse, one or the other, pulls up a chair next to Rose. I try not to pay attention, trying hard to focus on Johnny, but paying attention to him is just as awkward since when he's not talking, his aide is spooning food into his mouth, so I stand to get myself something from the refrigerator. When I return to the table, Rose is pushed up against it, and the woman is gently reprimanding her. Again, I'm uncomfortable sitting down while she's telling Rose she needs to eat if she wants to recover effectively, but it'd look more obvious if I walked away from the table again. So I sit and concentrate on eating my pudding. And, of course, I got three of them. One for Johnny, and one for Rose.

"Hey, thanks, Ben," Johnny says, his voice genuinely happy. "You mind feeding me this?" he asks his aide.

"Course not."

When Rose's nurse, or whatever she is, walks away, I place the chocolate pudding on her tray and give her nothing but a smile to go with it. There are a million things I'd like to say to this lost girl, but she's already so timid, and I don't want to scare her away.

"If you're not gonna eat that pudding," Johnny says, looking at Rose's untouched tray, "I'll take it."

It's humorous when Rose narrows her eyes just slightly. I can't read her mind, but I think Johnny throws her off. She doesn't know what to make of him just yet.

"Or I can lend you Marti here," he continues, referring to his lunch aide, "if you're having trouble eating by yourself."

I pull in my lips to stifle a laugh, because, well, that was funny, but my guess is Rose probably won't think so, and looking at her suddenly blushing face, I've guessed right. In fact, she looks embarrassed, and a couple seconds later, she reaches for her orange juice and takes a sip. Seeing this, I pick up her pudding, remove the foil lid, and put it in front of her. Sticking a spoon in it, I say, "The chocolate pudding is outta this world." And then in a softer voice, "If you're in to processed milk-type products."

Her chest moves. A silent laugh. But she takes the pudding cup and holds it between her hands. With a sigh, she looks down at it. Contemplatively. If I could just get inside her mind...maybe I could make her see how this doesn't have to be the end of her world. Then again, how would I know? I'm just a kid studying psychology. I still have a whole mountain of things to learn.

While Rose fights with the dilemma of whether or not to actually eat in front of us, I see her nurse walk in with another woman. In about six steps, they're at Rose's side, and Rose's eyes grow wide when she sees them. Well, when she sees the other woman. Rose's eyes tear up and the woman bends down to hug her. "Oh, Rosie. Oh, baby."

"Rose," the nurse woman says. "We'll push back your therapy for an hour. Let your mom sit with you a while."

The woman – Rose's mom, I guess – stands to thank the nurse. "Thank you, Nina. I won't stay long, I just miss my baby."

"Sure."

When Rose's mom spots Johnny, his aide, and me, she nods and says hello. We greet her back and then she says to Rose, "You mind if we sit over there?" she asks, pointing to the black leather couch area.

Very subtly, Rose shakes her head to the right and back, and her mother pulls her away from the table. After they leave, Johnny asks, "Why doesn't she talk? Is she unable to?"

I take a second before answering. "Nah. I think it's a choice."

"Who would choose not to talk? I don't get it."

Coming up short on an answer, I shake my head and shrug a shoulder. *Why* would *anyone choose not to talk?*

9

ROSE

I love my mother. I miss her so much. Being away at college, I'd pretty much only see her during the holidays and breaks and all, but being here – and the reason for being here – I miss my mother pretty bad.

But I wish she hadn't overheard that Johnny boy asking why I don't talk. It disappoints my mother. More than my missing leg, it breaks my mother's heart that I don't say anything anymore. I'm sure if she could have her way, she'd gladly have her smart-aleck daughter sassing back at her again. Not that I was all that sassy, but if I didn't like something, I made sure to have my opinion heard. That was just me. If it was on my mind, it was out of my mouth. In a polite way though; I always made sure to remain polite, even if I didn't want to be. Now...I'm completely different. I'm not polite. People talk to me; I don't respond. People give me pudding; I don't say thank you. Mother visits; I can't say, "I love you."

But I want to do all those things. It's almost as if my brain won't let me. Like if I start talking, I make this whole thing real. If I start talking, I'm giving in and accepting this fate. I don't want to accept it. I don't want to be a one-legged human being who can't dance anymore. Dancing was everything to me. How can I possibly survive without it?

"Rosie." My mom breaks my train of thought. "I contacted your friend Holly."

"No," I want to say, but I don't.

"It wasn't easy. She's not in the dorms this year, and the school wouldn't give me her new address, but...I went to that bar you mentioned. The one where you said she had gotten a job once. I took a chance, and fortunately, she's still working there."

I don't look at my mother. I close my eyes instead. *You did not tell Holly. Please say you didn't tell her.*

"She'd like to come see you."

No, Mom. No. I'm not ready.

"She's so sorry she hadn't made more of an effort to find you. She just thought you were busy with dan..." Mom drops her head. "I apologized for not reaching out to her sooner. It was hard for me..." Mom shakes her head, her eyes still cast on the floor.

I know, Mom. I know.

My mother sighs, and it's so loud I'm afraid the whole room heard her. "Rosie, let her come. Please," she begs, her voice wet with tears she's trying not to shed. "Maybe seeing her will help. Get you to talk again." My mother's hands are shaking. "It hurts to see you like this, baby."

I cover my eyes with my hand to block my own tears. I hadn't shed one since that day I screamed in the hospital, but ever since the other day, they seem to come so easily.

"I told her I'd ask you first, but...I'm kind of hoping she comes anyway. She seemed insistent on it." My mother nods, trying to keep this conversation up by herself. One-sided conversations are hard, I'm figuring. "I did tell her it was only fair to ask you, but you don't want her to come, do you?"

No. I don't. I don't want her to see me like this. I don't want her pity. Anybody's pity. Things will never be the same again. My breath catches at this thought.

My mother notices. She moves in closer and puts her hand on my leg. My good leg. I notice my mother won't look at my other leg. She doesn't want to accept this as much as I don't. To my face, she says, "Rosie, I want you to come home. But you can't until you know how to use your pros...your new...Oh, Rosie, just please do what they say."

She's crying now, she can't help it. "Please, baby, so you can come home. Please. I know you'll feel better when you're in familiar surroundings."

I blink for my mother. My acknowledgment of her plea. Then I lean forward to hug her. She takes my body in hers so fiercely I think I'm going to fall out of my chair.

"Please come back, baby," she whispers in my ear.

I give her a whimper. Because, really, I do want to come back. I just wish I could come back as a whole person.

When my mother pulls away, she wipes away her tears with a tissue and smiles. "Can we go into your room? I'd like to brush your hair."

Because it probably looks straggly and unkempt, is what she's thinking. It's bad enough Lou has to wash me. I can't expect her to spend time keeping my waist-length hair neat.

"I brought a pair of scissors too. Maybe I can trim it up, like old times?"

Mom always trimmed my hair. It's not like it's hard to do. I have thick, straight, one-length hair. She liked to keep it tidy for me, because it was so thick, it would tangle easily. Anyway, I offer my mom a simple nod. It's the least I can do.

I use my electronic controls to wheel myself to my room, so my mom doesn't have to push me. When we get to my room, she asks if I want to move to the regular chair. I shrug, not sure where I want to sit.

"You can stay where you are if you want."

My mother's gentle touch as she brushes my hair makes me sad. I'm not sure why, because even when I had two legs, I still loved when my mother would bring a brush to my hair. There's just something about your mother's touch. But now I feel sad. I think I'm always going to be sad.

I close my eyes and try not to think. Instead, I pay attention to each brush stroke and try to bring myself back to my life before.

51

But I can't.

It was so easy three days ago to sink into my past and leave this place, but now...I can't. I'm too much here...in the present. I focus on the wall in front of me, because sometimes that would work, but today it doesn't. *Dammit, I don't want to be here. I want to forget again. Just for a few moments.*

I sigh in resignation and let more tears fall.

Before I realize it, my mother has brushed and trimmed my hair. When I turn my chair around and look at the floor, all I see is red. Snapping my head up, I silently ask my mom why she cut so much off.

"It was all dead, honey. You haven't been conditioning it, or even hardly brushing it. It looks healthy now. Take a look."

She wheels me to the mirror that hangs along the bathroom door. My hair now comes to just above my breasts. I guess that means it falls right about to my bra strap in the back. But it does look healthier.

"I know I should have wet your hair first," my mother says, "but I think it looks nice. Don't you?"

I bring my hands up to touch it, and for the first time, I nod. A real nod. Accompanied with a smile. *I love you, Mom. So much.*

She kisses the top of my head, and starts braiding my hair. "Now, I know you don't really want to fuss with your hair while you're here, so if you just keep it in a braid, it won't get all knotty. Can you at least do that, Rosie?"

I nod. *Sure, Mom.*

Mom leaves, and I'm back in therapy with Nina, who says I look a little brighter since Mom came to visit. *Yeah, well, I love my mom.*

"If you're willing to try today, Rose, I have your temporary prosthetic." She looks at me, hopeful, and begs me with her eyes to be cooperative.

I'm the one who's been holding this whole process up. My temporary prosthetic was ready when I first got here, but the new uncooperative, impolite me refused to let Nina put it on. Allowing them to put this fake leg on me cements the truth. Makes it real. I'm so not ready for real. But I do want to get back home. And to begin the journey back home, I guess I have to take the first step. I shake my head at the pun and give Nina a distinct nod. *Why not?*

"You're shaking your head, you're nodding, which is it, girl?"

I nod.

"Good. Now let's get you on your feet."

My half-leg had already been prepared with a rigid dressing, but Nina slides on a couple of socks before she attaches this thing to me.

"Okay, we won't be needing this pillow underneath your hip," she says, as she removes the pillow that's been lodged under my hip to keep the lower part of my half-leg from hanging. "Well, we're ready to attach the prep to your stump."

I flinch. I cannot stand that word. I will not use it.

Nina knows I've tensed up. "I'm sorry. That's not the best word to use, is it?"

I don't respond, but Nina gives my thigh a rub.

"Let's get you upright." My metal leg is attached, and she helps to pull me out of my chair.

I'm standing on this plastic-looking foot that is attached to what looks like a metal paper towel tube. It's hideous, and I'm about to break down again. My breathing becomes forced, and I feel my heart pounding. *I can't do this. I can't do this. How can you expect me to live like this for the rest of my life?*

"Rose," Nina says calmly, holding on to my shoulders. "You got this. Don't break down on me again. Come on, this is temporary. Your real leg, it's gonna be prettier, I promise."

Prettier? Really? No.

"Please, honey," she begs again.

I lift my hands to grab onto her arms, and I squeeze. *Please don't let me fall.*

10

BEN

"Okay, kid, looks like you don't need that chair anymore."

"Thank heavens."

"But you do need to rest your leg quite a bit during the day," Craig continues. "I wanna see you sitting on that couch in there with your leg up. But I'm gonna keep your brace unlocked from now on. You're recovering nicely."

"Thanks."

"How's that pain, though?"

"It comes and goes."

"Still a shooting pain?"

I nod. "Yup."

"Hmmm." He pauses, looking worried.

"Craig?"

"We'll just keep an eye on it. I want you to schedule an MRI, though. Just to be safe."

"Okay, sure."

Craig continues to push me to my limited limits, and I have to laugh at myself. I'm on a treadmill, walking two miles per hour. If my teammates saw me now, they'd tear me up. "Will I ever be able to run again?" I ask Craig, half joking.

"Of course." He laughs. "One step at a time, Ben. We can't speed up the process. We want you like new again, and that's gonna take a little time."

"I guess." I continue on the treadmill another twenty minutes before Craig pats me on the back and tells me it's time for stretching. About ten different stretches later, I'm told to take a walk around the building and then get lunch.

I'm not sure how I feel about walking around the

building. Especially since Johnny can't. Don't get me wrong, I like standing on my own two feet, but I almost feel as if just by being able to walk around, I'd be rubbing it in to my friend who may never be able to walk again. When I met him, we were on level playing ground, so to speak. I feel guilty that I no longer need my chair.

At my usual lunch time, since I no longer need anyone to help me retrieve my lunch, I go to the cafeteria and get my food to go. As uncomfortable as I am to walk in front of Johnny, I enjoy sitting with him and don't want to give that up. He's one of the coolest guys I know, and I'm grateful to have met him. So I bring my lunch to the rec room and hope that he's just as cool with me being on my two feet permanently.

When I walk into the rec room holding my lunch, the first one to look my way is Johnny. He's already sitting with Marti. "Whoa, Ben. Look at you," he exclaims loudly. "Is that for good or just a little reprieve?" he asks when I'm at the table.

Setting my tray down on the table, I pull out my chair and sit across from him. "It's for good."

"Awesome." And he genuinely looks happy for me.

"Hi, Marti."

"Hi, Ben."

"Dude, you wanna watch a movie tonight?" I ask Johnny. "Lou was telling me we're not confined to our rooms at night." Usually I spend the evenings reading *Sports Illustrated* or some baseball book, but I feel like doing something different tonight.

"That'd be cool. I'm usually so beat, I'm sleeping by the time you get done with your last session, but I'll try to stay up tonight."

"No, don't worry about it. Was just an idea."

"I want to. I'll tell Jack not to put me to bed tonight."

"Cool." I eat my lunch while Marti feeds Johnny his, and in between bites we make small talk.

About ten minutes in, Johnny's head turns toward the door and his eyes grow twice their size. I turn around, since my back is toward it, and at the door, next to her therapist, who's holding a lunch tray, Rose *walks* in, with only a cane to assist her.

"Oh my *God*, she's beautiful," Johnny says, echoing my thoughts.

"Shit, yeah," I say, utterly blown away. It's amazing, really, but on two feet, standing at probably five foot five, with her hair pulled back in a loose braid, Rose looks completely different. As if her soul decided to come alive. There's still no smile on her lightly freckled face, but there's a soft peach glow to her cheeks and energy in her eyes. Before I realize what I'm doing, I wave two fingers backwards in silent invitation to join us. Her lip quirks, revealing a cute dimple on her right cheek. She ducks her head as she walks, and when her therapist walks over and places the tray to my right, Rose doesn't follow. Instead, she reaches for the chair to my left. It doesn't slip by me that her scar is on her left side. Though it doesn't take away from her beauty *at all*, I realize she's self-conscious about it. And she sits to *my* right, as opposed to Johnny's. This ignites a vain thought. *Could this sweet redhead be interested in me?*

Shit.

That'd be so damn cool.

When her therapist walks around to place the tray in front of Rose, I notice the tag on her scrubs says Nina. Nina the therapist. At least I know what her name is now. Nina tells Rose to feel free to walk around the room after lunch and she'll be back for her in an hour.

"Damn, girl, you look good on two legs," Johnny tells her in a non-flirtatious way.

I, on the other hand, attempt to flirt by leaning into her ear and whispering, "I think you're beautiful no matter what."

Her eyes get as big as Johnny's did a minute ago, and then her face turns a brighter peach and she looks down at her lap. I mentally kick myself, because maybe that was being too forward. With Rose, I need to take it slow. I know this. She's been through a traumatic event. I need to rein it in a bit, but damn, I couldn't help myself. She's beyond beautiful.

Rose's eyes dart around the table, but she hardly raises her head, and she never touches her food.

"Girl, I'm gonna sic Marti on you if you don't start eating."

Marti just laughs but doesn't respond to Johnny's comment.

Rose tries to ignore him, but her hands are fumbling over each other on her lap, and I'm pretty sure she's embarrassed right now.

"Hey, Rose," I say to distract her, "Johnny and I are watching a movie in here tonight." She turns her head to look at me. "You're welcome to join us...It gets boring sitting in our room night after night," I say as an afterthought.

She looks me in the eyes, and I may be wrong, but I think she wants to say yes.

To get her to seal the deal, I say, "There'll be chocolate pudding."

Her lips tuck in, but a small smile escapes. I made her smile, and if I'm not mistaken, the little rise of her chest tells me she's stifling a chuckle too.

"How 'bout seven?" I ask Johnny. "I have a thirty-minute session with Katrina at six thirty. Is that good for you?"

"Sure. They usually put me in my bed about six, because I work out like Schwarzenegger and I'm beat by then, but tonight, for you guys, I'll stay up."

"Good for you too, Rose?"

She nods. Just twice, but she nods. *Yes.*

Obviously Rose remains quiet while Johnny and I talk, but we do include her in the conversation. Once in a while I'll get a nod or a barely-there smile, but she does respond, and this puts a smile on my face so huge that it's pretty hard to keep it hidden.

"What's so funny?" Johnny asks.

"Nothing. Just...a joke I remember."

"Care to share?"

"Not really."

He shrugs and drops it.

Throughout lunch, I try really hard not to let on that I'm watching Rose, but because she's become somewhat of an interest to me, I can't help myself. I notice, though, that today...she eats. It's not a lot, and she even tries to hide that she's eating, but it's more than I've seen her eat on other days. Well, anything's more than nothing.

After Johnny's nurse wheels him away, and we've confirmed our plans for tonight, I ask Rose to take a walk with me around the room.

"Come on." I nudge her after she doesn't respond. "I heard Nina telling you you should. Besides, the room emptied out. It's practically just the two of us in here."

She looks down at her legs for such a long time that I think she's ignoring me, but then her hands cup the edge of the table and she pushes her chair away. My impulse is to take her by the arm, but I don't want her to think *I* think she needs my help.

Her small pale hand grips her cane and she steps to my side. I take the first step, and we walk together around the edges of the large room. I'm guessing the room is set up for walking, since the tables are set in the center of the room and the lounge area is off to the far corner, leaving adequate space for wheelchairs and recovering walkers to roam about the room. A month ago, I think I'd have laughed if someone asked me to walk around a room for recreation. I'm just saying, the room may be large, but it's no baseball field. None of that matters at the moment, though, because I'm walking with the most beautiful girl I've ever had the honor of walking with. So, yeah, I'm good.

11

ROSE

This is so awkward.

And embarrassing.

I don't even know what to think right now. My yoga pants are covering this fake leg, but it's not like Ben doesn't know. Besides, even if he didn't know, all he'd have to do is look down at the big plastic foot that sticks out from the bottom of my pants.

I'm trying. Really. There's nothing I want more than to be home with my mother, but...

Well, that's a lie.

There is one more thing I want more than to be home, and that's for this stupid accident to never have taken place so that I could still dance. But that dream was wrenched away from me, and that makes me sad. Yet I don't want to stay here forever, so I need to find it in myself to willingly cooperate and show some kind of semblance to my old self.

"So, I know you don't talk much," Ben says slowly, his hands stuck in the front pocket of his sweatshirt, "so you can just nod or shake your head...if you're comfortable with that, of course."

He pauses in his speech and his step. I force myself to look up at him but only for an instant. Then he continues to walk as he asks, "Do you like funny movies?"

I nod.

"Do you like horror movies?"

I shrug, because they're not bad, but I don't necessarily love them.

He seems to understand my shrug, since the next thing he says is, "Soooo, not reeeeaaaally a fan, but you'll watch it...if forced."

The way he draws out some of the words, I can't help but smile.

"Okay. What about action films...like...*Need for Speed* or *Fast and Furious*?"

I scrunch up my face and shake my head.

"What about...*Hunger Games*, *Twilight*, that kind of thing?"

I nod.

"Okay, okay, what about love stories? Like Nicholas Sparks and..."

I nod before he's even finished asking the question.

"Noooo." He throws his head back as we walk. "Okay, okay, I had a feeling, but...just wanted to be sure. I guess I'll see what DVDs we have to choose from, and I'll pick a love story or something funny.

He looks at me again and then says, "Probably something funny. I have a feeling Johnny needs to laugh."

Yeah. I'm sure he does.

Look at me, feeling sorry for myself having only one leg, when poor Johnny can't even move. I sigh, and a painful-sounding noise escapes my gut. Quickly, I cover my mouth, but not quick enough to hide the noise from Ben.

"Are you all right?"

I nod, but I'm terribly embarrassed, and I feel myself start to cry. In an attempt to be normal, I force the tears back. Though, in doing so, I'm sure I look like a complete idiot.

"Hey. Johnny's gonna be okay." He pulls a hand out of his pocket and takes my elbow. "And so will you," he whispers.

Did you ever really not want to cry in front of someone so badly that you try really hard to hold back your tears? Your throat hurts, your face freezes, your eyes go wide because if you close them you'll just release them faster.

That's me right now. And I'm sure I'm looking all kinds of foolish. But I can't help it. I'm not strong enough to barricade the tears, so I turn away from Ben and slowly hobble out of the room.

I don't have to turn around to know that Ben isn't following me. He's too polite for that. I've figured that much out about him already.

The hallway is a blurry mess in front of me, so I move to the side and lean against the wall, attempting to wipe away the tears that are causing it.

"Rose?"

I look up to see Nina in front of me.

"I was just coming to get you. What happened?"

The tears don't stop. Not at all. They rush out of my eyes like Niagara Falls.

Nina wraps her arms around me, but I push her away and slink to the ground. If I could run, I would, but I can't, so I sit.

"I'm gonna go get Dr. Rappaport."

A couple minutes later, Nina is back with Dr. Rappaport and they're both struggling to lift me off the ground. Not because I'm too heavy; I've probably dropped down to ninety pounds by now. No, they're struggling because I am fighting them with every deconditioned muscle in my mutilated body. Soon, there are two male aides, and I'm being hoisted up and onto a stretcher. But I fight that too, and before they can strap me down, I roll off and fall flat on my face, my hands and arms too weak to keep my nose from hitting the ground. Now I'm in physical pain on top of everything else.

That's when I do it.

That's when I let out all the emotions I'd been keeping in for the last two and a half months.

That's when I am finally able to speak.

And it's not just normal speaking.

I let out sounds so deep and so loud, that I can't believe they come out of my mouth.

From somewhere deep in my gut, I scream, "God, why? Why did you do this to me? Why? Oh, God, nooooooooooooo, noooooooooo, not me! Oh my God, no, no, no, no."

The words go on forever, and they echo throughout the hallway.

By the time I am done screaming, only Dr. Rappaport is left. And he is sitting by my side, rubbing my back. Someone brings a pillow and places it under my head. I don't know how long I was screaming, but at the end of my meltdown, I am exhausted. Physically. Mentally. Emotionally.

I am sitting in Dr. Rappaport's office sometime after, and instead of not speaking, like is usually the case, I've been yelling. In my old life, I never yelled. Never found the need for it. Now. Now, I'm this person I don't even recognize. Half a person. Who screams at the top of her lungs. Now. Is this who I'm going to be for the rest of my life?

"This is *not* who you are going to be for the rest of your life, Rose," Dr. Rappaport says in response to my question, which evidently I said *out loud*. "You're going through the second stage of grief. It took you a while to get there, but you're there now. And it's good."

"Second stage?" I ask, screaming the words at him, digging my fingernails into my folded arms.

"Anger. The first one is denial. The second, anger. You're making progress."

I shake my head. "I don't want to make progress!" I touch my neck. My throat is awfully dry. I'm on my third glass of water since I've been sitting in here. "I want this to never have happened," I yell, pleading for time to rewind.

"But it did happen, Rose, and now you have to make

a decision."

A decision? I just glare at the doctor.

"You have to make the decision to either take control of this situation, or let it control you."

I stand up, and let me tell you, it isn't easy, since I still don't know how to use this metal leg attached to me, and the new bruises I incurred from my fall are raw and aching. "God decided already," I scream. "He decided I should walk around life on one leg and never dance again. It isn't fair. It isn't fair." I sit back down, because I hurt and I'm exhausted. "It isn't fair," I whisper, punching both my thighs.

"It isn't fair, Rose. Not at all."

"And that's supposed to help me?" God, I'm being so fresh, but what am I supposed to do? This isn't the life I wanted. This isn't me. This isn't me. This isn't me. My tears find their way back, and I just want to go to sleep.

"Rose. You're beat. If you want to stay here and talk things out, then stay. If you want to rest, I'll have one of the nurses bring you back to your room. Besides, you really need to ice your face some more. I think that pack isn't cutting it anymore."

No, it isn't, since it's been lying on the chair next to me, keeping the chair nice and cold.

Nina helps me to my room and takes off my metal paper towel tube. Then I almost vomit when she takes off my protective socks and dressings. Usually Lou or Katrina does it, and I never watch. Gone are the days I can just mind-travel back to sunnier days and ignore the present. So when I see the mutilation that is my left leg, my stomach lurches, and I think I'm going to puke for real.

"I know today was rough," Nina says, looking up at me while she's tending to my missing leg, "but you should have been taught how to do this already, Rose. It was infected for a long time, so your incision is still healing. Don't think it can't get infected again, because it can. And then that will just prolong getting your permanent prosthetic. You need to care for your own stump."

That's when I hurl. All over my lap and Nina. I can't stand that word. *Stump*. It's an ugly word. It makes me feel ugly.

"Oh my God, Rose. Really?" Nina says, standing up, her arms held out, her face disgusted by the vomit spewed all over her Scooby-Doo scrubs.

Now we both have puke on ourselves, but only Nina can clean herself up. I'm stuck on the bed with no chair, no cane, no nothing to help me get up.

So, like the baby that I'm being, because I don't know how to act grown up with this deformity, I kick the side panel of the bed with my heel, and grunt something incoherent, even to myself.

Nina comes back in my room with Lou, and both of them tend to cleaning the vomit off of me. Afterward, I'm asked whether I want to be put in my chair, but I shake my head and pull the covers over my legs. The only thing I want to do is sleep. Even watching a funny movie with Ben tonight holds no appeal.

12

BEN

Johnny and I were disappointed when Rose didn't show up to watch a movie with us last night. Truth be told, I was the one disappointed. Johnny seemed uninterested in even watching the movie. The poor guy gets tired easily, and last night, he looked beat. His curtain is closed this morning, and it sounds like he's still sleeping, despite it being nearly eleven in the morning.

Saturdays are a little more laid back, and we only have one therapy session, so we're allowed to sleep in if we choose to. I chose not to and had breakfast in the cafeteria with a lot of the center's employees and the patients' visitors. There were some patients eating in the cafe, but I think most of them were outpatients. The inpatients usually eat in the rec center.

But after breakfast, I came back to the room to see if Johnny wanted to hang. Since he's still sleeping, I head down to the rec and promise myself I'll sit and rest my leg when I get there. It's hard to sit still, but Craig insists that I rest it, and because I still have some pain and weakness, I intend on obeying him. I grab a soda out of the fridge, sit on one of the reclining couches and give my mom a call.

"Benito, it's so good to hear your voice," she says upon answering.

"Hey, Ma. Miss you."

"Miss you too, Benny. How's pain?"

"Pain's not too bad. I'm doin' good. They unlocked my brace, so I'm walking around again."

"Oh, so good. When you come home?"

"Not sure. My therapist said another week."

"Good. Good. Papa and I come see you tomorrow, yeah?"

"Yeah, yeah. That'd be good. Listen, Ma, can you or Dad call the doctor? Craig said he wanted me to get an MRI on my knee, but I didn't want to call the doctor from here. So you think you can call?

"Sure. I'll call Monday. I don't think he's in on Saturday. I'll try though, yeah?"

"Yeah. Thanks, Ma. See ya tomorrow?"

"See ya tomorrow, baby. Love you."

"Love you too. Bye."

Just as I slip my phone into the pocket of my sweats, I see Rose walk in with one of the weekend nurses. The nurse is talking to her, and Rose is just nodding. When the nurse points over to the lounge area, Rose shrugs, and then she sees me. I hope this encourages her to sit here.

She looks down at the floor, but I notice she allows the nurse to lead her over here.

"You want to sit here?" the nurse asks, pointing to the couch that sits adjacent to mine.

"Rose, why don't you sit here?" I speak quickly, before she has a chance to respond to the nurse.

"Oh, you know each other?" the nurse asks, taking Rose by the elbow and guiding her in my direction. "Okay, if you need anything, just press the button on your pager."

"You have a pager?" I ask Rose after her nurse leaves.

I expect her to nod in response, but she presses her lips together then opens them and takes a breath. "I guess they give them to the patients who can't get around on their own."

Oh my God, her voice is soft, and sweet, and childlike. I nod and stare. And then I come back to Earth. "You have a sweet voice. You should use it more often."

Her peachy complexion turns more peach. "Thank

68

you," she says very softly.

"We missed you last night."

She just nods.

"Cat got your tongue again?"

She closes her eyes and shakes her head, but she does present me with a close-mouthed smile.

"I'm sorry. I shouldn't have said that. I was trying to make a joke, but...it wasn't funny. I'm sorry."

Again, her eyes close briefly, and she laughs one silent laugh.

"Please don't stop talking again on account of my being an ass. You have such a sweet voice. It's meant to be heard."

"S'okay." She barely opens her mouth, but at least she says something.

"Do you have therapy at noon too?" I'm trying to make small talk, but it's difficult. I don't want to say anything that might offend her or trigger her tears. I'm not sure what I said yesterday to cause them, but I'm afraid to do it again.

Now I know I have the option of just leaving her be. Not paying any attention to her. Hey, if someone doesn't want your friendship, why try to attain it? But I don't think that's the case with Rose. I believe with Rose, it's a matter of helping her see through this. It's not that she doesn't want me as a friend - it's that she doesn't know how to be a friend in her new body. She doesn't know how to exist in her new life.

Rose holds up her fingers, and at first I think she's telling me to, "Wait a second," but she's actually telling me she has therapy at one.

"Ah. Mine's at noon...obviously."

"Are...you here long? At...rehab?" Her voice is tiny, but it's beautiful. It flows, like a song.

"No. About another week. You?"

She shrugs. "Guess it depends on me." She frowns.

"On you?"

"I...I haven't been well behaved," she speaks under her breath; I can barely hear her.

"Well behaved, did you say?"

"Mmm-hmmm."

"You're the quietest girl I've ever met. I don't believe you have it in you to misbehave."

She closes her eyes again. Only this time, she keeps them closed, and I'm hoping I haven't caused her to cry again.

"Rose?"

She turns her head and looks at me. Right in the eyes. "I'm not a happy person. And I haven't been very cooperative."

"I'm sure it's not easy facing a substantial lifestyle change." While I'm speaking the words, I'm wondering if I shouldn't be saying them, but I want to get close to this girl. I know she intrigues me, but she also smells so. Damn. Good.

"It hasn't been. No," she admits quietly.

She's struggling. I hear it in her barely audible voice. I see it in the way her fists are tightly clenched. And I see it in the rigid way she holds herself.

"I have no way of knowing what you are going through right now, but I imagine you'll learn to adjust. Eventually."

She only nods. Her fists are still clenched so tightly, her knuckles are bright white. I'm also guessing her fingers are in an awful lot of pain as well.

"You're in good hands here. My coach thinks so anyway. He's the one making me be here."

I laugh at the confusion on her face.

"I had meniscus repair surgery. I could have recovered from home. Gone to therapy a couple times a week as an outpatient. But he's ensuring that I'm *fully capable to be back on the field for the spring season*. His words. Not mine."

70

"Baseball?"

"Yup. Pitcher."

She nods her approval.

I want to ask her if she does any sports, but thankfully, for a change, my mouth doesn't spew before my brain has a chance to register what it's going to say, and I refrain from asking her something that I'm positive would trigger tears. At the very least, resentment.

I'm just about to ask her what kind of music she likes, but there's a guy wearing athletic gear and an unbuttoned lab coat standing at the door, searching for Benito Falco.

"That's me," I answer, standing up.

"I'm your PT today."

"Oh." I look at Rose. "Hopefully I'll see you later?"

She just nods. But I get a smile. Complete with dimple and all.

13

ROSE

Thank God he left.

I couldn't stand talking to him.

It took all my mental strength to not scream or, and this is new for me, to not punch something.

Ben is sweet. He's funny. He's so darn cute. In my old life, I'd have loved every single moment he'd pay me any attention. But today. Now. Me being a total mess. Scarred down one whole side of my body. I couldn't *not* be preoccupied with how I probably look from his eyes.

Will I be this self-conscious the rest of my life?

Before the accident, I never gave a second thought about my appearance. Yes, I took care to look neat and put-together. And yes, I kept myself trim so I'd look good dancing on stage.

But I never.

Never.

Cared how I looked while having a conversation with another person.

Now.

It's all I can think about.

Poor Rose with her half-a-leg and Jack Skellington face.

I guess I'm more vain than I thought I was.

But before I'm able to slink too far into myself, the rec room phone rings, and the aide who answers it tells me it's for me.

I point to myself, unbelieving that someone would be calling on the phone for me.

"You're Rose Duncan, right?"

"Yes," I say, too low for her to hear, but I nod my head and use the arm of the couch and my cane to slowly come to a stand.

When the aide sees me struggling, she motions to help me, but I hold up my hand, to my surprise, in silent protest. *I got it*, my mind says, though my mouth doesn't.

"Hello?" I keep my voice low when I take the receiver.

"Rose? Is that you, honey? You're really talking again?"

"Mom?"

"Dr. Rappaport called me to tell me. Oh, baby, you don't know how happy that makes me. Oh, I want to come down today, but Daddy's so busy on the farm. But I told Dr. Rappaport if you needed me, I'd come."

"No. Mom...it's okay."

"Really? Dr. Rappaport didn't think it was necessary, but I wanted to check with you. You're sure?"

"Yes."

"Rose. He said you hit the anger stage."

I don't respond.

"It's okay, honey. He said it's healthy. You're moving forward. I'm so happy, Rosie. I can't wait 'til you come home."

"Me too."

"Okay, baby. I'll let you go. Call me if you want me to come down before Wednesday. Otherwise, I'll see you Wednesday. I love you."

"Love you too."

Just as I'm making my way back to the couch, someone calls my name again, and I recognize the voice immediately. I'm excited and agitated at the same time. Using my cane to help me, I turn around slowly, and without being able to help myself, I smile and cry at the same time.

"No. No. Rose. I didn't come here to make you cry."

Putting her hands on my shoulders and searching my eyes, she says, "I came here to tell you to wise the fuck up and get better already."

And right away, I'm laughing along with my tears. God, how I've missed her.

"Oh, Holly."

"What the hell, Rose? You trying to play hero by getting through this by yourself?" She pulls away, and I turn to lead her to a table. When we're sitting next to each other, she looks at me and says, "Why couldn't you just call me? I could have been here for you the whole time. And wait. Your mother said you weren't talking. You said my name. Are you cured?" She's teasing me. Typical Holly. I've missed her so much. She'd become my best friend and dorm mate on the first day of college three years ago.

"Far from it," I tell her.

"So why did your mom say you weren't talking?"

"I wasn't. I just...started."

"You just started talking? Since your accident?"

I nod.

"Rose. How long has it been? I haven't heard from you in months."

"June 12th."

"You speak so softly now, I can hardly hear you. June 12th? That's, like, what, a week after you got to New York, isn't it? You didn't even get to...Oh, Rose, I'm so sorry."

"It was three weeks before the show opened." My chest hurts saying this out loud.

"Your mom said it was a delivery truck?"

Again, I nod. Dr. Rappaport's been trying to talk about this for weeks, Holly visits, and she gets me spilling my guts. Sort of.

"Oh my God. What do you remember from it?"

"Not much. I remember pain and then waking up two months later."

"Two months? Holy shit."

"I need water," I say, pushing away from the table to get some from the water cooler.

Rose comes with me, holding my hand as we slowly make it over to the cooler.

"So two months you were in a coma?"

"A medically induced coma. I had a lot of infections and a bad head injury."

"Is that why you didn't talk for so long?"

"I think that was psychological. Something about it being selective or conversion," I say slowly, softly. "They rattled off so many reasons."

"Then why are you talking now? So low, but you're talking."

"I don't know. Doctor said I hit the next stage or something."

"Next stage?"

"Anger."

"You? Angry? I don't believe that. You don't look angry."

"I'm happy to see you, Holly, but I'm not happy," I admit, sitting back down at the table. "In fact, for the first time ever, I wanted to punch something today. Yesterday...I had to be restrained."

"Oh my God," she says of my being restrained. Then she looks down at my lap. "Can I see it?" she asks carefully.

Reluctantly, I fold up my yoga pants and show Holly my metal leg...plastic foot attached.

"It's not so bad, Rose. Your pants cover it. But, you can never wear shoes again?"

Shoes are the least of my worries. I can never *dance* again. "This isn't my permanent leg. I'm told that one's *much prettier,*" I say bitterly.

"At least you don't have to try to find a monster shoe to fit that thing into," she says, referring to the ugly foot attached to my metal robot leg.

Rolling down my pants, I say, "I can never dance again, Holly."

She closes her eyes, and I get the feeling she already realizes this.

"I don't know, Rose. People run marathons with *no* legs. I think if it's something you want badly enough, you can do it. Besides, I was researching online after your mother came by the other day. Did you know there was a double amputee on Dancing with the Stars?"

That's right, I'd forgotten about Amy Purdy.

"Yup. And then I looked some more. There are a lot of dancers who have one or no legs."

"Ballerinas?"

"I think so. Yeah." She looks me in the eyes and gets so close I think she's going to kiss me. "This isn't a prison sentence. You can still plan the life you wanted. You just have to change the way you go about it."

"When did *you* get so...encouraging?"

"Rose. I *love* psychology. *Love it.* The best decision I ever made was to switch from finance to psych and social services. I love...helping people, I guess you can say." Holly bops her head from side to side, smiling modestly.

"That's right. You wanted to switch last time I saw you. I forgot about that."

"You're forgiven. You had other things on your mind," she jokes, before turning all serious. "Cooperate, Rose. Your mom said you haven't been. I miss you. I want you back at school."

"School? I haven't even thought about it."

"It's probably the best thing for you. Even if it's one

or two classes to start. You can live with me and Griff."

"Griffin?"

"Yeah, I took him up on his offer to move into his house."

"In his billiard room?"

"No, no. Hurley moved out before the summer. I took his room. And then Braden transferred to Monmouth this semester, so you'd be able to have his room."

I start to clench my fists, feeling agitated at the thought of my future. "Holly. You're...you're going too fast for me. I'm just trying to find my way back home right now."

Seeing Holly makes me happy, but it's also making me sad and very edgy. She makes it sound so simple. It's not simple at all.

"Well, when you're ready...I'm gonna talk to Griffin, so...keep it in mind at least?"

"I will. Thanks."

"I love you, Rose," Holly says, taking me in a big bear hug, so different than she was last May.

"Love you too, Holl."

"They told me you have PT at one. Can I walk you there?"

"I'd like that. Thanks."

14

BEN

Dinner is quiet today. For me, at least. Many of the resident patients had visitors, and Johnny and Rose were nowhere to be found. Johnny wasn't in our room when I got back from PT, and I haven't seen him since. I thought Rose would be here, because, well, I just thought she would. Then again, maybe it was just me hoping she'd be here.

Instead of going back in my room for the night, I put on *Dumb and Dumber* in the lounge area and settle in to watch. The leather recliner couches are comfortable, and there's nothing better to do. I've been ignoring texts from the guys, because they're just busting my balls about being in an old folk's home, and I don't really want to be dealing with that shit right now. So, I decide to text Holly, who I haven't talked to since the last day of summer classes.

Me: Hey stranger. Whassup?

About fifteen minutes later, my phone pops.

Holly: Hey. Long time no see. How's the knee?

Me: Good. How's school? Meet any new psych majors as interesting as me?

Right away, she answers.

Holly: Are u kidding? No one holds a candle to u.

Me: Except that bartender of yours?

Holly: Well, he's not a psych major. Jealous?

Me: A little. Lol

Holly: We'll have to get you a hot chick.

Me: Found one. Just trying to get her to notice me.

Holly: How can she not notice you? You're HOT.

Me: Hot? Yeah, well, this one's got a lot of other things to deal with than some horny guy. Besides, she's...fragile.

Holly: Fragile? What's she made of...glass?

Me: No. But she has been sort of broken. I'd like to be the one to help put her back together. ;)

Holly: You pansy.

Me: STFU

Holly: You text your mother with that phone?

Just then, Rose walks in and takes a seat on the couch adjacent to me. I text Holly.

Me: Gotta go. TTYL.

I shut off my phone and stick it in my pocket. Then I get up and move to Rose's couch. "I can change the movie if you want."

"No. *Dumb and Dumber* is good."

"How'd it go today?" I notice her fists aren't clenched like they were earlier.

"Okay. Making progress."

"I can tell. You're speaking a little louder."

Her hand flies to her mouth. "I'm sorry."

"No, no," I remove her hand from her mouth and keep it in mine, "you're not talking too loudly. This morning, I could barely hear you."

She looks at our hands on the couch between us, and I wonder if I am being inappropriate, so I let her hand go.

"So...do you go to school? High school? College?"

Her straight, perfectly white teeth all show when she laughs. "High school? Do I look that young?"

Thank God she's not in high school. "Well, you do look young, but I was kind of hoping you'd say college."

Once again, a brighter peachy pink colors her ivory cheeks, making them look like she's been in the sun. I like watching her blush. "I'm a senior, well, supposed to be a senior, in college, this year."

"Now *that*, I wasn't expecting. You look younger than a senior."

"Thank you? Maybe?" She smiles.

"It's a compliment," I assure her. "You're an older woman. I like that."

"Older?"

"I'm a junior. I'm twenty-one. Well, on November first, I'll be twenty-two."

"I'm twenty-two. Won't be twenty-three until March."

"So you're not too much older. Can I ask what you're

studying?"

"Education. And," she looks down, hesitant, "and...dance."

She's a dancer.

With one leg.

Now I get it.

I don't want to say, "I'm sorry." That may make her feel bad. So, instead, I ask, "Elementary or secondary?"

"Elementary."

"Good choice. Little children are less evil."

"I don't know about that," she jokes, and I'm starting to get a glimpse of the real Rose. "What do you study?"

"Sports psychology."

"Oh. You're a baseball player. Makes sense."

"Can't play ball forever, right?" I hope that wasn't the wrong thing to say.

"Nope. Guess not. There's an age limit in Major League Baseball, right?"

I relax. She doesn't seem to be getting offended or teary or anything. "Pretty much. Once you've hit your late thirties, you're pretty much done. Although, Jamie Moyer pitched until he was forty-six, so..."

"Forty-six. Wow."

"But that's not the norm, so sports psychology is my back-up."

"You're pretty sure you're making the Majors, huh?" she asks quietly.

I shrug. "Not positive. No. I've been scouted though, so it's looking good. I'm not full of myself or anything, please don't get the wrong idea, it's just...well, it's all I really wanted most of my life."

She nods. "I get it," she says quietly.

"I realize things can change." I feel like shit right now. The last thing I want to do is bring her down now that she's

81

finally smiling a little.

"So, you'll be Dr. Falco, the sports psychologist?"

I laugh, partly from relief from the ball-playing thing, partly...no, just relief. I'm relieved she's changed the subject. "Or just Ben. By the way, how'd you know my last name?"

"I heard the guy say it this morning."

"Ah. What's your last name?"

"Duncan."

"Rose Duncan. Nice."

"Actually, it's Rosalie. But everyone just calls me Rose."

"Rosalie's a pretty name."

"Thanks. It's okay...Benito."

"Are you making fun of my name?"

She shakes her head, but smiles. "No."

"You're in a good mood tonight."

She shrugs. "Faking it."

"Really?"

"I don't know. My friend came to see me today, so..." She fiddles with her fingers, and I notice she still hasn't clenched them all night.

"And you were happy to see her? Him?"

"Her. Holly."

"Holly. Really? I have a friend named Holly. That's who I was texting when you came in."

"Yeah? Can't be my Holly, she doesn't know any Bens."

This makes me laugh for real. "Oh. You know every person your friend knows?" I ask jokingly.

"Well, in the past three years I've known her, she's never mentioned anyone by the name of..." She pauses, her face scrunched up in thought. After several seconds, she says, "Wait a minute. Ben. Psychology. Did you take a psychology class this summer?"

Shit. "I did. Hunter Hill?"

"Oh my God. Are you...a 'nice' guy?" she says with quotes. "Like 'apple-pie' nice?"

I crack up. Slap my thigh and laugh out loud. "Holy shit. Holly. Yup." I shake my head at the reference of apple pie. Holly always thought of me as the all-American boy. "Gotta be the same Holly."

"Holly Buchanan?" we both say at the same time.

"Oh my gosh, she was just here. She didn't say...does she know you're here?"

I shake my head. "No. She knows I had surgery. Knows I'm recovering. She doesn't know I'm here though."

"Wow," she says, still fiddling with her fingers. "So you guys met in psych class?"

"Yeah. Actually, we met online during registration."

"Oh. I think her text said something like that. Back in June..." She trails off and shakes her head. This time I notice her fingers stop fiddling and disappear inside her fists, which are rested on her lap. "She texted me that she met you," she continues, her eyes glassy. "I think she was excited to have you as a friend." Rose smiles even though her eyes are still bubbling over. "Otherwise she never would have mentioned you." Now she chuckles. "Holly's like that. Only the real important stuff is worth her breath."

I nod. "That sounds like Holly."

Rose is fighting back emotions, but I give her courage for staying on the couch. Like she said before, she's making progress.

"So...you and she have been friends the last three years?"

"Yeah, she was my dorm mate and became my best friend." She nods, sitting still and unnerved. The only thing giving her away is her unmoving and tightly-clenched tiny hands.

"Cool."

"Did you live in the dorms?"

"No. I lived in a house with some teammates. This past summer, though, I rented a bedroom from some old lady."

"Really? Did your teammates bust you about that?"

"They didn't know. As far as they were concerned, I went home for the summer."

"Oh."

"That's how I became friends with Holly. All my friends were gone for the summer."

"Got it."

"So you live in the dorms when you're in school, where do you live otherwise?"

"Wantage."

"Wantage? Is that in New Jersey?"

She hesitates. "Up North. Near PA."

"Oh. I'm near PA, but I'm more toward Philly. Cherry Hill."

Her fists are still, but her knuckles are stark white. It's starting to make me nervous.

"Tell me about Wantage."

"Um..." She shakes her head no. "I..."

"It's fine," I cut her off, recognizing her discomfort with the subject. "You can tell me about it another time." I'm stumbling over what to talk about. I can't move too fast; she's vulnerable. Still trying to make her way back to normalcy. So I bring the conversation back to *Dumb and Dumber*. "You know, we've missed a lot of the movie. Are you up for starting it over? Watching it uninterrupted from the beginning?"

Rose doesn't answer right away, but when she does, she says yes, and I'm just happy to be sitting in silence next to her. Under normal circumstances, I may have tried to hold her hand or slide my hand behind her on the couch so I can slip it over her shoulder.

But these aren't normal circumstances.

And I don't want to push her away.

15

ROSE

I hate being so emotional. He only asked about my hometown.

But I want to be home so badly, I couldn't bring myself to talk about it. He must think I'm such a freak.

At least I didn't run away again. I'm trying. But it's hard. Especially because he's so cute. I sat down, purposely, on the left side of the couch, hoping I could lean my elbow on the armrest to cover the scar on my face with my hand. But then Ben moved to my couch. And in order to look at him, I had to turn my body. Which meant I couldn't lean my elbow on the armrest, leaving my ugly scar uncovered. I could have held my hand over my face, without leaning against anything, but I was aware that would have made me look even sillier. So I sucked it up and tried not to think about it.

Now that we are just watching the movie, I'm able to lean my elbow on the armrest. Not that it matters anymore anyway. I wish I could put makeup on to cover it, but I don't think anything I have at home is strong enough.

The movie is funny enough to alleviate any tension I put between us, and the rest of the night is actually enjoyable. We laugh at the same jokes, and I even notice Ben shift a couple of times to move closer to me. At least I *think* that's what he was doing. The fact that he hasn't seemed turned off by me yet makes me feel a little less self-conscious. Toward the last half of the movie, Ben pauses it to microwave some popcorn, and when he comes back, he's sitting so close to me that only the bag of popcorn is between us.

Now I'm feeling things I haven't felt in a long time, and I'm self-conscious in a different sort of way. *Why is he being nice to me?* Is it just because here, I'm the only girl his age? There's Kimberlee, but she doesn't spend time in the rec room. She has so many doctors looking after her that she's too busy to hang out.

"I'd have suggested chocolate pudding," Ben jokes, "but popcorn's more a movie thing."

I laugh, and we both stick our hand in the popcorn at the same time, but I move my hand before his touches mine. And once that happens, Jim Carrey and Jeff Daniels become invisible to me. Sure, I'm pretending to watch the silly movie; I laugh when Ben laughs. But my stomach is in knots, because suddenly he's become more than just the cute baseball player with a knee injury. He's become the cute baseball player with a knee injury whom I wish I could date.

If only I had two legs.

Liking a guy who may like you back usually results in a date. A date, into dating. Dating, into an intimate relationship. Which means sex. How could I have sex with only one leg? And it's not even the physical awkwardness I'm thinking about. *It's that a boy, whom I like, would see me...like that.*

Before I'm even aware of it myself, Ben says, "Shit, Rose, you're bleeding."

I look down, and there's blood on the cuff of my white shirt. My fingernails were jammed so far into my palm that I broke the skin. And now...on top of being self-conscious...I'm mortified.

I hadn't even realized Ben had left, but he's back with a few tissues and standing in front of me. He goes down on one knee and takes hold of my right hand to cover the nail marks with the tissues.

Feeling too tense and uncomfortable, I pull my hand back, and he gives the tissues to me instead of taking care of it *for* me.

"It doesn't look bad," he says, sitting back down on

the couch.

Pressing the tissues to my hand, I tell him, "I think I better get back to my room."

He nods and stands, but tucks his hands in his sweatpants pockets.

I crumple the tissue, hold it inside my bleeding hand, and lift myself off the couch with the help of my cane.

Ben stands there, looking unsure if he should help me, so I just say, "I'll see you tomorrow or something. Thanks...for the movie."

His smile is awesome, and I would kick myself, if I could, for being so wishy-washy. I hate wishy-washy. But currently, I don't even know which way is up. I'm at a total loss about who I'm supposed to be right now. Being friendly and normal is not on my radar.

I hobble back to my room and call the night nurse to help me take off my tube, since I'm not supposed to sleep with it on. My irritability level has skyrocketed in the last fifteen minutes, and when the nurse doesn't come quickly enough, I roll up my yoga pants and start yanking off the tube from my leg. And hurting myself in the process. The pain in my shin is unbearable and freaks me out.

Because my shin isn't even there!

I've had phantom pain before. They tell me it's normal for...people like me.

But this time.

I can't handle it.

The latches on my robot leg are not cooperating, and I'm using force to rip it off.

In no time, and after an unsuccessful attempt to dislocate the metal from my leg because I never paid attention to how to do it, I'm kicking the plastic heel against the side of the bed and screaming.

Pain is everywhere.

My non-existent shin.
My stupid nub of a knee.
My whole left side.
My chest.
And that's the worst pain of all.

Why did this have to happen to me?

Why couldn't I have just gone back to the apartment with Jordan when she forgot her cell phone? Then none of this would have happened. None of it.

My God, why are you doing *this to me?*

It's a new nurse, and when she sees my state, she calls for help. At least I think that's what she does, because moments later, I'm being pricked with a needle. And while I'm still screaming.

16

BEN

Rose walked out upset, and I'm embarrassed by how that made me feel.

Like I was dumped.

In the middle of a date.

I know, I know - unreasonable.

For God's sake, I just met her. We're in here to recover. Not to date. But I tell you, it started to feel like a date.

Maybe because I'm attracted to her?

Maybe because I'm feeling something from her too?

But we are here to recover.

Rose is, especially.

I can't be thinking about her in that way.

But I am.

So I text Holly.

Me: You'll never guess who I met?

Holly: Mike Piazza.

Me: Mike Piazza? Really?

Holly: He's the only baseball guy I know. If it's not him, who?

Me: I'm not that obsessed with baseball. Anyway...the girl I kinda sorta like?

Holly: The girl made of glass?

Me: Yeah. Her name is Rosalie. Rose for short.

Instead of the popping sound of a text alert, my phone rings. I press answer and hear, "Where the hell are you?"

I can't keep from smiling. "I'm at Orange Rehabilitation Center."

"Ho.Ly.Shiiit." She draws out the words. "You met Rose."

Sighing and smiling, I say, "I did. And Holly, I need your help with her." I keep my voice quiet, even though I'm the only one in my room.

"What do you mean you need my help?"

"I'm not sure if I should even be pursuing her. She has all this shit going on. She's so...distant and..."

"And fragile?" Holly finishes.

"Yeah." I pause and run my free hand through my hair, and realize I need a haircut. "Am I crazy? She should be the furthest thing from my mind right now. I mean with baseball, my knee, and the whole fact that she's far from healed emotionally from her accident." I stop talking, waiting to see what Holly has to say.

"Well, you're definitely not crazy. Rose is the best. It's just..." I hear her sigh. "Right now, you're probably best to just...be a friend."

"Well, that's all I want to be right now, but maybe...maybe she just wants to be left alone."

"It's true that Rose is going through something we can't understand...I don't know. I wish she had a phone so I could call her, or at least text her."

"I hadn't even thought about that. You're right. I haven't seen her with a phone."

"Her mom told me it was crushed in...well, anyway.

I'll try to get there this week. I just have to find someone to cover for me at work. She needs a friend. She's going through this all alone."

"I'm here."

"You know, I really wish her mother tried to contact me sooner." Holly ignores me. "I could have been there this whole time."

"Can you come tomorrow?"

"I work tomorrow. I can see if Donny can cover, but...I'll try."

***

Holly does come on Sunday to see Rose, only to be told that Rose isn't here.

"Rose signed herself out late last night. Her mother came and took her home," Holly tells me after she asks the front desk if she can visit with me instead.

"But why?" I ask, wondering why her mother would take her before she finished therapy.

"The woman couldn't tell me. Patient confidentiality and shit," Holly says, waving her hands in front of her as if they fed her bogus information.

If I weren't so worried about Rose, I would have laughed. "Damn."

"If she went home, I can just go there and see her."

I nod, agreeing she should go visit her friend. I want to say, "But where's that leave me?" but I don't. Instead, I say, with an ache in my chest, "Please keep me posted on how she's doing."

Holly reaches for my forearm, and while she's rubbing it, she tells me, "Oh, honey, I definitely will. I'll text you every time I know something. Okay?"

"Sure."

She reaches in and hugs me. "Since Rose isn't here, I'm gonna get back to work. Donny wasn't too happy to pull two shifts. I'll talk to you tomorrow?"

"Please."

***

Monday and Tuesday are quiet. Rose is gone, and Johnny hasn't been back in our room since Saturday morning. At first I was afraid to ask about him, but now I'm getting worried. So, on Tuesday afternoon, during my afternoon PT session, I ask Craig.

"He had to be taken to the hospital Saturday afternoon. He has pneumonia, and for someone in his condition—" Craig shakes his head "—it's not good, man."

Suddenly, I don't feel like finishing my session. I sit down on one of the benches and drop my head in my hands.

"It sucks," Craig says.

I look up at him. "Craig. I...Do we have to finish here? Today?"

"No, man, we don't. I was going to tell you this at the end of the hour, but...you get released on Thursday."

"Really?"

"Yup. But you have to go for that MRI. Did you tell your mother?"

"Yeah, yeah, she's supposed to be making me an appointment."

"Good."

I get up to go back to my room, but Craig stops me.

"He's at Saint Barnabas. Johnny. If you want to see him when you get out."

"Yeah. Thanks."

***

On Thursday, I'm released, but not relieved.

The first place I have my mother take me is to Saint Barnabas Hospital to see Johnny. He is someone I started to feel close to in such a short amount of time. I don't know if it is his wit or that he could look quadriplegia in the eye and laugh at it, but Johnny is a man of integrity. And one I'm proud to call *friend*.

I'm only allowed in for five minutes. He's in ICU, and I'm lucky they're even giving me *that* much time. He's awake, but tubes are coming out of him everywhere.

"Ben? What the...hell...you doing...here?" he says, barely getting the words out between breaths, when he sees me standing alongside his bed.

"It's me, dude. What the hell are *you* doing here?"

"Eh. Shit happens." His voice is warbled, and even though he has tubes sticking out of his nose, his breathing seems labored. "What are you...doing out...of rehab?" he asks slowly.

"Got released today."

"Going home...excellent."

"Are you gonna get better soon so you can get outta here?"

"Yeah." He pauses, but I know he's just trying to catch his breath. "Any day now."

"Good. Good. Hey, I don't have a phone number or address or anything for you." I pull out my cell. "What's your address?"

Johnny gives me his address, which is in Totowa, and, so he tells me, not too far from Hunter Hill.

"And...Mom's getting me...this voice...recognition computer...when I get out...of rehab...so we can email."

"Cool."

"I have a cell phone number too."

"You do?" I ask, not expecting him to be able to use it.

"Sure. I use voice rec for...that too...and Bluetooth."

"Well, you're all set then, aren't you?"

I punch in his number and promise him I'll call.

"Hey...call it now...leave me...a mess...age. This way I'll...know it's you."

He's struggling to get the words out, so I tell him I'll call and then I tell him to hurry the hell out of the hospital.

And then I walk out of his room, shedding the first tear I've shed in a long time.

***

I settle into home easily enough. Since Dad, Maria, and Dominic are at their respective jobs, and it's just Ma and me at home, it's pretty quiet, and I find myself bored right away. The highlight of my days are when Holly calls to fill me in on what's happening with Rose. The first few times she tried, Holly couldn't get in touch with Rose's family, but after about a week of calling, Rose's mother finally answers her call.

"She's in a mental ward, Ben," Holly tells me over the phone, her words muffled by her tears.

"Oh shit."

"She's really depressed, her mom said. She thought going home from Orange would make her feel better. She really wanted to be home. But...her mom said she got even worse. Crying all day long. If she wasn't screaming from nightmares, she wasn't talking. She sank back into her mutism; just refused to talk again."

"Did she...did she go willingly?" I ask, because I'd hate to think she was dragged to a mental facility.

"Her mother said she had a really bad nervous

breakdown and went to the hospital in an ambulance. She's at a regular hospital, but they have a psychiatric ward there. I mean, maybe she wants to be there, since she's old enough to sign herself out."

"Not if she was forced to go."

"It didn't sound like that."

"Thanks for calling, Holl. I think I gotta get going."

"Sure. I'll call you when I hear more."

"Thanks."

When you hear sad news about a friend, it makes you sad. Sometimes, it even makes you cry. But hearing this about Rose...well, it hurts. Right where my heart lives in my chest. That's when I realize, I must have really fallen hard for her, and I hadn't even seen it coming.

***

Monday, more than a week after I am released from Orange, I go for my MRI. My mom keeps making the appointment; I keep canceling. I'm not in the mood to deal with lying still that long, and I really haven't felt the need to go. But my mom put her foot down by Monday and threatened to cancel the cable *and* the phone if I didn't go. So it's Monday, and I'm here. The process takes about forty-five minutes, and I get to listen to my new Walk the Moon album.

Most of my time at home I think about Rose and wonder if she's getting any better. But I spend the rest of the time either doing my at-home physical therapy or going in the backyard and practicing pitching without bending my knee. Not an easy task, but it makes me feel like I'm moving forward a little bit.

Johnny enters my mind quite often as well, but being that more than a week has gone by since I've seen him, I call his cell and hope someone answers it.

On the third ring, it's Johnny's voice who answers. "Ben, how's home treating you?"

"It's boring. How 'bout you? You outta that hospital?"

"Yup. Two days ago. I'm actually home now too."

"Really?"

"Yeah. They're afraid of germs and stuff, so...got a private PT coming to the house a few times a week. My mom might hire me a full-time nurse if insurance covers it."

"That's great, dude." Is it? I really don't know how great it is to be in Johnny's shoes. I admire how he's holding up. "Can I come visit you, or will I bring in more germs?"

"No, no. Sure you can visit. My mom'll make you sterilize yourself before you come in, but if you don't mind taking a bath in boiling water when you get here, then you'll be good."

"Sure," I say, laughing. "What's a few third degree burns for a friend?"

"When can you come?"

"Shit. How 'bout tomorrow?"

"Cool. You got the address, right?"

"Yup. I'll put it in my GPS. See ya tomorrow, dude. And hey, you need anything?"

"Legs or arms that work if you can find them anywhere."

There is no response to that; I can't even laugh, and I know he is joking.

"Hey. Kidding. See ya tomorrow."

***

The next day, I borrow my mother's Accord, because my Civic is manual, and I'm not supposed to be using a clutch just yet, in case I jam my knee in the process of shifting gears. It feels good being back in the driver's seat, and the route is familiar, considering it's the same one I take to get to school.

A young woman, who looks older than she probably is, opens the door to Johnny's house.

"Ben?" she asks, greeting me with a smile and, after confirming I am in fact Ben, a hug.

"Hi," I say over her shoulder, trying subtly to break the embrace.

"Oh, Ben, thank you for coming today. You don't know how much this means to him...and to me, of course."

"Oh...it means a lot to me as well. He's a great guy." She shuts the door behind us and leads me in to the foyer.

"Please don't tell him I told you this." Her hand is now firmly on my shoulder. "But...oh, he likes to put on this act in front of people. In front of me even...but..." She has to stop to catch her breath and wipe her tears with a tissue she takes from her sweater's pocket. "When he's alone in his room," she continues, "and he thinks I'm out of earshot, I hear him sobbing."

I had a feeling, but I'd never say that to her. "I guess...it must be so difficult...to be...."

"To be a teenager who can't move," she finishes my thought.

"Yeah."

"He talks about you all the time now. I'm so happy he has you." She wipes her eyes again. "His other friends...I don't think they know *how* to react."

I nod, understanding completely. I have no clue, myself, how I would act if I had known Johnny before. But I had the good fortune of meeting him after, and so it was easier to not even have to react, but to just...act.

"Let me stop talking. He's so excited to see you. Do you mind though?" She holds out a huge bottle of Purell.

"No, of course not." I take off my sweatshirt, lay it on a bench in the foyer, and lather on the antibacterial hand gel. I rub it up my arms and everything.

"Johnny's in the family room," his mother tells me as she parades me through the kitchen.

"Hey, dude. Is that the way you greet your best friend when he comes to visit?"

Johnny's chair turns and he faces me. "Hey. You made it."

Walking over to him, I purposely knock him on the side of his knee with my hand. "Course I did. How they hangin'?"

"Who the hell knows? I can't stand up to see if they even do," he says jokingly. "So what's goin' on, Benny? Gettin' back in the groove?"

"Eh. No groove to get back into yet. Thinking about traveling with the team to Florida on break, but...that just might bum me out."

"Cause you can't play yet?"

"Yeah."

"I hear ya. Too loudly."

I cringe. "Yeah. I guess you would. Sorry."

"Don't be sorry. It is what it is. Can't change things."

"I...uh...I thought you...thought you'd...um...get better and shit."

"And shit's more like it."

Sagging into the couch, I let the severity of his depression sink in - he's given up. "Dude." I want to say more, but what? Telling him he might get better are just words that may as well come out of my ass. They mean nothing.

"I'm accepting it," he says, closing his eyes.

We look at each other for a few seconds too long, so we shift our eyes comically, to find someplace else to look.

Then Johnny blurts, "Hey, you got Words With Friends on your phone?"

"Um...no. I can get it, though. Why?"

"Wanna play?"

I must be giving him a blank stare, because he laughs.

"I mean with me. Play it with me. I have it on my iPad and...you wanna play?"

"Sure." I find the app in the app store and start the download. "But...how? How can you..." I point to him in the chair, but I don't finish the sentence.

"With this." He puts his mouth on the second straw-like thing that sticks out from his chair extensions and lifts it up, pointing it at the iPad he has sitting on an electronic tray. The end of the stick has a rubber tip.

"That's some chair," I say, impressed.

"Yeah, and here before this, I only wanted a mere Mustang," he jokes.

I know he's not trying to make me feel guilty for opening my mouth, but I do.

"Hey, don't feel bad. I see it on your face. I gotta make jokes. It's how I cope. And you're allowed to laugh. In fact, I would like it if you would laugh."

I nod, but I drop it and say, "App's loaded. Now how do I play this shit?"

Johnny laughs and rolls next to me. "They'll give you a bunch of letters and you gotta make a word out of them. Like Scrabble. You ever play Scrabble?"

"Oh yeah."

"Good." He rolls his chair back over to where he was and we play.

"Hey, that ain't a word," I say of the *word 'djin'* that he just played.

"It took my letters, and it's fifteen points, so that means it's a word."

"Well I think it's cheating."

"Nope. If it takes the letters, it's not cheating."

100

Laughing, I call it "...a lame-ass game."

As we get into the comfortable groove of playing Words With Friends and hanging, I decide to bring up Rose.

"John," I start, looking at him while he decides what letters to play, "I was thinking of finding Rose."

He looks up at me, surprised. "Finding?"

"I found out she's in some mental ward in some hospital."

"Mental ward?" With his rubber-tipped stick, he lowers the iPad tray. "Why? What hap..." He stops. It registers. "She can't make jokes."

I shake my head and put down my phone. "No joking."

"She must be really depressed."

Nodding, I agree.

"Then find her."

"Find her?"

"She needs to laugh. Make her laugh, Ben."

"Make her laugh? I'm not that funny."

Johnny cracks up. "Then joke about me. Find *something* funny to talk to her about."

"Funny? You think joking about your situation is funny?"

"Isn't it? Isn't it hilarious that at seventeen, I'm less active than my ninety-two-year-old great-grandmother? That's funny shit, Ben. If you consider cruel irony hilarious." Though his shoulders can't shrug, his eyes do. "What can you do?"

"Is this...all bullshit, John? You can't really be okay with this, are you?"

He looks at me.

Stares at me.

"I'm sorry for being so blunt, I just don't get it."

He finally speaks. "What choice do I have? If I let it

101

get to me, what happens? I end up in a mental ward like that pretty little girl of yours? Shit, I can't even kill myself to escape this."

His eyes start to tear.

My heart starts to break.

"I'm stuck like this with no choice, Ben. So...for my mom's sake, I laugh."

I nod, sadly understanding a little better.

"I'm all she has. Besides her gram. So...I'm gonna be the next Stephen Hawking and make enough money to pay for people to help her. Since I can't."

"Well...you do have a high IQ, right?"

"Damn straight. 156."

"Impressive. And you're still in high school?"

"Mom didn't want me to lose out on a real childhood. I'm in all AP classes though, so...I'm still ahead when I start college."

"Cool."

"If I don't get pneumonia again and die."

"Dude."

"I came close. That's why I couldn't go back to rehab yet. It's gonna take a lot to get my immune system up."

"Shit."

"Yeah." He picks up his straw with his mouth and elevates his iPad. "Let's get back to the game."

We get back to Words With Friends, but my thoughts are swirling all over the place.

Will Johnny really be okay?

Will Rose?

Do I go find her?

Or do I let her be?

In the end, I let her be – for now.

17

ROSE

Returning to the normal world isn't as easy as I thought it would be. Not that hanging home all day is considered normal for a girl my age. I should be studying or partying or enjoying life in my twenties, I'm told. But I haven't found my bearings yet.

While in the mental ward of the hospital, I did get my breaks to work on my physical disability and I did get fitted for my permanent artificial leg, which I'm wearing right now. It's not as robotic as my metal paper towel holder, so it's prettier to look at. Relatively. It's still not the real thing. But at least I can wear my own shoes with it, and it looks like a real leg. And oh yeah, they fit me for a second leg too. A leg to use when I, believe it or not, dance. That leg's really robotic looking, but it's supposed to be highly effective for dancing. And it does have a petite foot, so it still fits in a ballet shoe.

I know what you're thinking - "You can still dance?"

It turns out, yes, I can. But I haven't tried it yet.

My new therapist, the one for my brain, not my leg, allowed me to go online during some of my sessions and research dancers with amputated legs. During one of my early sessions, Denise asked me what I planned to do about dancing. I looked at her like *she* was the one who'd lost her mind.

"Was that not an appropriate question to ask?" she said in response, as if she couldn't see I only had one functioning leg.

My inclination was to keep staring, but my stomach rumbled with the urge to release a scream. So without raising my voice, I sarcastically pointed out that, "I seem to be missing an essential instrument for dancing."

"I beg to differ."

"How's that?"

"You're a dancer. You don't watch *Dancing with the Stars*?"

I rolled my eyes. Amy Purdy. Holly had brought her up the last time I saw her. "On occasion."

"Have you ever heard of Amy Purdy?"

"Vaguely."

"She was a double amputee. That didn't stop her."

I let that sink in.

"And...I've gone poking around the Internet. There are others."

Really?

"I don't think this is the end of your dancing career, Rose. I believe it's the beginning. A new start...a new challenge. Are you up for the task?"

Was I?

***

After that session, Denise and I spent a lot of time researching dancers with disabilities, and we found that there are actually academies that specialize in dancers with disabilities, including them with their non-disabled dancers.

***

So I'm home now.

It's Halloween.

And I still have disparaging thoughts about myself.

One of them being how fitting this holiday is for a one-legged *Skellington* like me. I don't answer the door for trick-or-treaters. My mother or sisters do that. I stay in my room and read. And answer Holly's texts every now and then.

My mother presented me with a smart phone as a welcome-home gift. She must have told Holly I had a phone again, because all day long she's been texting me. Most of them about how hot Ben Falco is and how he'd be perfect for me. I don't encourage her by agreeing, because I really don't want to talk about him. She can be relentless though. The texts have slowed up tonight, though, because the bar is probably slammed with customers. Part of me wishes I were there. I miss my old life.

It's about eight forty at night when I get a text from an unfamiliar number.

TEXT: Hi, Rose. Thinking about you. Hope everything's cool. *Ben

Ben?

Holly must have given him my number. My mother doesn't even know he exists. I don't think she was paying much attention the day she came into Orange, and we were sitting together.

Do I respond?

I don't know.

I toss the phone onto the bed and open my book, not knowing what to say to him right now. The words on the page of *Gone Girl* run together in one long fuzzy train of letters. Putting it aside, I pick up my phone and stare at Ben's text.

After several long minutes, I text back.

ME: Hi.

I know. Lame. But...*Is everything cool?* Not really. *Did I want to say, "Thanks for thinking of me?"* No.

So...Hi. That's the best I can think of. Maybe I suffered more brain damage than they think.

Right away, I get a text back.

BEN: Hi. :) I'd like to see you soon. Going stir crazy in the house. My mother's driving me nuts.

ME: Oh.

So lame. So lame. So lame.

BEN: Can I visit?

Shit.

I guess I don't text him quickly enough, because I get another ding.

BEN: No pressure. I'll use my imagination to remember your face.

ME: Please don't.

Uh oh. He could take that the wrong way.

BEN: You don't want me to visit?

ME: I don't want you to remember my face.

BEN: It's a beautiful face.

ME: It's a scarred face.

BEN: Scars are beautiful. Especially on you.

ME: I look like Jack Skellington.

BEN: You have a broken mirror. You look like a princess.

ME: Thank you.

BEN: You're welcome.

A few minutes go by and I think we're done texting, so I pick up *Gone Girl* but keep the phone next to me. "My throat was clenching and unclenching like a heart," is all I keep reading. I can't get to the next sentence, because I'm hoping so much that Ben texts back. Maybe I should just text him and say, "You can come up."

Fortunately, I don't have to make such a ridiculously easy decision that I'm nearly incapable of making, since my phone dings again, and it's Ben.

BEN: So. Is tomorrow good?

ME: To visit?

BEN: No. To fly to Naples.

ME: lol. Naples? Did you just tell me to go to hell?

BEN: What? No. Why?

ME: Doesn't Finabala or something like that mean go to hell?

BEN: lol. It means go to Naples, yes, which essentially means go to hell. But that is NOT what I said

AT ALL. BTW, you know Italian?

ME: Just some bad words.

BEN: I don't believe that. Then again, you are friends with Holly.

ME: Who do you think taught them to me?

BEN: Ah. Anyway, can I visit YOU tomorrow?

ME: Do you know where I live?

BEN: I was hoping you would tell me.

ME: Ok.

BEN: Thank you. Is noon okay?

ME: Yeah. Noon is good.

BEN: Good. Now I just need your address.

ME: 83 Brown Road

BEN: Great. I'll GPS it.

ME: Good luck. It's in the boondocks.

BEN: 83 Brown Road, Boondocks. Got it. ;)

ME: lol

BEN: Goodnight, pretty lady.

ME: Goodnight, Ben.

I set my phone aside, lie down on my pillow, and smile at the ceiling.

Ben wants to see me.

Ben knows what I look like, and he still wants to see me.

I can't keep myself from feeling warm inside, and I fall asleep, for the first time since early June, with a smile on my face.

***

I'm a shattered mess this morning. Everything in my closet is too big, which makes me look even frumpier than I am now, and I can't get my hair to do what I want. My sister Beth is lying on her stomach on my bed, and she's cracking up while I have an adolescent nervous breakdown.

"Calm down, Rose. He obviously already likes you, so don't try so hard."

"Easy for you to say...you don't have a hideous zipper covering the left side of your face."

"Rose. He's seen your scar. Yet he's still coming. He saw you at your worst. Something tells me that you could be wearing a potato sack and have no hair, and he'd still come."

"Right."

"Rose, wear your jeans and your ivory American Eagle sweater. You look nice in ivory."

My stomach hurts. How do I make myself look halfway normal?

"And wear those cute red cowboy boots you have."

"My boots?" I look at her like she's crazy. "I've only ever worn sneakers with this thing."

"They fit the foot to your size, right?"

"Yeah, but those boots were tight to begin with. I don't know if I'd feel comfortable walking in them."

My sister bites her lip and gives me one of those, "I'm sorry" head-tilts. "The sneakers will look cute, too," she says, the sound of her voice indicating she feels bad for bringing it up. "I'm sorry, Rose."

Pulling the sweater out of my antique dresser, I tell her not to worry about it. Then, when I turn and face her, I whip the sweater at her leg. "Get out now. I need to get dressed."

Beth sighs, disappointed at the change. Before my accident, my sisters and I always dressed in front of each other. If one of us was taking a shower and the other had to use the bathroom, we'd just walk in on each other. But now...Mom told them they need to respect my privacy and not walk in on me. I'm just not ready for anyone to see my leg. I can barely look at it myself.

Staring at my reflection in the mirror, my chest pounds, and my stomach ties into knots. I try really hard to keep from crying, but I scream for Beth instead.

She comes running into my room, hysterical. "What? What's the matter?"

"My face." I'm holding my face with my fingers, wishing that I could wake up from this pathetic nightmare.

Beth looks at me through the mirror, her hands on my shoulder, and says, "Your face is beautiful, Rose."

"Stop lying. I need you to cover this."

"I'm not lying." She leaves my room and comes back a minute later, holding her makeup pouch and the chair from her room.

She pulls her seat up next to mine, places the makeup pouch down on my vanity, and rummages through it. "I'm not gonna cover it too well, cause that'll just look phony, and he already knows you have the scar."

"So what're you gonna do?"

"I'm gonna lessen it. Take the red out. Downplay it."

"Just make me look like I'm not wearing a Halloween costume."

She slips her fingers through some strands of my hair. "It's not as bad as you're making it out to be, Rose. It really isn't."

Her fingers tap lightly on my cheek as she spreads concealer along my scar.

"Now I'm going to put a light foundation over your whole face to blend it all in."

"Will it be noticeable?"

"The scar or the makeup?"

"Both."

She laughs. "Neither will be," she assures me as she pats loose powder on my cheeks, chin, forehead, and nose.

"Now what're you doing?" I ask as she comes at me with a pencil.

"I just wanna line your eyes."

I back away. "Please don't. I just want the scar covered."

"Okay. But let me do your hair."

"Nothing fancy."

Beth stands, grabs my brush, and runs it through my hair. When she's finished, it's hanging long with a few strands pulled back, hippie-style, and secured in the back with a small butterfly clip.

"You look beautiful, Rose," my sister says from behind me now, staring into the mirror with me.

My hand naturally reaches for the scar, and instead of seeing an ugly red zipper, a flesh-colored scratch sits in its place. "Wow."

"Looks good, right? Now stop touching."

"What if it...comes off?"

"There's not that much on, Rose. Your scar is not that bad. It didn't need much."

"But..."

"It's not going to come off," she reassures me. "Now come on. I heard a car pull up."

Oh my God. "Oh my God," I breathe out loud.

"Rose. It's not like you haven't had boys come over. Come on. Nothing's changed."

Everything's changed.

18

BEN

My fingers were tapping about ninety-five miles per hour on my thighs while I waited for the door to open. I'm usually an extremely calm guy. Not much gets me flustered. But today? Forget it. You can power a whole baseball stadium with the nervous energy I'm putting out.

A blonde girl about Rose's age answers the door. "Hello," she says, smiling. "You must be Ben." My hands continue to drum my thighs, so I force them into my front pockets.

"I am."

Without hesitation, she yells, "Rose," but as she turns to yell again, Rose and another blonde are already walking down the stairs.

"We heard you, Patti," the other blonde says.

"Hi." Rose's smile is soft. Tentative. Unsure. I get the feeling she's as nervous as I am.

"Hi."

"Thanks," Rose says to her sisters, and motions, with the tilt of her head, for them to leave.

"Nice meeting you, Ben." The first blonde closes the door behind me.

"Likewise." I smile, but turn my attention to Rose. "You. Look. *Amazing.*" I pull my hands out of my pockets to give her a quick hug and a kiss on the cheek.

"Thank you." Her voice is still as soft as I remember, but she doesn't seem as sad.

"Sit." There are two ivory couches and an old rocking chair in the front room. Rose sits on the rocking chair.

So I sit on the couch closest to her, even though I was

hoping she'd choose one of the couches to sit on. I'm guessing it wasn't by accident that she chose the single chair to sit on.

"So," she starts, fiddling with her fingers while her hand sits on her lap.

"So...you have a great house. I mean...is that all your property out there?" Lame-ass thing to talk about, but I'm not sure where to start.

"Uh. Yeah. Most of it. From the front of the drive all the way...it's about five acres."

"Wow."

"My dad's a farmer. He's got animals all over the place." She nods. "Anyway, you're not back in school yet, right?"

"No, no." I shift on the couch and lean back, attempting to appear comfortable. "January. Knee's still healing. I am getting bored though."

"Yeah." She sighs and leans back in her chair too. "Me too."

"Yeah? You goin' back in January?"

"No." Her answer is quick. Definite.

"Maybe next fall?"

"Maybe." With the toe of her sneakers, she pushes off the floor to rock her chair.

"So...how is...everything? Are you still doing PT?"

She nods. "Yeah. It's okay. I go three times a week. What about you?"

"Same. But I might give PT a rest soon. Over winter break, I'm going to Florida with the team. Hopefully I'll be cleared to play by then."

"Oh. Good for you." She looks down at her lap for several seconds. When she looks back at me, she says, "I'm sorry. I'm not usually this...awkward." She shakes her head and sucks in her lips. Then..."I think they're lying when they tell me I didn't suffer any brain damage." She chuckles. "It's like I've forgotten how to be human." She stands up, quite nimbly, and smiles. "Can I get you a drink or something, or...does your knee hurt to walk? We can take a walk around the farm."

And just like that, the tension's lifted.

"A walk sounds good."

"Let me grab my coat."

While Rose finds a coat, and since mine is still on, I take a look at all the photos that hang in the front room. Tons of them. Many of Rose - Rose wearing short denim shorts, an ivory lace crop top, and red cowboy boots, sitting atop a beat-up red tractor. Rose in a black leotard, sitting and bending over to tie her pink satin ballet shoes. Rose in a short black dress, side straddling a white horse. There are other photos, with her sisters - I recognize the two who I met before. Another blonde graces some of the pictures too. But what strikes me most is not that Rose is the only redheaded sister, or that she is by far the most beautiful of the four; it's her legs. They are the color of light cream. They're firm.

And there are two.

I suddenly feel sad again for her.

"My mom's a photographer in her spare time. It's a hobby of hers. That, along with cooking and knitting." I turn around to see Rose standing in the doorway.

Immediately, I am drawn to her red leather coat. "Does that go with the boots?" I point to the picture of her on the tractor.

"I'm so embarrassed." Her cheeks redden just a little. Well, not red so much as that bright peach color they turn.

"By what?"

"All the pictures. Mom loves her camera."

"I think they're sweet."

As we head out the door, she grabs a bamboo cane

and says, "Yeah. It goes with the boots. They were a Christmas present."

"I like it. The coat *and* the boots."

She shrugs. "I can't wear the boots anymore though." She looks down and kicks the ground with her left foot. "This foot doesn't fit."

"Ah."

"It's made to my size, but...those boots are snug, so..."

"So you need a new pair."

She laughs. "I'm not worried about it."

There's a long gravel road that goes beyond the house, and Rose takes us along it.

"You're getting good at it." Jutting my chin toward the ground, my eyes point to her foot. "With the leg." I don't *want* to bring it up, but I don't want it to be the elephant in the room either.

"Yeah." She pulls her sweater out from the cuffs of her jacket and tucks her hands inside, repositioning her cane as she does.

"You cold?"

"No. Just...Yeah, it's getting easier. Walking. I still bring the cane, though, just in case. I trip a lot. I'd hate to fall."

"I don't blame you. Is it...easy to get on and off?" I lay my hand on her shoulder. "If I'm being too forward or you don't want to answer, just tell me to shut the hell up."

Rose smiles and looks at me while we continue walking. "It's not too bad getting on and off." She tsks. "I feel like such a baby, the way I acted at Orange. So...selfish. Those people were trying to help, and I...I just..."

Thrown off by where she takes the conversation, I'm stunned into silence.

"I couldn't handle knowing I...you don't want to hear this."

116

I slip my fingers around her sweater-covered hand and stop walking. "Rose. I wanna hear everything you have to say about anything. Please don't be afraid to share what's on your mind. And don't ever feel silly or *like a baby*...What you went through...are going through...it's life-altering. There is no right way or wrong way to react."

"Thanks. But I *was* a brat. You know who I think about a lot?"

Me, I hope.

"Johnny." She gazes up at me, smiling. "He was never sad. He can't move, yet...I don't know. I think about that and...I was a brat. Still am."

"You're not a brat. And Johnny? He's not always happy. He's...resigned."

"Resigned?"

"He's accepted his fate...but only 'cause his mother has no one else. And who's to say keeping all your emotions in like that is the right thing? I'm not so sure it's all that healthy."

"You sound like my therapist."

"One day, I hope," I say, laughing.

"That's right. Dr. Ben."

"Yup."

We continue walking the gravel path through the massive farmland. On the right side is a huge red barn and some stables. On our left is flat land covered in hay-colored grass. Four horses are roaming the field, including the white one that was in the picture with Rose.

"So...how *is* Johnny? Do you ever hear from him?"

"Yeah. He's home. He ended up in the hospital with pneumonia."

"Oh...my goodness."

"He's okay now. But he's...his immune system is low, so they don't want him back at rehab yet."

"Geez."

Her head is down, but we're still holding hands. Which I am very happy about.

"So when did you leave Orange?" she asks as she gently tugs me to the left.

"A few days after you."

Rose bites her lip and nods, then reaches her hand over the wooden fence she brings us to. "Come 'ere, Cloud," she says, signaling to the white horse galloping toward us.

"Cloud?"

"Yeah." Cloud lowers his nose for us to pet. "He's mine. I named him. He's white and fluffy..."

"Like a cloud," I finish.

"Yup." As she continues to pet Cloud, she says, "I had to get out of there."

I don't say anything, hoping she'll continue.

"I couldn't handle it anymore."

"Orange?"

"Yeah...it...it wasn't the place. I just...I didn't have time to adjust...to my leg...to my scars...I don't know. I got so...I'm sorry. I don't know why I'm bringing this up." She takes her hands from Cloud, and from mine, and turns to lean her butt against the low fence, and rest her hands behind her on the rail.

"Like I said...I don't mind." I stand against the fence and mimic her stance.

After a mirthless laugh, she says, "I ended up in a mental hospital." Her eyes dart to mine, gauging my reaction?

I don't let on that I know. I try not to show *any* reaction.

"I couldn't even handle it at home."

"And now?" She seems better. Talkative. More confident.

"Still struggling, but better. Much better."

"That's good."

With her head down, she kicks at the grass with her...injured leg. "It is good. I just wish it were...I wish it'd just be great, you know?"

"It'll get there."

Her foot stills, and Rose shifts so that she's turned toward me. "I don't think so, Ben."

"And why is that? Why can't things be great?"

She continues her gaze downward and kicks her foot again. "What if someone told you you couldn't play ball anymore, and you'd never make it to the Majors?"

"Fair enough. But...Rose?"

"Yeah?"

"I guess dancing was a big part of your life? You told me you studied it, but you never went into detail."

"It was a huge part of my life. I didn't study it at Hunter. I only studied Education there. But...I belonged to a pretty prestigious dance academy. I had been rehearsing for a part in a Broadway show. It was my dream...to be up there on Broadway." She looks me in the eyes and keeps her gaze there. "I lost my leg three weeks before the show opened."

"I'm so sorry."

"That's why...I'll never get there. Not anymore."

"That's tough. I'm sorry."

"It is what it is, I guess, but...oh, anyway, let's get off this subject. Come on, we can go back for something to eat. Are you hungry?"

"A little."

She smiles and takes *my* hand. "You ever ride a horse?"

"No."

"Maybe one day you can come ride Cloud. Or one of the others. I don't think my sisters would mind."

"You each have your own horse?"

119

"Doesn't everybody?" she jokes. "Yeah. And we each take care of our own too. Well, Beth has been taking care of Cloud for me while I've been gone, but...my dad wants me to get back on the proverbial horse and start scooping poop again." She laughs again, and I must say, I'm really enjoying the sound of it. "He says he'll give me today and tomorrow off, but come Monday, I gotta get back out there."

"I think that's a good idea. Do you?"

"I do. I miss it anyway."

"Good for you, Rose."

Her smile is big and bright as she flashes it at me. She squeezes my hand and says, "Thank you for coming here, Ben. I haven't seen any of my friends in so long, and...well, it's nice."

"So I've made it to friend status, have I?"

Nudging me with her elbow, she says, "I think so."

***

Back at Rose's house, I sit at the huge white table in her kitchen while she fixes us ham and cheese sandwiches.

"Rose. Can I ask you something?"

Her hand stills while she spreads the mayonnaise on the bread. "Um...oh...kay."

"You seem to be getting around well...physically...and I can't tell for sure, but emotionally, you seem like you're getting better. Why aren't you going back to school in January?"

She finishes preparing the sandwiches, slides a plate in front of me, pours some iced tea into two glasses, and sits down across from me. "I'm afraid," Rose says, running her finger along the rim of her plate.

"Of what?" After I ask, I take a bite of my sandwich, and with a mouth full of ham & cheese, I exclaim, "Holy hell, this is awesome." I swallow before continuing. "The ham. It's...wow."

Rose laughs. "Yeah, well...it came from our farm."

"What?"

"We live on a farm. My dad raises farm animals. That there sandwich was probably Missy."

I push my plate away. "What?"

"I'm joking."

I pull the plate toward me.

"We don't name them."

"Wait. What?"

"That's my father's business. We provide meat to the local butchers." She must notice the expression on my face, because she says, "It's all organic, if that helps. I'm sorry. Should I have not told you where the ham came from? I thought you knew it came from pig."

"Uh...yeah...I guess it threw me for a moment."

"If it bothers you, I can make you something else."

I laugh now. "No. I'm not a vegetarian. I eat meat. I just never knew anyone who *knew* their ham before they ate it."

"You sure it doesn't bother you?"

"I'm sure." I get back to my sandwich then, "Why are you afraid, Rose, to go back to school?"

She runs her hand along the back of her neck.

"You don't have to answer that." Maybe it makes her nervous to talk about it.

"I don't know why I'm afraid." Her fingers tap the edge of her plate. "Maybe I do. I don't know."

I continue eating while she contemplates why she's afraid.

"It's gonna be all different. People will look at me differently. I don't know. I've never worried before what people thought of me, but..." She doesn't finish her thoughts.

"I think that's something you aren't going to be able to work on by staying hidden on your father's farm."

"Would you like another sandwich? Or...a piece of cheesecake?" She effectively ignores my comment by appealing to my stomach.

"Cheesecake's perfect. Unless, of course, you killed something to make it?"

"Oh my God." She laughs. "I scarred you for life, didn't I?"

"You did. By making me eat poor ol' Porky."

She shakes her head but continues to laugh. "We just used Chicken Little's eggs. Oh, and my mom made cheese from Lady's milk."

She's got to be joking.

"Lady's our cow. And no, Mom didn't make her own cheese, but she did get the eggs from our chickens."

"Your last name isn't Ingalls, is it?"

"No. It's Walton."

"You think you're quite funny, don't you?"

She hands me the slice of cake she just cut.

"None for you?" After I ask, I realize there are only two bites taken out of her sandwich.

"Nah. I'm good."

"This is...amazing."

"Yeah. Mom's a good cook."

"You don't cook?"

"No. I'm not sure you even put eggs in cheesecake. Beth's the one who takes after my mom."

"Who's the oldest out of you and your sisters?"

"Beth. Then it's me, Patti, and Terri. We're all just about a year apart."

"Wow. That must have been crazy when you guys were younger."

"Dad says the hardest was when we all hit puberty."

"Oh I'm sure. Four teenage girls in the house? God bless him."

I love the sound of Rose's laugh. It's something I'm getting very used to. Plus it's good to know she's reached the point where she can laugh again. I hope she reaches the point where she can feel confident again, and no longer afraid of whatever it is she's afraid of.

"Are your sisters in school?"

"Beth graduated, but she still works with my dad on the farm. She got a degree in agriculture, so...it's actually what she wants to do. Patti and Terri are still in school. Patti goes to County. Terri's up in Syracuse."

"Cool. So..." I take the last bite of my cheesecake and get up to put my dishes in the huge white sink.

"You don't have to do that," Rose says as she gets up to stop me from making my way over.

"I don't mind." I walk around her and do it anyway. She's standing next to me with her plates. As I take them from her hands, I ask, "So what do you do for fun around here? Is there a movie theater nearby? We can go to a movie."

"Really? Um...I haven't been to a movie in so long."

"Then let's go."

"I...I...well, I just got home yesterday. Maybe I should...maybe another time?"

I try to hide my disappointment. I'm not so sure I succeed.

"There's a drive-in theater not too far from here. Maybe we can go next week?" she asks.

"A drive-in? They're still around? I thought they died out in the sixties."

Rose grins. "No, silly, there are still some around."

I step close to her and run my hand up her arm, "So...can I take you next Saturday night?"

Her hand grazes my chest before she snaps it away.

"I'd like that."

"Good. It's a date."

"Do you have far to drive?"

"I do. About two and a half, three hours, but I got my music."

She finds the hem of her shirt, plays with it, but sticks her hands in her pockets instead. "You sure you want to go to a movie at night next week? By the time you get home, it'll be late."

"I'm a twenty-two-year-old guy. I sleep during the day."

"You're not sleeping now."

"Because I have a reason to be up."

Rose tucks in her lips and blushes. "Are you one of those sweet talkers?"

"No, actually, I'm not," I say seriously.

"Oh."

"Listen, I know you just got home yesterday. I wasn't thinking about that when I asked if I could come up. I'm sorry if you're tired and need..."

"No, no. I'm happy you came. I didn't mean it like that before. I meant, I just shouldn't go to a movie tonight. I'm sure my mom would be more comfortable if I stuck nearby. That's all I meant."

"Hey. You don't have to explain." I take her wrist and lift her hand from her pocket. Her hand is small and warm in mine. "I should let you get settled and I have a long ride home." I'd drive for days, though, if it meant being with her. "But next week...the drive-in...you and me."

She smiles, squeezes my hand, bites her lip, and nods. "Yeah. That sounds nice."

When a twenty-two-year-old boy stands twelve inches away from a beautiful girl, it takes all his resolve not to whisk her in his arms and kiss the shit out of her. Right now, I'm testing that resolve.

"Wait a minute," she says, unwittingly helping me along. "Before, you said you were twenty-two. I thought you were twenty-one."

I raise my brow.

"November. You said your birthday was November something, but today is only the...oh my God, Ben, today's your birthday."

"Yeah, well."

"Happy Birthday." She tugs my hand and kisses my cheek.

"Thank—"

"Why...I mean...I can't believe you came all the way up here on your birthday. Why?"

"I can't think of anywhere else I'd rather spend it." Lame. Pathetic and lame. True story, though. I can't think of anywhere else I'd rather be...because I can't think of anyone else I'd rather be with.

19

ROSE

At Sunday morning's breakfast table, Mom is wearing a goofy grin. She wants so badly to ask me about Ben, and I'm trying to ignore her, but I don't know how long I can hold out. Last night she tried to ask, but I excused myself in the middle of dinner, feigning fatigue.

I don't want to talk about Ben. Yesterday was wonderful. Being with Ben was comfortable and fun, but I'm not sure I want to take things further. He'll be going back to school, baseball, getting back to his life. I'll be here, feeding the chickens and picking up poop. The only thing on my mind will be what Ben is doing and who he's with. He's an athlete with a life. Ben might be showing interest in me now, but it's probably because he's bored. Whether it's schoolwork, practice, baseball, or two-legged girls, he'll have plenty to keep him busy once he's back in school.

"So...you like Ben?" My mother asks anyway.

"He's okay. He's just a friend."

Beth narrows her eyes, and I subtly shake my head for her to keep quiet.

"Oh. I was under the impression it was more than that," Mom says.

"Nope."

"But..."

"Sam, leave her alone," my dad insists. "She doesn't wanna talk about him."

Thanks, Daddy.

Mom doesn't pry anymore, but she looks hurt. When things are going well, I'm very open to talking to my mother, but when I'm not sure where things stand, I'd rather keep my thoughts to myself. I hope Mom understands that.

***

After a fairly boring Sunday spent mostly in my room, on Monday morning, I get back on the farm, my brown work boots unfamiliar on my feet. It's been so long since I've worn them. Getting around the farm is tricky with my new leg. The divots and mud holes cause me to trip. But I manage, using my cane when I have to, and by the end of the day, I'm exhausted.

Back in my room, I take off my prosthesis to care for my leg - I still can't say the S word. I haven't quite accepted the whole truth yet, and looking at it still curdles my stomach. I grab the crutches I keep next to my bed and step into the bathroom to take a shower, where I'll sit on the chair my mother bought me so I don't fall while showering. I undress and wash in the dark, not ready to look at my scar whole. Bits and pieces are hard enough.

When I'm clean and dressed in my flannels, I slide into bed, without dinner, and turn on *Friends*. At least I'll laugh at Chandler and Joey's slapstick.

At about seven, Mom walks in with a piece of pie. "You didn't come down for dinner."

"I know."

"Why?"

"Not hungry."

She sits on the edge of my bed, blocking my view of the television. "I don't want you sitting up here all the time. It's not good for...Stop rolling your eyes at me, Rose. I don't want you alone this much."

"God. I'm not alone a lot. I was outside all day. I'm tired."

"It's not good for...for your...depression." She says

127

depression like it's a bad word.

"I'm. Not. I'm tired."

While she's sitting on my bed, I tilt my head to look around her so I can see the TV.

My mom huffs and gets up, but says nothing as she walks out and slams my door.

Sometime during another *Friends* episode, I get a text from Ben.

BEN: Hey. How's John Boy Walton today?

This makes me laugh.

ME: John Boy? Do I look like a John Boy to you?

BEN: Not. At. All. I just don't know any other Waltons. Should I have said Laura Ingalls?

ME: Better. ;)

BEN: Seriously. How'd your first day back on the farm go?

ME: It went. Tiring.

BEN: I bet. Did you cook any more of your pets?

ME: OMG. You make us sound evil.

BEN: Kidding. But it does freak me out a little.

ME: LOL. Pansy.

Ben: </3

ME: Haha. What did you do today?

BEN: Went to the doctor. Check-up.

ME: And?

BEN: Eh. They need to send me for a CAT scan.

ME: Why? :(

Oh my God. I shouldn't have put the sad face. That's implying I like him.

BEN: Don't be sad. It's just routine.

ME: Good. Can you play ball yet?

BEN: No running, but Coach wants me back for practices.

ME: When?

BEN: Now. I'm thinking of going back this week. Getting bored.

I can't respond right away. I'm thinking of all my earlier reasons for not wanting to get involved. And it's happening sooner than January.

BEN: You still there?

I lay my phone down and pick it up, repeating this several times before I text him back.

ME: Sorry. I'm here. I think that's great you're going back.

BEN: Thanks. It means I'll be closer to you too.

ME: Good.

BEN: We still on for Saturday?

ME: Sure.

BEN: Cool. Do you know what's playing?

ME: The new schedule comes out on Thursday.

My phone rings mid-text and I don't get to send it. It's Ben.

"Hello?"

"I wanted to hear your voice, and my thumbs are getting tired."

"Hey." My cheeks feel hot at the sound of his voice.

"You mind I'm calling?"

"No," I lie. I may want to talk with him, but before I know it, I'll be dating him and worrying who else he's seeing.

"So...what're you doin'?"

"Talking to you."

"Yeah but before I called."

"Texting you," I joke.

"Funny. From *where* were you texting me? Your bedroom?"

"Yes, actually." I laugh.

"You weren't sleeping, were you?"

"No. Just lying in bed watching *Friends*."

"*Friends.* Yeah, I heard it's funny. Like *How I Met Your Mother,* right?"

"Funnier. You have Netflix? 'Cause you should watch it."

"Maybe I will. Maybe I can come over and watch it with you."

"Maybe. You *are* one of those sweet talkers, aren't you?"

"I am so not one of those guys, Rose. I swear. Yes, I'm flirting with you, but only 'cause I really *do* want to come over and be with you...to watch anything. Even *Little House on the Prairie.*"

"I don't watch *Little House on the Prairie.*"

"Ok. *The Waltons.*"

"I don't watch *The Waltons* either." I clutch my stomach to stop the betraying butterflies.

"Rose?"

"Yeah?"

"Can I come over to watch whatever the hell it is you watch?"

My cheeks burn again, causing me to pause in my response.

"Should I take that as a no?"

"No, I don't mean no. Yes...I'd like that." My brain kicks itself for making my mouth say yes.

"Do I have to wait until Saturday? Can I come up sooner?"

"What about your team? Won't you be involved with them?"

"Maybe I'll wait 'til next week."

"You can do that? I thought your coach wanted you back."

"Didn't give him an answer yet. I'll just tell him I have to finish my therapy."

"You'd do that?"

"To be with you I would."

"Ben?"

"Yeah?"

"Why?"

"Why? Because I like being with you. You're...interesting."

"Interesting? I'm boring."

"What? You're not boring. I never met anyone who picked up shit for a living."

"Haha. I pick up *poop* for a college educa...tion..." I digress.

"I never met anyone who made a *sick* ham and cheese sandwich the way you do," he continues when I don't.

"Right." I chuckle, despite the recent revelation that since I'm not going back to college, I do indeed pick up *shit* for a living.

"Do I have to have a reason why, Rose?"

I don't respond.

"I like you. I met you, you intrigued me, and you still do. I want to get to know you. Is that okay?"

I squirm under the covers. "Yes."

"Good."

"But can we wait until Saturday?" I ask. "There's so much to do here...for my dad. And, well, would you mind?"

"No. Saturday's fine." His voice sounds deflated.

"I'm really sorry."

"No, don't be. Saturday's good. I'm looking forward to it."

"Me too."

"Well, listen, I'll let you go. Get some rest."

"Okay. Thanks."

"Bye, Rose."

"Bye, Ben."

Hanging up with him at that point seems wrong, premature, but I shut off *Friends*, turn off the lights, and place my phone on the nightstand, putting the conversation, and my hesitation, out of my mind.

The following morning, I wake at the call of the rooster and take my coffee to go. With my mug in hand, I head out to the barn and drink it with Cloud.

"You wanna ride?" my father asks as he enters the barn.

"What?" I ask, confused. "No. 'Course not," I whisper.

"Cloud misses you."

I look at Cloud, then to my dad. "I'm right here." I run my hand along Cloud's coat to prove my point.

"You know what I mean. It's been ages since you took him out."

"Yeah. Been kinda busy and all."

"You're not now."

Stilling my hand on Cloud, I ignore my father.

"There's no reason you can't ride, Rosebud. It's all in your head. That new leg o' yours is perfectly fine for riding."

I can feel my father's stare, but I won't turn toward him. I concentrate on breathing in and breathing out, and returning to petting Cloud.

My father pats Cloud's side. "Cloud here'll getcha feelin' like yourself again."

I'd love to feel like myself again.

"Come on. We're takin' him out," my father insists.

"Not today, Daddy. Maybe tomorrow, 'kay?"

"No." He walks away, but I know he's coming back.

My stomach rumbles, knowing he went to get my saddle. When he comes back, I'm standing against the side of the stall, afraid to move. I loved riding Cloud. Before. What if my leg doesn't move the same? What if Cloud misreads my instructions? Will I fall? Will I get hurt even worse? I don't think I could live through another serious injury.

Dad comes back with the saddle and flips it on to Cloud's back. "I know you like riding bareback, but I think we should start again with a saddle. Just for now, bud."

"Not today. Not today," I repeat and walk out of the barn.

***

In my room, in a box on the floor of my closet, is the leg my parents paid for to get me dancing again. Aside from testing it out in the doctor's office when it first came in, I haven't put it on. The leg sits in the box, a high-tech promise to give me back my dignity.

I don't believe in promises.

Not anymore.

I don't trust them, nor do I make them.

My future on Broadway had been promising. We've seen how that turned out.

I finger the machine-like leg and decide to take it out of the box. Mom's at the grocer, Dad's doing his thing on the farm, Beth's out getting new accounts for Daddy, and Patti's at school. It'd be the perfect time to try it on and maybe dance.

No.

Not yet.

I put it back in the box and tuck it away in the closet.

Then I climb under the covers and take a nap.

When I wake up two hours later, I'm too late to feed the animals. I'm sure my father took over when I ran out, but after I pick up the poop, I lug some bales of hay over to the barn. The day is long, and I suspect each day from now on will just get longer.

20

BEN

My ass hurts.

My whole body hurts.

I thought the only pain I'd have after practicing with the team for three days would be my knee. No such luck. I may not be running bases, but I *am* playing the field and I *am* pitching and damn, am I out of shape.

I got here Wednesday morning, happy to be back on the mound. Coach is making me take it easy, but I'm itching to just play a whole game again. Enough is enough already.

Tonight the guys decide to go to the bar. I'm not one for drinking much, and I certainly don't spend much time in bars, but since I have nothing to study, and they agreed to my suggestion to go to Donny's, I tag along. I'd really like to see Holly.

***

"You're looking good out there," my first baseman says on our way to Donny's.

"Thanks, Jax. Didn't realize how out of shape I was. Shit."

"Eh. You'll be back in no time."

"Yeah."

"So, Donny's? You never come out with us then you go and recommend a bar? 'S'ere a girl there?"

"No." Just her best friend. "I mean, I do have a friend who works there, but it's not like that."

"Right." He smirks. "You know, we never do see you with a girl. You go the other way, man? I mean it's cool if you do, but..."

"I'm not. Gay."

"Do you have a girlfriend?"

"No. Not since high school. I date. Not frequently."

"Why not?"

"More into the game than anything."

"Think that knee's messed up your chances?"

"To get into the Majors? No. The doctor said I should be a hundred percent by spring."

"Good. I know it means a lot to you."

"Means everything. It's all I ever planned for."

When we get to Donny's, Tony, Chris, Carlos, and Matt are already sitting at a table.

"Yo, Jax, Falco," Matt calls.

"I'll be right there," I tell Jax, then grab a seat at the bar.

"Ben," Holly yells when she sees me. "Oh my God, I didn't know you were coming." She pours me a Coke and slides it in front of me.

"Maybe I was having a beer today."

She laughs. "So what're you doing here and why haven't you called me?" she asks in one breath.

"Been busy. I'm back in my apartment with the team."

"You're all healed?"

"Not completely. But I was released with restrictions."

"Cool. So you're here. Those your friends?" She points to the rowdy table, where Adam has now appeared.

"Yeah. That's some of us."

"So you really are here to have a beer." Holly winks.

"Maybe."

She starts filling a mug with something on tap and pushes it at me, saying, "It's on me."

"Thanks."

Holly takes care of an order the waitress gives her,

then comes back. "Why you still sitting here, stud? What's on your mind?"

"Who do you think?" I take a drink of my beer while she grins.

"I love it."

"What?"

"You and Rose."

"Don't love it too much. I'm not sure she likes me."

Holly looks around, "Are you staying 'til closing?"

"Not sure."

"Why don't you? Hang with me while I close up. We can talk."

"Sure. Why not. Thanks, Holl." I take my beer and my Coke and sit with the guys.

"Looking good out there, Falco," Brian says as he sits.

"Thanks."

Drumming his fingers on the table, Adam says, "Jax, here, says you picked this place. That little bartender why?"

I drum my fingers back. "No." I mean, yes, Holly's why, but they'd never believe she's just a friend.

"So, Falco, how's the knee?" Matt asks, concerned.

"Not bad."

"Pain's gone?"

"For the most part."

"Shit, that's great. We need you, man. I mean Steve is good, but he's not you."

"True dat," Jax says.

"Hey, little lady," Brian says to the waitress, whose name I believe is Tabitha. "You my server tonight?" he asks, dipping his eyebrows up and down.

"Not if you talk to me that way. We reserve the right to refuse service. You may just find your ugly ass out on the street tonight."

"Ooh, Bri, she called your fat ass out," someone at the

table says, while the rest of us bust out screaming in laughter.

I look at Jax. "Didn't she take your orders already?"

"Not Brian. He just sat down."

"Right." I forgot.

"Hey...Holly's friend, right?" the waitress says to me.

"Yeah. Tabitha, right?"

"Yup. Been a while since you've been here."

"Ah...so the bitch is the chick," Adam says, referring to why I suggested Donny's.

I ignore him, keeping my attention on Tabitha. "Yeah, took the semester off. But I'm back in January...for school. I'm back now for baseball."

"Cool. It'll be nice seeing your cute face in here again."

Tabitha walks away, and the whole table starts on me about her.

"I'm tellin' you. She's not the reason. I like it here. The bartender's my friend and that's all."

"Yeah right." No one believes me, but they drop it and our conversation throughout the night is generic.

Many burgers and beers later, the bar signals last call, and the guys decide to call it a night.

"You comin', Falco?" Jax asks.

"No. I'm gonna catch a ride with Holly."

"So it *is* the bartender," Jax jokes.

"It's not the bartender. I'll catch you later."

***

"So what's going on, Ben? What do you mean Rose may not like you? Did you tell her you like her? She might not realize it."

"She knows. I don't know. I'm getting mixed signals."

Holly moves to the sink to wash glasses, so I slide

down the bar.

"She may not be ready for a...to date," I say. "Maybe I should back off for a while."

She raises her eyebrows at me, but continues washing. "Maybe. I feel bad I only texted her once this week. With school and work, it's been crazy, so I don't even know what she's thinking these days."

I just sit there thinking instead of responding.

"I can talk to her if you want," Holly suggests.

"No. We're not in high school."

"Eh...college kids need reinforcements too."

"What?"

"Nothing. I can be indirect about it if I talk to her."

"No. I'll deal with it. I'm gonna be busy now with ball, so...we'll see how tomorrow goes and I'll take it from there."

Holly moves on to drying the glasses. "You're seeing her tomorrow?"

"Yeah. Made the date last week, but..."

"Then she likes you."

"Ya think?"

"Rose is sweet, but she's not a pushover. She does what *she* wants. She may not want to hurt feelings along the way, and she'll find the most compassionate way to let you down, but...she won't lead you on just to spare your feelings. That's not Rose."

"Well that's good...I think. But I'm not sure we're dealing with the same Rose you knew before her accident."

"Whaddya mean?"

"I didn't know her before, so I wouldn't know, but *this* Rose is lacking in self-esteem. People who lack confidence tend to do things that make *others* happy...not themselves. At least that's what *I* think."

"Yeah, I forgot. You're farther along in your psych degree than I am."

We laugh together then she moves on to turning over chairs. To the music that still plays on the jukebox, together we turn chairs onto tables, and then I watch her mop.

Tabitha comes out of the kitchen, wearing a dirty apron and yellow rubber gloves. "Hey, gorgeous, you're still here?"

"Looks that way."

"Leave him alone, Tab, he's a *good* kid."

"He don't look like no kid to me."

With a soundless chuckle, I grab my coat from the bar stool and put it on.

"You're leaving?" Holly asks.

"Yeah, I'll talk to you later. I need to think," I say before heading toward the door.

"You sure it's thinking you need, stud," Tabitha says. "'Cause if it's something else, well, I'd be happy to oblige."

I come to a dead stop.

"You interested?"

This is why I don't come to bars and this is why I don't drink. Because I do things impulsively.

"Falco," Holly exclaims. "Get your brain outta your dick. Tabitha, he's not gonna be one of your whores tonight." I walk out the door and shake it off.

On my way up Pompton Road, Holly's white Mercedes pulls up next to me. "Get the hell in."

I do.

"Why you walking? You could have just waited for me."

"I told you. I needed to think. Besides, good thing I didn't stay. I might have taken Tabitha up on her offer."

"What? No. You don't want Tabitha, she has major problems. Besides, you want Rose, don't you?"

"Of course I do. I just meant for tonight."

"Guys. You think with your dicks, I swear."

140

"Make a left," I spit out.

"Oh. You live up here?" she asks, making the turn.

"Yup. The big house on the left."

"Nice. The whole team lives here?"

"Most of us. Thanks, Holly." I open the car door and get out.

"No prob. Let me know how tomorrow goes."

"'Kay. Bye."

Tomorrow never goes.

Saturday morning, I get a text.

She's canceled.

21

ROSE

I'm a chicken. I belong on Daddy's farm.

I text Ben I'm not feeling well and will have to take a rain check. He knows it's a lie. His text back is a mere, "Okay."

My heart is disappointed, my brain doesn't care. The thing about tonight? It would've been a date. If it went well, which I surmise it would have, we'd go on a second date. Soon, we'd be dating regularly. And besides all that *what's-he-doing-with-who-at-school-without-me* crap, dating leads to sex.

The first time having sex with me would be Ben's last time having sex with me. Sure, there's the option of doing it in the dark, but when his hand explored my body, there'd be a huge chunk missing. Dark or not, his imagination would see what I don't want him to see.

I'm not ready.

Not now.

***

Life on the farm is monotonous. Growing up, it was fun. School always came first, my mother made sure of that, but our chores had to get done. Since most of our friends' parents worked regular jobs and had no access to horses and cows and farm life, it was exciting for them to come over after school and ride - horses, tractors, whatever was ride-able. It made me proud. And once I went away to college, because I'd be away from it for chunks at a time, I treasured the weekends I'd come home to help Daddy.

Now it's all I do.

And it makes me sad.

Since the day I canceled on him, Ben stopped texting me - I deserve it.

Part of me wishes he would have fought harder, but why should he? He can have anyone he wants.

Holly texts me a few times a week, but she's been too busy with school, work, and her relationship with Mick to get into any real conversation. Not that I'd open up. I don't do that anymore.

I'm so bored that I pull my dancing leg out of the box again. I don't know why, I just do. I start touching it. Again. It's so foreign. With my hand, I bend the foot at the ankle...back and forth...side to side; it actually moves effortlessly, unlike the one I'm wearing, which is more rigid in its motions. I stare at it for God-knows how long, but that just makes me mad.

Why? Why can't things be simple? What's Your purpose for doing this to me? I just don't understand.

I stare at this thing that's now in my hands, and I curse it. Loudly. Then I put it back in its box. Again.

***

The following week, at least, is the start of our busy time, so there's a disruption of our regular farming schedule, which makes it a little less dull and a little less boring. This Thursday is Thanksgiving, so Daddy is busy preparing our turkeys for the butchers. I'd forgotten how busy it gets at the end of November.

Mom is watching me from the window. Every half hour or so, I look up at the house and see the curtains move.

Yes, Mom, I'm okay.

She worries too much. All I want though, is to be left

alone. This is my life. It is what it is, and if I've accepted it, then Mom should too.

"Why haven't you used your dancing leg yet?" she asks every chance she gets.

"Because, Mom, it's not what I want anymore."

"Then go back to school. You walk like everyone else. No one would even know."

"*Everyone* will know, Mom. They've heard about the accident."

"Then go to a different school. We can apply online."

"Sam. Enough." Dad always ends the redundant conversation.

***

"Rose," my mom says when I walk in the door, exhausted from bringing the last of this season's turkeys to the butcher. "After you take a shower, get dressed in something other than your pajamas for a change."

"Why? I'm only gonna be helping you bake pies for tomorrow."

"Yes, I know, but...well...we're having company for Thanksgiving and they're coming tonight."

"Tonight? Who?"

She sucks in a breath and I know right away I'm going to be pissed.

"Who?"

"Holly and her boyfriend."

"And her *boyfriend*? Mom, why?"

"And your friends Griffin and Cali and someone named Nathan."

"Oh my God, Mom, why? I don't want to see them now."

I storm up the stairs as best I can and slam my

bedroom door behind me.

Maybe if it were just Holly visiting I wouldn't be so upset, but she invited all of them. Why? Doesn't she get it? I want to be left alone.

I text Holly and beg her not to come, then I detach my leg, go in the bathroom, and undress to take my shower. When I'm done, I slip on yoga pants and a baseball jersey and reattach my leg. Not bothering to dry my hair, I braid it wet, stick my phone in the waistband of my pants, and go downstairs, saying nothing to my mother while we slice and peel apples for the pies.

"You look especially pretty tonight, Rosebud," my father says when he comes in.

I mumble a quick "Thanks" but return to my brooding.

Patti and Beth walk in from their two-day trip to Syracuse to pick up Terri.

"Terri," my mother squeals. "Oh, I've missed you." They embrace in a long hug and then Terri looks at me.

"Hi Ter," I say, smiling before I hug her.

"How are you, Rose?" Her tone is full of pity and verging on condescension, with a hint of sarcasm.

"Don't."

"What?"

"Don't talk to me like that. I'm fine."

"I know," she says wide-eyed. "I just..."

"Rose, she just hasn't seen you...since..."

Since the accident, or at least since I entered rehab.

"Still. I'm fine, Terri. Please treat me like normal."

She nods.

"Then why don't you act it?" Patti mutters.

"What?" I spin around to face her.

"You heard me."

"Girls," my mother chides.

145

"No, Mom, she's gotta know," Patti continues. "You mope around this house like your life is over instead of being grateful every day that you're still alive. My God, Rose, when you were lying in that hospital bed with all those machines and tubes sticking out of you...we thought you weren't gonna make it." Her voice breaks. "I thought I'd never get to talk to you again, and here you are, perfectly capable of talking and walking and going to school, and you can still be anything you friggin' want, but you sulk. And it's like you're dead anyway. Get over it already. So you have one leg. Big fucking deal. You're here. You're here, goddammit..." She can't finish because her tears have become too much.

I look at everyone and they're all just staring at me, their eyes bubbling over.

"You all feel this way?" I ask, barely breathing myself.

Every single one of them nods. Even Terri, who hasn't been here to properly give her two cents.

I huff.

And dramatically, I puff. I want to scream. I want to blow my top. *Has any one of them even come* close *to being in my shoes?*

With my two hands held up in defense, I shake my head and walk out, but not before grabbing my phone and the keys to my father's old truck.

The gas tank is empty and I have no money. I didn't even think to grab my driver's license. Because I'm in no position to run out of gas, I head up through a private trail in the woods not too far from my house and park, turning off the engine despite the cold.

My mind is all over the place - what if this? Or what if that? I know that playing the what-if game is a dangerous road to travel, but I can't help but wish I could turn back the clock five and a half months.

Then my thoughts go to Johnny. I don't know much

about what happened to him, but I do know how he ended up. Yet he never let anyone see him down. Ben says it's the thought of his mother keeping him going, but I don't understand that kind of selflessness. All I think about anymore is myself. And why this had to happen to me. It's not who I *want* to be, it just is.

I do the last thing I expect to do - I call Ben.

"Hello."

"Hi," I say much too quietly.

"Rose? Are you okay?"

From out of nowhere, I cry.

"Rose. What's going on? Are you hurt?"

Oh my God, I can't stop crying long enough to get the words out.

"Are you home?" he asks.

"No." My tongue mimics the word but it barely comes out.

"Where are you, Rose?"

I close my eyes and concentrate on breathing, while willing the tears away.

"Rose." Ben's voice loses its urgency.

"Mmm."

"You good?"

"How's..." I swallow what feels like glass in my throat. "How's Johnny?"

"Johnny?"

"Mmm."

"He's...okay. I spoke with him last week, Rose, what's going on?"

"No...no one understands."

"Understands? Understands what?"

"Me."

"You. No one understands you?"

I shake my head.

"Rose, what don't they understand?"

I hear him breathing and it's quite heavy.

"That you're having a hard time adjusting to your new life? Because, honey, I understand. I understand completely. This changes your dream. I get it. I do. Is that what they don't understand?"

I nod, even though he can't see me.

"Because *I* do. And it's okay to feel this way. It's okay, Rose. Do you hear me? It's okay."

Silence consumes us for a couple minutes before Ben speaks again. "I'm only asking this as a friend, Rose, nothing more, but do you need me to come up? I'm in Haledon still, so I can be there in less than an hour."

"No, no, that's okay, I'll be all right." My breath hitches, a belated effect from my sobbing. "Wait a minute. Are you alone? For Thanksgiving?"

"I'm fine, Rose. I just want to know if you need me to come. If not, I'm good."

"Oh."

"Rose. Are you home?"

"No."

"Where are you?"

"In the woods somewhere."

"In the woods? Jesus Christ, Rose. You're alone?"

"Yeah. But I'm in my dad's truck."

"Go home, Rose. You can't sit in the woods, even if you are in a truck. Please go home."

"Yeah."

"Will you text me when you get there?"

"Yeah."

"Yeah? You promise."

"I don't make promises. I don't believe in them anymore."

"Rose. Text me when you get home, okay?"

"Yeah."

"Better yet, put me on speaker while you drive. This way I'll know you got home."

I sniff some leftover tears.

"Rose, you're not drinking, are you?"

"I wouldn't...I wouldn't drink...and...drive."

"You don't sound okay. Are you driving?"

"No...the car is off."

"Start the car, Rose. Am I on speaker?"

I put the phone on speaker and lay it on the seat. "Yes." I do as he says and start the car, but all the crying has exhausted me and I feel like I'm going to fall asleep.

"Now head home."

I step on the gas and go forward in search of a wide enough space to turn around.

"Are you on your way home?" Ben asks, intruding the silence.

"I...I...no. There's nowhere to turn around."

"Ro...Ca...Back."

I can't hear him.

"Rose...find a...out?"

"You're breaking up."

"Ro..."

Stepping on the brake, I pick up the phone from the seat. No service and a blinking "Charge Battery" message. Instead of continuing forward, I try a k-turn right on the trail. As I put the truck in reverse, it dies. "No no no no no." I start it again, it goes. *Thank God.*

I press on the gas, it dies again.

Oh my God.

I try one more time, but I'm on a slight incline and the truck won't start. Frantically, I search the glove compartment for a flashlight.

Nothing.

"Daddy," I call out in the dark. "Come on."

Under the seat, in the cushions, under the dash. I search everywhere and find nothing to light my way back home. In the woods, it's pitch black. The light of the moon can't penetrate through the thick blanket of trees. I've traveled these trails so often in my past, but without a light, there's no way I'd make it home.

Alone without even a coat to keep me warm, I lie across the seat and decide to sleep until the sun comes up.

No sense in fighting the darkness.

22

BEN

I drum my fingers on the steering wheel all the way up to Wantage. Rose has me worried sick. She's in the woods with no phone. Common sense tells me she found a place to turn around and she's home safely in her house. My gut tells me she never got home. My overactive imagination tells me she's lying in a ditch somewhere dead.

Odds are, common sense has won, but what if?

That's why I am racing up Route 23's two-lane highway at double the speed limit. Kudos to my Honda for breaking a hundred miles per hour.

When I pull up, every light in the house is on, including the front porch light. My panic has me rapping on the door harder and faster than I should, especially since with my other hand, I'm ringing the doorbell.

"I'm coming, I'm coming." The voice on the other side sounds just as panicked.

"Ben," Rose's mother cries as she opens the door.

Even before I ask, I know the answer, but I ask anyway. "Mrs. Duncan, I'm just making sure...is Rose here?"

"No. No."

We're bombarded at the door with the rest of Rose's family...and, "Holly?"

"Ben?"

"Do you know of any trails around here where Rose would go?" I ask quickly.

"Trail?" the man, who I gather is Rose's father, asks. "Do you know where Rose is?"

"She called me from some trail. Her phone died and...and I have this feeling."

"Come with me, son." The man grabs a set of keys off a hook on the wall and leads me off the porch. "I'm Bruce, Rose's dad."

"Ben, sir. Rose's friend."

We get into a huge F350, and Mr. Duncan peels out of the driveway.

"You sure she said trail?"

"Yes. And she didn't have room to turn around. Then her phone went dead."

"Hopefully she's where I think she is. We didn't know where she went. She wasn't answering her phone. I mean...we weren't worried at first, but then my wife saw her purse was still in her room and I knew there was no gas in the old Chevy. I don't know why she took that clunker and not this truck, or her mother's car, but..." He glances at me. "Sorry, I couldn't get a word in edgewise in the house with my wife yappin' it up. Sorry."

"No need to apologize, sir."

"Call me Bruce. Please."

We turn up a dark road paved only with what seems to be huge rocks and small logs. Rose would have had to have taken a truck to pass through this. My car would never have made it.

About two miles up the trail, we spot the truck. Both of us make a run for it, because from where we are parked, it looks like no one is inside. The doors are locked when we get there, but when Bruce shines his flashlight in the window, we see Rose curled up on the seat, sleeping.

Bruce bangs hard on the glass. "Rose," he yells. "Rose."

The banging startles her awake, thank God, and she unlocks the driver's side door. "Daddy," she says when he opens it.

I'm standing to his side and she doesn't see me yet.

"What the hell, Rosebud?" He's half yelling, half laughing.

"I'm sorry, Dad. I ran out of gas and my phone died. It was too dark to walk, so I...Ben? Ben, what are *you* doing here?"

"Thank God he *is* here," Bruce answers instead. "He's the one who told us where to find you."

"I'm sorry."

"Come on, let's get you home. I'll come back in the morning to get the truck. No one'll be driving up here tonight."

"Do people actually drive up here normally?" I ask as Bruce helps Rose out of the truck.

"I'm good, Daddy," Rose says, climbing out of the truck herself.

"Not normally," Bruce says in answer to my question. "Unless of course you're my daughter."

I open the passenger-side door and Rose says, "I can't believe you came. Thank you."

"I was worried."

She hops up using her right leg and slides in to the middle of the bench. My hand not-so-accidentally grazes hers, but it's so cold, I reach for her other hand and hold both inside mine. "You're so cold."

"Not too much." But I see her straining to keep her teeth from chattering.

"Why, Rosebud?" her dad asks while backing his way off the trail. I like his nickname for her.

"Ironically, I didn't want to run out of gas."

"But you did."

"That's why I said ironically, Dad."

"Sorry they all ganged up on you before. I shouldn't have let it get that far."

"It's okay."

153

Her father keeps glancing our way after he's found a spot to turn around, and I can tell he wants to say more, but my presence is probably keeping him from it.

"You warming up?" I ask Rose quietly.

She nods and her fingers move inside my hands. I squeeze tighter, assuring her they're just fine where they are.

"I still can't believe you came," she whispers, sounding amazed.

Trying to keep my voice low, even though I know her father can hear me anyway, I say, "You call me, crying alone in the woods, and then your phone dies. That's a scene right out of a Stephen King novel. What did you expect me to do?"

"Yeah. I guess that would sound scary," she says above a whisper, "but I used to ride Cloud up here all the time. I know these trails like I know my own house. It's just..."

"It's just pitch black here in the winter, and you can't tell your ass from your eyeballs out here," her father finishes, making no sense but causing us to laugh despite that.

"Yeah. That," Rose deadpans.

***

We're back at her house, walking up the stairs, when she asks her father, "Are they all in there?"

"Your sisters or your friends?"

"My...my friends?"

"Only Holly. The others left when they found out...that you ran out."

"Didn't she get my text?"

Her father shrugs. "She didn't mention no text."

Rose bows her head and stops before we go inside. "So everybody knows I had a hissy fit."

"No, bud. Everybody knows you're struggling. That's

all."

"But Patti...did she, like, tell them..."

"No. I wouldn't let her bring that up again."

Rose nods and looks at me. "I'll tell ya later."

Her father leads the way in.

In the kitchen, standing around the island where Rose made me the ham sandwich, Holly, Rose's mother, and Rose's three sisters are chopping things.

"Hey." Holly's the first to run over. "You mind I'm here?" she asks before squeezing the shit out of Rose.

"No, I'm glad you're here. You didn't get my text before though?"

"No. I didn't. What did..."

"It doesn't matter," Rose says, practically into Holly's shoulder.

When Holly lets Rose breathe again, the sister who answered the door the first time I was here says, "I'm sorry, Rose. I shouldn't have said that."

Rose shrugs. "It's fine."

Holly tilts her head at this, then she looks at me.

I shrug, having no idea what she's trying to relay.

The sister I haven't met is rolling her eyes and pursing her lips.

I can't even fathom what was said before Rose took off in her father's truck.

Holly tugs my sleeve. "Let's give them some privacy."

Running my hand on the back of Rose's arm, I tell her I'll be in the other room.

"You were right," Holly says when we're in the front living room. "We aren't dealing with the old Rose."

"How can you tell already?" I whisper.

Barely above a whisper herself, Holly says, "When her sister apologized, the old Rose would have said, 'It's okay, but...,' and proceeded to tell her exactly why she didn't like

155

whatever it was her sister had said. This Rose just shrugged it off."

"But is that bad?"

"I don't know. To me it is. It's a sign that her self-esteem, wait...you told *me* this a few weeks ago."

"Yeah. Yeah. You're right. I wish I knew her before, just to see."

"Maybe it's better that you didn't. Maybe Rose likes it that way."

I'm contemplating that when she asks, "So why are you here, anyway? Did Rose invite you? What's been going on?"

"No, she didn't invite me. I haven't even talked with her since that night you dropped me off."

"Are you kidding me? Then what are you doing here now?"

"Out of the blue, she just...called me. Crying." I move to the farthest side of the room and sit on the loveseat I sat on last time. Holly takes the rocker. "She barely said hello before she started crying."

"Really?"

"Then...I don't know. I shouldn't talk about it behind her back. Not like she won't tell you herself. Not that she even told me anything."

"Wait. You're rambling. Why are you *here*?"

"Her phone died right after she told me she was alone in the woods with no place to turn her truck around."

"Oh." Holly's mouth turns into a cocky grin. "Man, you got it bad. You come running up because her phone died?"

I roll my eyes at my insanity. "I thought she may have been in trouble or something."

"Hey." Rose walks in.

I stand.

"You okay?" Holly asks.

"Yeah. Just feel like an ass," Rose says. "Ben, I'm really sorry you had to come all the way up here."

"I didn't mind at all." Sticking my hands in my pockets, because I'm just so nervous all of a sudden, I repeat what Holly asked. "You sure you're okay? What happened?"

"Something stupid. Do you want something to drink, Ben? Coffee, tea, cider, anything?"

"I'm good, Rose." I sit down, patting the space next to me. "Sit down."

"I feel bad that Mick and them left," Rose says to Holly.

"No. We came 'cause your mom asked. Mick actually felt funny coming anyway. And Griff and them, they only wanted to help."

"Why did my mother even ask? That was stupid."

"She's worried about you, Rose. She said all you do is farm work." Holly hesitates. I think she's waiting to see Rose's reaction.

Rose just darts her eyes to me every now and then. We don't know each other well. I'm thinking I shouldn't be here.

"Rose," Holly says. "Come back to school. Live with me at Griffin's. We'll have so much fun."

"And get to be lifelong friends," Rose adds, and Holly and she laugh at something I'm not getting.

Holly winks at me and says, "It's a line from the movie *Grease*."

"Ah. Never saw it."

"We used to watch it in the dorm," Rose adds with a chuckle. Then she looks at me. "I'm sorry I called you like that. It wasn't fair."

"I really didn't mind. But...do you mind if I ask what prompted it?"

"I can leave," Holly suggests.

"No. It's...it was nothing like that." Rose leans back against the couch. "My sister laced into me for not being grateful I'm alive...and for moping around and acting like I'm dead anyway." She looks embarrassed admitting this.

"Oh, Rose." I take her hand and squeeze it.

"I reacted sorely. I just should have shrugged it off."

"Do you think your sister is right?" Holly asks.

"Maybe. Yes."

Rose's eyes dart to mine again.

I'm still holding her hand when I say, "Really, Rose, I can leave if you want to talk to Holly alone."

"No. I don't. I want you to stay. My mom's setting up a bed for you in the back room."

"Oh, I don't need to stay."

"Please." Her eyes bore into mine and I can't help but comply. "I feel bad you had to come up; I'd hate to see you drive back down so late. Besides, it's Thanksgiving. My mom makes a ton of food."

"I'll stay."

"Yeah. He can drive me home tomorrow night," Holly adds.

"Sure," I tell her.

"Why don't we..."

"Rose." She's interrupted by her mother. "Why don't you all come in the kitchen? I put some coffee on, and we're all sitting around the table."

The three of us look at each other.

Rose shrugs and says, "You guys mind?"

"No," Holly and I both say.

We're sitting at the table about fifteen minutes before her sister Terri suggests we play Monopoly. So we do.

I'm pretty competitive and usually stop at nothing to get Park Place and Boardwalk, but I notice that Beth gets sore when I purchase Boardwalk, so when I land on Park Place, I pass on purchasing it. Making enemies with Rose's family is not my goal tonight. Terri, on the other hand, seems to find it funny that I ruined Beth's plans and broke up the two premium spots. When Beth lands on Boardwalk, I offer to sell it to her.

"Don't you dare, Ben," Terri says, leaning in close to me on my right. "Don't let her make you feel guilty. It's good for her to finally have some competition."

"Thanks, Ter," Beth says sarcastically.

I shake my head and sell her Boardwalk anyway.

"So, Ben," Terri says, rubbing my forearm before she rolls. "Are you my sister's boyfriend?" That's some question to ask while rubbing my arm, but I don't know Terri well, maybe she's just a touchy-feely kind of person.

I hesitate to answer, but I do look at Rose first. Staring into Rose's eyes, I reluctantly answer her sister. "No. I'm not." *But I'd like to be.* Saying that out loud may be a bit premature though.

Rose and I are still looking at each other when her sister asks, "Are you dating anyone?"

"No. I'm not," I say again.

"Would you like to be?" Terri continues her inappropriate line of questioning.

"Terri, stop," Beth reprimands her.

"What? I'm just interested in our new friend," she says coyly, and I'm starting to feel uncomfortable. When I look at Rose, she looks pissed.

"So, Patti..." I say, to break the sudden tension, "wanna sell me Tennessee Avenue?"

She laughs. "And let you have a complete set? I don't think so."

I end up rolling three doubles and put myself in jail.

"You ever in a long-term relationship?" Terri asks, so

oblivious to the tension she's causing for Rose.

I consider not answering, but now everyone's looking at me, including Rose. So, with my attention on her, I say, "Yes. Once. In high school."

Rose doesn't react.

"How long?" Terri asks.

"Three years," I say as unemotionally as I can. I really don't get why she's asking me all this now.

"Why'd you break up?" This question comes from Rose, and she asks it so low, I'm not sure the rest of the table heard it.

So, only looking at Rose, I tell her, "I became serious about baseball, and she wanted nothing to do with it."

Rose nods.

"Have you dated since?" Terri asks.

"Yes."

"Are you a player?" She winks this time when she questions me.

"Only baseball."

"I don't believe that," she says.

"You don't have to," I say, and I don't hide the fact that I'm getting annoyed.

"I wonder if Rose believes you." No point in having enemies when you have a sister like Terri, I suppose.

"*Does* Rose believe me?" I ask Rose.

"Yes." She does.

"Okay, enough with the getting-to-know-Ben shit," Patti says. "Rose, it's your turn."

Rose rolls the dice, and not so subtly, I move my chair closer to her.

23

ROSE

"What the hell was that?" Holly says to me once we're alone without my sisters and out of earshot of Ben.

"I have no idea. She probably wants to get her claws into Ben."

"More like into *you*. That was definitely something personal against you, Rose."

I don't bother responding to that, because I have no idea what to say.

Ben walks up and puts the last of the dishes into the dishwasher, and I plop in the pod and start it up.

"So where am I sleeping tonight?" he asks.

"You can take my spot in Rose's room," Holly offers, hopefully jokingly.

Ben and I both laugh, and I show him to the back room, where my mother pulled out the couch and made up the bed. "You want one of my dad's t-shirts or something?"

"No, Rose, I'm good. Thanks."

"Okay. Well, if you want a change tomorrow, I can find something."

"Sure."

Before I walk out, I want to make sure he knows how much I appreciate his concern tonight. "Uh. Ben?"

"Yes?" he asks, sitting down on the bed.

"Thank you again for coming tonight. I really...it was just so nice of you. Thank you."

"I'm just glad you were okay."

He smiles and the way his eyes smile with it, nearly knocks me off my feet. It's going to be harder to resist him than I thought.

***

In my room, Holly makes a big stink about how much Ben must like me because of how worried he was.

"He's just a really nice guy. He'd worry about you the same way."

"Maybe," she agrees, "but I know for sure he's crazy about you."

"He's crazy if he likes me, that's for sure."

"Tell me what really happened tonight, Rose," she says seriously now, sitting down on my bed, her paisley pajamas on her lap.

"Pretty much what I told you."

"One sister doesn't like how you're behaving and you take off? I don't buy it."

"Well...the rest of them agreed with her."

"Rose. What's going on? You're perfectly healthy. You're fuckin' cute in your little leg. I swear, it doesn't affect how beautiful you are."

"But it affects how I dance."

"That's what this is, isn't it?"

I don't answer right away. First, I go to my dresser and pull out a pair of plaid flannels and a tee-shirt, and then I sit on the bed next to her and roll up my left yoga pant leg. As I unclasp my prosthetic, I say, "The dancing is why I get depressed. I will never be what I was, and that makes me beyond sad...You can't even imagine." I lay my leg on the floor and kick it under the bed. Then I show Holly what my leg looks like without the prosthetic. I slide the sock off, keeping my own eyes from looking. "And *this* is why I can never date Ben...or anyone."

Holly's quiet for a moment while she stares at my...thing...my leg. "Rose. Why should this matter?" She touches my knee. The left one.

I look at her face in amazement. "That doesn't gross you out?"

"Gross me...Rose, of course not. Why would it gross me out?"

"Because it grosses *me* out."

She rubs my leg and hugs me with her other arm. "Rose, you're beautiful. This—" she squeezes my knee "—adds character. You survived, Rose. Be proud."

Sometimes I wish I hadn't.

"But I don't get it," Holly continues. "Why don't you want to date Ben? What's your leg got to do with that?"

I hesitate to answer at first. "Eventually...we'd have to get naked." I shrug. "I don't want him to see me like this...It's ugly."

"It's not ugly. It's just part of who you are now."

"One big ugly scar. That's what I am now."

"Rose. A fucking delivery truck hit you, and you're still fucking gorgeous...not to mention alive. Again...be proud." She pulls me into her arms. "Maybe your sister was right. You *should* be grateful."

I nod. *Of course I should be grateful.* But I'm having trouble getting there.

***

When we enter the kitchen in the morning, Ben, donned in a pair of sweats and one of my dad's t-shirts, is standing at the counter, pouring a cup of coffee.

"Good morning, sleepyheads," my mom says to us from the other side of the counter.

"Morning, Mrs. Duncan," Holly says. "Smells good."

"Thanks. Making the stuffing right now. Grab some coffee and a biscuit. Make yourself at home."

"Thanks," she says, all smiles.

Ben already has two more mugs he's pouring coffee into. "Milk?" he asks.

"Please," I say, grabbing the sugar bowl. "Sugar?"

"No thanks."

"Yes, please," Holly answers.

"Regular or maple?"

"Maple? No thanks, regular sugar is good for me," she says.

"Where'd you get the clothes?" I ask Ben. "You said you didn't need any, so..."

"I didn't. But then Terri knocked on my door and gave them to me, so I thought, 'what the heck?'"

Holly and I pass a glance to one another, before I say to Ben, "I'm sorry. I would've gotten them for you."

"No, Rose," he says, touching my elbow and pulling out a seat for me to sit, "I really didn't need them..."

"Wait a minute." Holly points a finger at Ben. "You don't find it odd that Terri came into your bedroom last night?"

"Well." Ben nods his head from side to side. "Not really. She just...well, she brought in the clothes and sat on the bed, but I told her I was beat. She left right away."

Shit. She sat on the bed?

"Uh, Rose?" Holly's eyes are raised. "How do you feel about that?"

"Holly," I whisper, inconspicuously shaking my head.

"It was nothing, Rose, really," Ben adds.

"It's okay," I say, pretending to shrug it off as if I don't care that my sister went into Ben's room late last night.

"Sounds like *she* wanted it to be more than nothing," Holly says sarcastically.

Ben's hand is suddenly on my knee. The left one. That's when it occurs to me that I forgot to sit on his left side.

"I don't *like* her, Rose," he whispers.

I nod. "Okay."

His fingers move along my thigh, and in no way is he being fresh, but I'm finding it uncomfortable because it's my left leg.

What must he be thinking while he's touching it?

Is he curious?

Is he wondering what it looks like?

Is his stomach churning from the grossness of it?

"These biscuits are awesome, Mrs. Duncan."

"Thank you, Holly."

Holly gets up to pour more coffee.

"Rose," Ben says quietly, his hand still grazing my leg. "When you called last night, you asked about Johnny. We didn't get too far with the conversation."

"Oh...I'm sorry."

"No, no. I'm just wondering...would you like me to take you to visit him?"

"Really? He takes visitors?"

"Of course he does. I think he'd love to see you."

"Really?"

"I have practice tomorrow morning, but I can pick you up at two."

"Oh...um...okay."

"Okay what?" Holly asks when she sits back down.

"We're just talking about a mutual friend."

"You two have mutual friends...who aren't *me*?"

"Ha ha."

"Someone we met in Orange," Ben says.

***

After breakfast, we all shower and change, then help

my mom in the kitchen with preparing dinner, while my sisters help my father with the animals.

"This is some spread, Mrs. Duncan," Ben tells my mom while he peels potatoes.

"Doesn't your mother cook a big meal on Thanksgiving?" my mother asks.

"Oh, sure, it just doesn't look like this. We usually have a turkey, but it's her lasagna that usually takes center stage on the table," he jokes.

"Lasagna? On Thanksgiving?"

"Mom, Ben's Italian."

"Ah. That explains it, then. What about you, Holly? What's your Thanksgiving table look like?"

Holly laughs. "Bare. We eat at the country club every Thanksgiving."

"Wow," my mother says, not at all expecting someone to say they don't cook their Thanksgiving meal.

Once we're done with the food, we set the table and call everyone to take their seats. This time, I remember to sit to Ben's left. And again, Terri sits on the other side of him.

Throughout dinner, I see Terri eyeing Ben and me. I want to say something, but I don't. Now's not the time to ask her why she needed to bring Ben clothes in the middle of the night.

"Mom, dinner was out of this world."

"Thank you, Patti."

"Yes, Mrs. Duncan, it was delicious. Thank you for having me," Ben says.

"Ditto for me too, Mrs. D."

"Oh, don't mention it," Mom tells them.

"Trevor sure was tasty," Dad adds.

"Trevor?" Ben leans in to me and asks.

"Trevor...our turkey," Dad says with a straight face.

Ben's hand flies to his mouth.

"Don't tell me you don't know where turkey comes from, son."

The whole table erupts in laughter.

"Dad. Ben doesn't like to think about that."

"What are you sayin', Rose?" Dad jokes.

I shake my head. "I'm sorry, Ben."

"I thought you didn't name your animals."

"We don't. Daddy's teasing."

"Trevor was tasty, Mr. D." Holly thinks she's funny.

Ben leans in to me again. "Your family's gonna cause me to go vegan."

I chuckle and apologize simultaneously.

"Don't laugh. I'm serious."

"Benny," Terri says, after overhearing him talking to me. "I think it's cute that you care about animals."

"I think it's more that I don't want to know I'm eating them."

"See? Cute," she continues. "So last night...in your room." Her voice is all seductive now. She's gotta know I like him. "Did you sleep well after I left?"

Holly chokes on her water.

"Uh...yeah...thanks for the clothes."

"Terri's grin is as wide as her ass," Holly whispers from my other side.

I laugh beneath my breath.

"Did anyone show you the farm, Ben?" Terri asks, her smile cunning.

"Yes, actually. Rose did the last time I was here."

"Oh," she says, her grin still wily.

"By the way, Bruce," Ben addresses my dad. "Tomorrow, Rose and I are going to visit a buddy of mine. I was wondering if you'd mind if I took Rose out on an official date afterwards."

Oh my God.

"Oh my God," Holly says.

"Oh. My. God," I hear Terri say under her breath.

"Of course I don't mind. As long as Rose doesn't."

My stomach gurgles. "I don't mind," I whisper, looking at Ben.

"Good," he says, looking back at me.

***

We're all cleaning up the dishes after dinner when Dad pulls Ben aside and says, "You like football? Let's go watch the game."

Holly pulls me aside, away from the sink and the others, and says, "Ben did that for you, you know. He totally dissed Terri for your sake."

"That *was* pretty cool."

"So."

Speak of the devil.

"I thought you two weren't dating?" Terri asks snidely, her face contorting in a sneer.

"Well...we weren't."

"And...now...you *are*?"

I don't know what her problem is. "I guess."

"God, Rose. Yes or no? Make up your mind," she says.

"*Obviously*, he doesn't want you," Holly says to my sister. "He wants Rose. Hence, the date tomorrow night."

"Ugh." Terri stomps off.

"Is she a brat or what?"

"She's really not," I tell Holly. "I don't know why she's acting that way."

"Well, don't let her near Ben. But she is right about one thing...Shit or get off the pot, because you know Cali's friend, Tabitha?"

"Yeah?"

"She made a move on him too."

"What?"

"Nothing happened. She suggested, he declined...eventually."

"Eventually?"

"He was leaving the bar and she invited him to go home with her. He stopped, thought about it, and I kicked him out."

"So, like, he would've gone with her?"

"I don't know, Rose. Probably not, but if you don't let him know you like him...he is getting other offers."

"When was this? When Tabitha seduced him?"

"Uh. I don't remember...I drove him home that night. Oh...he said he was going out with you the next...day...uh. Oh."

"November eighth?"

"It could have been." Holly shakes her head.

"So he had a date with me the next day and he was considering going out with Tabitha?"

"Having sex. Not going out."

"Oh. Helpful."

"Well, they're two different things."

I toss my hand towel onto the table and walk out the back door.

Holly follows. "Rose. He's a guy. That particular night, even though you guys had a date, which you canceled, by the way, he wasn't getting a vibe from you. He said he really wasn't sure how much you really liked him. Did you ever even tell him?"

"Well...no."

"See. He also said he thought maybe you weren't ready to date yet. That you were still struggling with the accident...and maybe he should stay away."

169

"He said that?"

"I don't remember exactly, Rose, but something along those lines. If you don't like him, that's one thing. But if you do, let him know you're ready."

"Shit."

"Or get off the pot."

"You're a freak."

"I know. But hey, you said yes to tomorrow night, so that's a start."

As we're walking across my backyard, I realize I haven't even asked how things with her have been. "Holly. I'm such a bad friend. How is Mick? I haven't even asked you, and then you had to go and send him home. Is he eating alone today?"

"Of course not. He's with his sister and his niece. He's good. Griffin and Cali are eating at Griffin's dad's restaurant. It's all good."

"But how are things with you and Mick?"

"They're great. I like having a steady boyfriend."

"Good. I'm glad."

"Yeah. You can have that with Ben too, you know."

"One step at a time, Holl."

"We're gonna have to do something about your sister, though. She's horrible."

"She's not. I'll talk with her. Something's up. She wouldn't just steal him out from under me."

"Ooh...kinky."

"Freak."

"Geek."

"There you are." Ben is standing on the patio when Holly and I return from our walk. "Your mother said dessert's on the table."

"You mind leaving right after?" Holly asks Ben. "I'd like to go see my boyfriend tonight."

"No problem. I have practice early in the morning, anyway."

Holly makes her way inside while Ben holds up his hand and silently asks me to stay put.

"Are you okay with what I said back there at the dinner table? About tomorrow night?"

"The official date. Yeah...I'm okay with that."

Ben sticks his hands in his pockets and bends his neck to look into my eyes. "I may have asked your father in front of everyone to deflect Terri's...advances? But I really had intentions of asking you out after we visited Johnny."

"Thank you. For deflecting *and* for asking."

"I'm not wrong, right? Thinking there's something between us...you and me?"

I shake my head. "No. You're not wrong. I just...I'm..."

"We'll take it slow. You need to get your life back, find the old Rose...I get that. One step at a time. Can we do that?"

"I think so."

"But can I tell you? This new Rose is pretty special. And so beautiful."

His hands still in his pockets, he bows in embarrassment. Something tells me he really isn't one of those sweet-talking guys.

"Thank you for spending the day with us," I tell him. "And for worrying enough to come up last night. It made me feel...it made me feel good." I blush under the admittance. "Let's go have dessert. My mother makes a mean pumpkin chocolate cheesecake."

"That's right...using Molly's eggs."

"Chicken Little's eggs," I correct him.

"Chicken Little's eggs." He laughs, takes my hand, and walks me into the kitchen where everyone is already indulging in Mom's desserts.

We sit next to each other, our hands still joined, understanding that something just changed between the two of us. I know I want there to be something between us, but that doesn't change the fact that I still don't want him to see me naked.

One step at a time.

We'll try it his way.

***

After Ben and Holly leave, the first thing I do is approach Terri. "Got a minute?" I ask her up in her room.

"Yeah," she says, not making eye contact.

"What was that about? You flirting with Ben."

Now she looks at me. "He said you weren't his girlfriend. So I made a move."

"What were you expecting to happen last night...when you brought him Dad's clothes?"

"I don't know. I like him. He's cute." She doesn't sound sincere.

"Yeah, well, I like him too, so...find someone back at college."

"He's not your boyfriend. He's fair game."

"When did you become such a brat? He was here for *me*. You know damn well he was."

"Still...all's fair, right?"

"Oh my God. What happened to you? You were never like this."

"Yeah, well...get used to it. We can't all cater to the poor cripple." Her eyes pop. She didn't mean that to come out, but she's not apologizing, so I do something I've never done before. I slap her.

"You fuckin' bitch," she yells.

"No. I believe that title belongs to you." I walk out and slam the door, my hand stinging, not from pain, but from guilt. I should have had more restraint. She's my sister, for goodness' sake. But, dammit, she called me a cripple.

I just get into my room when my door slams against my wall. "I can't believe you fuckin' hit me, you bitch. You think you can do anything your disabled little body wants, but..."

I sit on my bed, and with strained composure, I say, "Get out of my room. Now."

She comes at me with her fists clenched, but stops short before she swings.

"Go 'head, Terri. Hit me. But just know...this is not how we should be treating each other."

"Ugh. You're such a goody-goody."

"Terri. I'm not quite sure what has you so angry, but I never asked anyone to treat me differently. That's all you."

"No. It's *you*. Just like Patti said, your moping makes Mommy pity you, so we're all supposed to walk on eggshells around you. It sucks."

"You haven't even been home for more than a day. How would you even know?"

"Because it's all Mommy ever fucking talks about when she calls me. I can't stand it anymore."

"Then blame Mommy, not me."

"No. I blame you. Until you're back to normal, Mommy's gonna continue to baby you."

"Well, I'll never be back to normal, so just get out of my room. I don't want to talk about this anymore."

Terri stomps out of my room, leaving me to stew over her insults and my family's *real* feelings.

I take off my leg, feeling heavier than I did all day. This time, though, I don't leave in my father's truck. I stay put and fight the urge to break down.

***

I'm already about a mile down my road, just my bamboo cane and me, when I see Ben's Honda. Limping off the side of the road so he can see me, I wave for him to stop.

His car barely comes to a stop before he's out of it and at my side. "Rose, what the hell are you okay what happened?" His words rush out without a pause between them.

"Ben. Ben. I'm fine." I flatten my palms against his chest. "Calm down."

"What the..."

"I just needed to get out of the house. So I walked."

"Rose, your house is like a mile away. Why would you..." He pauses and his expression goes from eyes wide in surprise to eyebrows dipped in concern. "How's your leg?"

I hold up the cane. "That's why I brought this. But, yeah, it hurts." Walking so far on an unpaved road was stupid.

"Come on. Let's get you in the car." He wraps an arm around my waist and helps me into the car.

While he makes a k-turn, he asks, "What was so bad you had to leave the house?"

"Nothing. It's not a big deal."

"It's not a big deal it's silly? Or it's not a big deal you don't want to talk about it?"

"Both. Kinda."

He nods as he keeps his eyes on the winding road. I feel silly about why I walked out, but it feels wrong not to tell him why I stormed out of my house again. "What kind of music you like? I'm not sure what stations work up here," Ben says, fussing with the knobs on his radio.

"Pretty much nothing works up here."

"I can put my CD back on..."

174

"I bitch-slapped my sister last night."

Ben turns off the radio and takes my hand. "Let me guess...Terri?"

"Correct."

"Oh boy. She must have done something bad to cause *you* to lose your temper."

"I'm no angel, Ben. I do get mad. I usually don't resort to violence, though."

"So...what made you resort to it this time?"

Leaning my head against the passenger window, I close my eyes and sigh. When I open them, Ben's eyes are on me, not the road.

"Ben. The road."

"Oops."

I laugh and then tell him. "She called me a cripple."

His shoulders droop and he closes his eyes for a second, shaking his head as he opens them.

"You better keep your eyes on the road, Falco. I can't afford to lose another leg," I joke. Kinda sorta.

"Sorry. I can't believe she called you that. What was she thinking? And why the hell would she say that?"

"Evidently," I say slowly, "my sisters resent me."

"All of them or just Terri?"

"Patti and Terri."

"Why would they resent *you*?"

"Right? Ol' Peg-leg here."

"Oh no. I did not mean it like that. I only meant...you're having a hard time. Why would they resent that?"

"They resent my parents' treatment of me. And Terri's sick of hearing all about me."

"That sucks."

"Yeah. This morning there was this huge fight. Terri was yelling at my mother, saying she didn't even make a big deal about her making the honors band or something at school, 'cause all she could talk about was, 'Poor Rose, she can't even dance anymore,' 'Poor Rose, she's afraid to go to school,' 'Poor Rose, blah, blah, blah.'"

"I'm sorry, Rose. What's your dad say about it?"

"Well, he doesn't help, 'cause I've always been kinda his...not really favorite, but...we have a bond. Maybe it's 'cause I have red hair like him. I don't know. But...he made them cut it out this morning."

"Them?"

"Well, Terri got Patti going. Terri told them I slapped her and Mom didn't defend her. Instead, she asked what Terri did to get slapped."

Ben starts cracking up. "So what happened when you told her what your sister called you?"

"I didn't."

He looks at me longer than a person driving should.

"The road, Ben."

"Right." Bringing his attention back to the two-lane highway in front of him, he asks, "Why didn't you tell?"

"There was no need. I know she only said it because she was mad. Besides, I slapped her. She wanted to *punch* me, but she thought better of it. Which made me more mad, because I bet if I had two legs, she would have."

Ben says nothing, but he does nod.

I'm not quite comfortable sitting in silence yet with Ben, but I'm also uncomfortable sharing more of my drama, so I think of the first thing that comes to mind. "So did you really break up with your high school sweetheart because of baseball?"

He shrugs. "She hated how much time it took away from her. I mean, I was a teenage boy. I enjoyed the time I spent with her, but...she wasn't worth giving up my dream, so..."

"You dumped her."

"Actually, no. She dumped me. I was willing to stay in the relationship. I liked her. A lot. But she gave me an ultimatum, and I couldn't give her what she wanted."

"So you haven't had a girlfriend since?"

"Not really. I've had dates. I go out with girls here and there, but until..." He takes his eyes off the road again to look at me, "Well, until you, I haven't really been too interested."

Okay. I'm not blushing too much right now. Hopefully he can't tell. I gaze out my window until I feel the warmth in my cheeks dissipate.

"What about you?" he asks. "Did you have a high school sweetheart?"

"No. My father wouldn't let us date until we were sixteen, so I didn't even start seeing anyone until...my senior prom was actually my first date."

"Really?" He sounds surprised.

"Yup. But like you, most of my time was spent dancing."

Ben chuckles.

"Not that you dance, but...you know what I mean."

"Yeah. You were committed to something other than the opposite sex."

"Right."

For a moment, he looks like he's going to ask something, but he shakes his head and the look's gone.

"Were you always a pitcher?"

"Pretty much. I like being the center of attention."

"You? That doesn't sound like you."

"Just kidding. I have good focus. Besides, I suck in the outfield."

"What about batting? You good at that?"

He nods. "Again. Good focus."

"I'd love to see a game."

177

"We start scrimmaging in February. You can come to one of them if you want. The real games start at the beginning of March."

"Yeah. I'd love to." Then I remember that there will be other people at a college baseball game, so I quickly change the subject to avoid confirming a concrete date. "When will you be done with college?" Duh. He's a junior. He'll be done next year.

"Next June."

His phone rings from the dash. "Incoming call. Mom."

"I'm sorry. She'll keep calling if I don't get it. Hi, Ma."

"Benito. Are you driving?"

"Yeah, Ma. I told you, it comes out the speakers. My hands are on the wheel."

I swallow a laugh, not wanting to embarrass him.

"Benito. Did you make that appointment with the..."

"Ma. I got a friend in the car. I'll make the appointment. Been busy with baseball."

"I know, Benito, but you need that scan. I can call..."

"Ma. I promise *I'll* call. 'Kay? Right now I'm heading to Johnny's. I'll call Monday."

"Okay, Benny. Say hi to Johnny."

"Will do, Ma. Love you."

"Love you, Benito."

"Sorry about that," he says to me. "So...what about you? Are you going back? To school?"

I don't respond immediately. I would be graduating in June if I didn't miss this semester. "I don't know. Your mom sounds nice."

"Thanks. Overbearing, but nice. You're a senior, right?"

"Yeah. I love her accent."

"Yeah. Thank God I don't have it though. So you can

always finish online if you're not up to going back."

"Yeah." I didn't really think of that.

"At least you have options, right?"

"I guess." I contemplate this. Options. Do I finish online even though I'll be working my dad's farm for the rest of my life? Is that really an option? Seems like a waste of more money to me. "You have a best friend or anything?" Lame question, but I have to get off the subject of me.

"I got my team, but they're not really what you'd consider best friends. More like buddies. I like talking with Johnny. And of course Holly. She's cool. I never had a girl as just a friend before."

"Yeah. Holly is cool. But she's *my* best friend, Falco. No stealing."

"Right. I'd never do that." He holds up two fingers. "Scouts' honor."

"You were a boy scout?"

He laughs. Really hard. "No way. But isn't that what you're supposed to say when you're telling the truth?"

"Or 'cross my heart, hope to die,' but I like 'scouts' honor' better."

"Okay," he says. "Now I gotta pay attention. I've never gone to Johnny's from this way."

"You got it on GPS?"

"No."

"Falco, Falco, Falco," I tease, hoping he doesn't see that I'm really a bundle of nerves. That sitting so close to him for this long, just the two of us, is making me feel all sorts of tingles and nervous energy.

24

BEN

"Well, Duncan, why don't you take my phone right there and open the map app and help me?" he jokes.

I take the phone out of its holder and laugh. He gives me the address and I punch it in.

"Oh. We're close. Two more blocks make a right and then...a left onto Washington Place."

"Thanks."

When we pull up to the small crowded cape, the first things I notice are a makeshift wheelchair ramp and a gutter filled with old leaves.

"What a cute house," Rose says as I turn off the engine.

"Yeah."

Rose hasn't quite gotten out of the car when I reach the other side.

"You okay?" I ask, wondering if her legs still hurt from her walk.

"No, no. I'm fine. Just slow moving. I am a little nervous though."

"Don't be. He's happy to have you here."

"You told him."

"Oh yeah. I never wanna show up unexpected."

His mother answers the door, runs us through the sanitizing routine, and brings us to his room in the back. "Isaiah is with him now, but they're done with therapy."

"We can wait," Rose suggests.

"Nonsense. Isaiah's great. He won't mind at all."

"But Johnny?"

"No. Johnny won't mind either. He's coughing a lot

again, so just keep a little distance. With his oxygen, he doesn't really cough, but he's stubborn and won't use it while you're here."

"Oh."

"His lungs struggle, but he's okay."

"If it's a bad time..." I start to say, but she stops me.

"Please," she says almost desperately. "He *needs* to see you."

"Of course."

Johnny is staring out the window while his therapist sits ankle over knee on a recliner.

"Dude. Is that how you greet your guests?"

He spins his chair around and smiles when he sees us. "Wow, Rose." His greeting is interrupted by his cough. "You look amazing."

"Oh, thank you, Johnny. I'd kiss you, but your mom said..."

"Don't listen to my mother, she's just protective." Johnny wheels himself over and Rose kisses him on the cheek.

"Hi. I'm Ben."

"Isaiah."

I sit on the couch alongside the wall. "How's it goin', John?"

A couple coughs later, "Not bad. You meet Isaiah?"

"Yeah."

"Hi," Rose and Isaiah say to each other.

"These are my friends Ben and Rose."

Isaiah nods.

"So, Rose," Johnny coughs. "How's recovery going? You're walking so well." Johnny's tone almost sounds as if his sentiment isn't genuine.

The slight drop in Rose's shoulders as she sits confirms she recognizes it too.

"Recovery's going okay," Rose answers. "What about you?"

"Eh. You know."

"He's doing wonderfully," Isaiah says. "Had some movement in his fingers."

"Really? Dude, that's excellent."

"Yeah. Look what I can do." The middle finger on Johnny's right hand slowly rises off his hand pad.

"Nice," I say before flipping him off and cracking up.

Rose looks like she doesn't know how to react.

The tension has lifted and Isaiah excuses himself, informing Johnny he'll be in the next room.

"Does he stay with you?" I ask. "Is he your PT or is he a nurse?"

"Both. He's my nurse, but he does therapy with me too."

"He lives here?"

"No. I think Mom wishes he could though."

"She could use the help?"

"That. And I think she likes him."

"That bother you?"

"Nah. I mean, she needs *somebody* to take out the garbage." He laughs. Again, Rose isn't getting Johnny's humor. Not that I think he's laughing on the inside though.

"Don't be so quiet, Rose. What's going on?"

"Not much. I hang home most of the time." She pauses. "Actually, all of the time."

"You don't go out."

"No. To the butcher and back, that's about it."

"The butcher? You like meat that much?"

This gets her laughing.

"Get this," I say. "Her family eats their pets."

"Oh my God, we do not. We don't, Johnny, he's just..." She elbows me.

182

"Do you or do you not own your animals?" I joke.

"Stop." She laughs.

"Do you or do you not kill these animals and cook them?"

"Shit," Johnny says.

"Johnny, my father's business is raising livestock for the local butchers, restaurants, and markets. It's an organic farm and we don't eat our pets."

Johnny cracks up. His laugh is accompanied by hacking coughs, but if he could throw his head back in laughter, he would.

The joking continues until finally Johnny says, "So, Rose, what the hell you doin' staying on the farm? Ben says you're a senior. Don't you want to graduate?"

Rose looks at me.

"Hey, we're friends, we talk," I say, explaining why Rose came up in my conversation with Johnny.

"I don't know," she tells him.

"You afraid of what people will say?"

She shrugs. "Maybe."

"I'm afraid too."

"You are?"

"But you don't let that hold you back, right, man?" I ask.

"No. I don't let what people *think* hold me back. I let my own noodle legs do that."

"That...Hmmm." Johnny's different. "I was telling Rose how you're gonna be the next Stephen Hawking. Gonna make millions for your mom, right?"

Johnny's silent for once in his life. Then he starts coughing. When he doesn't stop, I get up and locate the tubes that weren't attached to his chair last time I was here.

"How's this thing work, dude?"

"I don't need the oxygen, Ben."

"Won't it help your cough?"

"I don't really give a fuck," he says between hacks.

"Dude, what's going on? Do you not like Isaiah hanging around?"

"I love Isaiah hanging around. My mother needs him."

"He's your nurse."

"But he's a man. Who happens to laugh at all my mother's lame-ass jokes."

"What's the problem, then?"

"I'm tired. Rose, you got two working legs. You may not have been born with one of them, but they work. Get the fuck off the farm."

Rose writhes in her seat and nods.

"Don't give up, dude," I tell him. "You sound like you're giving up."

"Don't worry. I'll still be here next week, next year, a decade from now...if God doesn't quit this cruel joke of His."

I look at Rose, uncomfortable now. Bringing her here was a mistake. Maybe Johnny just needed *me* here today.

"Hey, bud. Why don't I bring Rose home and come back?" I look at Rose, who is nodding in agreement.

"No. No. I'm sorry. It's..." He can't finish this time, because his coughing gets out of hand, so I go grab Isaiah and bring him back.

"John. I knew this would happen. I shouldn't have allowed you to take it out."

Isaiah turns on the machine and sticks the tubes up Johnny's nose.

Rose walks over to Johnny and sits on the coffee table in front of him. "It's getting to you," she acknowledges.

He blinks.

"Your life's not what you'd planned. It's like someone slipped the rug out from under you."

"Yeah. And now I have no way of getting up."

"You say my legs work, but I feel the same exact way as you do. I had plans. Now I don't."

"Rose. Make new plans. I get it. You were a dancer, right? Well...now you can't dance. But you can live. You can sit, you can stand. You know what? I can stand too. Watch this."

Johnny maneuvers the mouth tube on his chair with his tongue and he slowly rises. His chair stops when it reaches full height and he's nearly in standing position. "I can fucking stand. How 'bout that? Now what can I fucking do with that?"

Rose drops her head.

Johnny comes back down. "I'm sorry, Rose. It beat me. I was trying, you know, for my mother's sake."

For the first time ever, I see Johnny cry. It doesn't take long for Rose to follow.

"What made you...so happy before? If you don't mind my asking."

"Hope."

"You don't have it anymore?" she asks.

After some heavy inhales, he says, "I can't even flip a decent bird. Chances are I won't get much movement past my fingertips."

"What about the whole Stephen Hawking thing and your hi-tech computer?" I ask.

"Mom needs somebody to pay the bills."

"And?"

"Maybe Isaiah will take that place," he says seriously. I realize his garbage comment was not a joke at all.

"So what? You just sit here 'til the end of time? How's that any better?" Now I'm mad.

"I can't even play my fucking video games. They set me up with this thing—" he looks down at some square thing on his chair "—but I gotta fuckin' blow into it to make moves, and it's so fucking slow it's lame. Maybe I'll just write movie reviews. All I do is watch movies all the damn time."

"Then write fucking movie reviews. Don't just sit here and give up."

"Easy for a two-legged, perfectly capable baseball player to say."

"Okay," Rose chimes in. "Let's not do this, please."

"I'm sorry, Rose," Johnny tells her.

"Yeah. Sorry," I repeat. "Johnny, let me bring Rose home and you and I can hang out. Can I crash on your couch tonight?"

"Really?"

"Yeah."

About fifteen minutes later, Rose and I are in my car pulling away from the curb.

"I'm really sorry about canceling our date tonight, Rose. I just think he really needs a friend right now."

"Please don't apologize. I think he needs a friend too. I feel so bad. I wasn't...well...you told me how together he was, so I wasn't expecting him to be like that, but truthfully...that's how I would have originally thought him to be. It amazed me that he wasn't."

"Really? You think he's acting normal?"

"In my opinion, yes. I mean look at me...and like he said, I have two working legs...yet I still can't get over it. I'm glad you're his friend, Ben. He needs someone like you."

I am sad the whole car ride home and I think Rose feels it, because she doesn't talk much and neither do I. Our date tonight is important to me, but something tells me Johnny's life is at stake here. He doesn't have the means to end it, but I could see in his eyes that he wants to. I'm pretty sure Rose suspects something like that too, but we don't talk about it. We ride in silence instead. Not even the radio is turned on.

Back on the last stretch of road that leads to Rose's farm, I remember that things weren't going too well with her sisters. "Rose, are you gonna be okay at home? It just occurred to me that you and your sisters had an argument."

"I'll be fine. It was just a sister thing." She pats my hand on the gearshift. "Please don't worry about me. Worry about Johnny. He really needs you. I'll be fine."

In her driveway, I put the car in park and turn toward her. "I really do want to take you out on a date, you know."

"I know," she says, smiling. "We'll get there. This is important."

"Yeah."

"Ben?"

"Yeah?"

"You seem...very compassionate for a college guy. Maybe that's why you're in the field you're in and all...but...I don't need for you to...*fix* me. I hope that's not why you're here."

I shake my head. "No, not at all."

"I mean, you came to my rescue the other night. That was sweet. You saved me from a cold night in the truck. But please don't feel obligated to be with me like you do Johnny."

"I don't feel obligated to be with Johnny. Not because he needs fixing or I feel sorry for him. I like him. Isn't that what friends do? Aren't friends there for one another when they need them?"

"Of course. Of course that's what friends do. I'm sorry. I am. About saying that about you being obligated. I didn't mean that. Just...please don't try to heal me." She pauses, but then says, "I might not want to be healed."

I nod, not quite sure how to take that. Why wouldn't she want to get better?

I open my door to get out and walk her to the porch.

"I don't want to fix you, Rose. That's not what I'm about. But...when I care for somebody, I can't help it if I want to take care of them."

She nods, hopefully in understanding.

"Can I take you to dinner tomorrow night?"

"Yeah. I'd like that."

I reach for her hands, hold them, and kiss her goodbye. Letting my lips linger a moment or two.

She goes inside, closes the door, I walk back to my car, and I drive back to Totowa in silence, stopping home only to pick up a pair of sweats and my toothbrush.

***

When I get to Johnny's, he's staring out the window again, while Isaiah is reclined watching a movie.

Isaiah is first to acknowledge me. "Hey, Ben."

"Isaiah. Hey, John."

He circles around and he blinks.

"What movie you watching?" I ask them both, figuring they started out watching the movie together, before Johnny lost interest.

"Mission Impossible," Isaiah says. "Netflix."

"Never saw it."

"Neither'd Johnny," Isaiah says, showing no expression. "But I've seen enough. Johnny, if you need me, just beep."

"Beep?"

"He's got a button there on his chair pad to call me."

"Oh."

I toss my bag in the corner and sit on the couch near Johnny. "What's going on, man? Why the sudden change?"

"It's not sudden. I just don't have the energy to pretend anymore."

I nod. "Do you talk to someone about it?"

"I meet with someone. She comes in three times a week. Do I talk? No."

"Why?"

"Talking's not gonna make my arms move. God. Not having use of my legs I can deal with, but do you know what it's like to be in a straitjacket twenty-four seven? That's what it's like. A fucking straitjacket."

I nod again. What more can I say? I don't know what it's like and if I did, I'm sure I'd be as angry as he is. Rose is right. This has to be the normal reaction to his situation.

"You ever think about being caught in a burning building?" he asks, and I'm sure it's rhetorical, so I don't answer. "Well, I do. 'Cause I dream it every night. Every night, I'm trapped. Behind some huge block of steel. Flames are blazing around me. I have nowhere to go. I'm trapped. And I can't get out. I watch the flames creep toward me. It feels like the sun crashes on friggin' top of me. The sun. That's how hot it is. Every night I get caught on fire. Every. Single. Night. I catch on fire. It's like a goddamn episode of Groundhog Day. Only I don't get the girl at the end."

By now, streams of tears are running down both our faces. We're too caught up in emotions to worry about showing our vulnerabilities to each other.

Silence surrounds us and I'm at a loss for words still. A bird trapped in a cage. With no room to flap his wings. It must be torturous, and I don't even know how to ease his pain.

"I'm so sorry," I finally manage. "Just. So sorry."

"I didn't mean to bring you down. That's why I didn't want you to come back. I'm too tired to pretend it's gonna all get better."

He stares at me. "If you weren't such a good guy, I'd ask you to put a pillow over my head tonight after Isaiah puts me to bed."

My body tenses. I don't know how to respond to that.

"Don't worry. I wouldn't ask that of you." I hear the disappointment in his voice.

"This may sound absurd, but why don't you go to college like you planned?"

"It is absurd. College is not a place for someone like me."

"That's not true. You already have a daily nurse. Let Isaiah help you to classes. I see people in wheelchairs all the time at school."

He blinks his eyes.

"You're so fucking bright, John. The technology is there. Look at the way you maneuver that iPad. Give it a try."

His eyes are cast down, but I can tell he might be thinking about it.

"Take one class in January. Don't matriculate. See if you can handle it."

"I can't."

"Why not? Give me one good reason."

"'Cause I'm still in high school."

"Oh, geez. That's right. You still have your tutor?"

"No."

"No? What happened?"

"I stopped learning. I stopped responding to her. When it finally sunk in that I wasn't getting any better."

"Get her back, John. You still have a brain that functions on the genius level. You can do so much with that. You can still be an engineer. And homework will keep you busy, and you'll...you'll still have a life."

"You make it sound so fuckin' easy, Ben. I'm a goddamn cripple. It ain't gonna be sunshine and roses for me. *Ever*. Just...stop trying to make things better. It's not gonna happen."

I shrug it off. I guess I am simplifying his condition. Rose's too. Maybe I'm not supposed to fix things for the people I love. Maybe I just have to sit here and agree with them. *Yup. Your life will be nothing but suffering. I agree. Your life sucks.*

I have a lot to learn.

Until I walk in their shoes I guess...

25

ROSE

I have no idea why it's bothering me so much tonight, but it's killing me to know. Maybe it's what Johnny said about making new plans. Maybe it's because Ben looked so disappointed when he realized Johnny had lost hope. Maybe it's just finally time. I really don't know, but tonight, I pull out that box, take the leg out of it, and put it on. Tonight, I'll know for sure.

Even though it's the middle of the night, with my dancing leg clasped on, I make my way to the studio my dad had built several years ago in the basement. It's complete with ballet barre, wood floor, and floor-to-ceiling mirrors. My own haven once upon a time.

The small stereo sitting in the corner is dusty, and my dance compilation CD is still waiting in the player. I turn it on and let the music fill the room, hopefully finding its way back into my soul.

My mind wanders all over the place as I stand at the center of the barre. I do some quick warm-ups and stretches while my dancing life flashes before my eyes. Taunting me is my first recital. My first solo. My first honors performance. My first time competing. My first appearance on Broadway - a rehearsal - the farthest I will ever go.

When the images stop, I catch sight of myself in the murky mirror. With my hand, I streak it, and see the tears on my face. I hadn't even realized I'd been crying.

Sucking in my snot, I go over to my bin of dancing shoes and pull out my old ballet slippers. With trembling hands and a shaky breath, I slide them on my bare...feet? Does a plastic foot count as bare?

My heart races as I stand, looking at my feet. Can I do this without breaking down?

Stepping into the center of the floor, I close my eyes, take a deep breath, and wish to God I could travel back in time and go with Jordan to the apartment instead of heading to rehearsal by myself. I may not believe in promises anymore, but a part of me would like to believe in magic.

My eyes still closed, I bring my new foot toward the inside of my good knee and attempt a fouetté turn.

I complete three in a row, but I'm rusty.

I do three more with my right foot on the floor before attempting one on my left.

Just lifting my right foot off the ground causes me to lose my balance, but I right myself and try again. This time, I tuck in my core, breathe deep, and envision myself doing one before I actually do it. Inching my right foot up, I place it into position and...

Fail.

I fall when I attempt the turn.

My ass on the floor, I drop my head in my hands and wonder why the heck I even try.

A few minutes more of sulking, I pick myself up and go to the barre. And practice the fouetté turn without the spin. When I don't get it exactly right, I move on to some easier positions, but not without major disappointment. I spend nearly an hour in the basement, with nothing to show for it, so I take off my slippers, turn off the music, and get back to my room before anyone wakes up and realizes I've been down there. I put my dancing leg away, lotion up my leg, and cry myself to sleep.

***

I know something is wrong the minute I open the

door.

His hands are sunk deep into his jeans pockets and his smile lacks mirth.

"Hey, beautiful," he says and kisses me on the cheek.

"Hey," I say back.

"Mind if we keep it low-key tonight?"

"Not at all. You okay? We don't have to do this."

He takes my hand, walks me to his car, and says, "Are you kidding me? Knowing I was seeing you tonight was the only thing keeping me going."

We get in his car and start driving. "I Googled some places around here and found this cute little cafe upstate. It's about thirty minutes away."

"Oh yeah. The Treemont."

"You've been there?"

"No. Beth has. She's mentioned it a few times."

"Good. Your first time will be with me."

Goodness gracious, this makes me blush.

I think he realizes what he just said, because I see him tuck in his lips, and his cheeks look red.

"Are you okay, Ben? You seem sad."

He nods. "I'm okay."

"Things aren't good for Johnny?"

He shakes his head. "No."

"It's gotta be hard."

"Yeah. For you too, I guess."

"For different reasons. But...I don't want to talk about me."

Ben turns on the radio and fusses to find a clear station.

"You're not gonna find much."

He presses a button and One Republic's "Ordinary Human" comes on. "You mind listening to this?"

"No. I like *One Republic*."

194

That's the last thing we say to each other until we're seated at The Treemont, where the lights are dim and I don't have to worry if he'll see all the makeup covering my scar. "It's nice here. Feels like we should be somewhere in Vermont."

"Yeah. It does. Like one of those bed and breakfasts."

"Definitely."

We look at our menus, and I realize things have become awkward. Maybe it's because I didn't want to talk about me, but I was being honest. He wants to make things better for me. He wants me to just be grateful. Just like my sisters. But I'm not grateful. All I ever wanted to do was dance for an audience. And once I'd fulfilled that, I wanted to teach dance. Now I can't do either. Especially after proving it to myself last night. So I'm going to sulk. Might not be mature of me, but it is what it is. I'll learn to be content on the farm, but I don't want anyone to try and convince me that my life can still be fulfilling. If I can't dance, it won't be.

The waitress takes our order, and now we're sitting there staring at our beverages. I have to cut through the tension. "So...you'll be going to Florida next month. You excited?"

"Well...I'm not excited, but I am looking forward to it."

"Did you have practice this morning?"

"Yeah. Coach finally let me run bases." He smiles.

"Good. How'd that feel?"

"Invigorating." After he says this, his smile drops.

"Something wrong?"

"No, no. It felt good to let loose again."

"Knee's good?"

He shrugs. "Pretty much, yeah. What'd you do today?"

I show him my nails. "Patti insisted we all go for a

manicure."

"Peach. They look pretty. Did you all go?"

"Yup. Terri too. To make peace."

"Good. Sisters shouldn't fight."

I crack up. "That's all sisters do. But...we also make up. You have siblings?"

"One sister, one brother. Both older."

"Oh. Nice. What are their names?"

"Maria and Dominic."

"Nice Italian names."

"Johnny wants to die," he blurts, his face sullen again.

"Oh my God."

"He wanted to ask me to put a pillow over his face."

"Oh my God."

"If I wasn't so nice a guy, he said."

I just stare at Ben in disbelief.

"Of course, I can't. I wouldn't do that, but...you think it's that bad that death would be *better*?"

"I don't know, Ben. There was a time I wanted to die. Sometimes...still...I...entertain the idea."

"Oh my God, Rose," he says loudly. "No. You are perfectly healthy and..."

"Ben. Johnny...let's talk about Johnny."

Ben drops his head in his hand and doesn't look at me.

"Ben. Look at me."

He does.

"I don't know what to say about Johnny. I don't even know what to tell you to do."

"Yeah."

Fortunately, the waitress brings our food and we don't have to talk for a bit. I eat my omelet in contemplation of what to talk about to change the mood between us. But then he reaches for my hand. "Don't consider this our first date,

Rose. We can do much better."

"It's not so bad."

"It is. And not because of you. Please know that. I just...I can't stop thinking about Johnny. I can't imagine being so depressed."

"Did you know him before rehab?"

"No. But I liked him right away. He's funny. Joked all the time."

"Can I get you anything else?" the waitress asks, picking up our plates. "Dessert? Coffee?"

"Rose?"

"I'll have a cup of tea, please."

"I'll have...coffee's good. Long drive home," he says to me. "Rose. What are you doing tomorrow? Can I come up?"

"Really?"

"I promise. I'll be happier."

"I don't mind if you're sad. I wish you weren't, but..." I trail off, nowhere really to go with that.

"Does that drive-in show movies during the day?"

"Well...no...not dark enough."

"God. I'm so stupid. That's right."

"Plus. I think they stopped showing them now, since it's too cold."

"We can go bowling. Do you bowl?"

"Um...not since...I don't know. We can rent a movie," I suggest. I really don't want to do anything remotely athletic.

"Renting a movie sounds good. Where? I thought rental places were gone."

"Well...we can demand a movie. But can you believe we still have a place that rents movies?"

"What?"

"Yup. At The General Store."

"You have a general store?"

"Yes, sir."

"You really do live on Walton Mountain."

"I don't think the Waltons had video rentals at their general store."

"Ooh...this town's hoppin'," Ben jokes.

"Thank you," we both say to the waitress when she brings our coffee and tea.

"A movie sounds good. I got a load of laundry to do in the morning, I can come up about one...or two, if I sleep late."

"Or...you can do your laundry by us and come up for breakfast. Sunday mornings Mom makes a big breakfast, and Terri's going back tomorrow so she can only flirt with you for an hour or two." I laugh so he knows I'm kidding. Kinda. Sorta.

"Your parents won't mind if I'm there?"

"No. They like you."

"Okay. I can do my laundry at night, though. I won't bring it."

"You can, you know."

"That's okay. What time's breakfast?"

"Usually 'bout ten. After Dad feeds the animals and stuff."

"Sounds fun."

"It isn't, but..."

Ben laughs, then finally takes a sip of his coffee. I'm almost finished with my tea.

"So," he says, "you like One Republic. What other bands you like?"

"Well. Don't tell anyone. Holly would stop being my friend, but...I like country music."

"Of course you do, half-pint."

"A Laura Ingalls' reference now?"

"I'm teasing. But it makes sense you like country

music up here in farmland."

"Most of us hillbillies do."

"So who are your favorites?"

"Keith Urban. Hands down. But...I really like them all."

"I've heard of Keith Urban. He's that guy on *Idol*."

I laugh. "Yeah. That's him."

"Who else?"

"Tim McGraw, Zac Brown Band, Eric Church."

"I've heard of Tim McGraw. The dude married to Faith Hill."

"Yup. Who do you listen to...besides One Republic?"

"I'm pretty mainstream. Not too big into music, but I like..."

"Wait. A college guy not into music? That's like a college guy not into booze and sex."

When he raises his eyebrows, it clicks.

"You're not a normal college guy, are you?"

"I think I am."

"You don't drink?"

"I do. I don't make it a routine though."

"And sex?"

"Occasionally, but...I'm not a freak, I promise. I just have a definitive plan for my future, and those things get in the way."

"And that's making it to the Majors." I don't ask, I state. I know this is his plan.

"Yes. And then when I'm done there...psychology."

"To sports dudes."

"That's the plan."

"Do you ever wonder what you'd do if you don't make it?"

"No," he says as a matter of fact. "That would distract me. Putting doubt there. I can't have doubt. That's just a recipe for failure."

I just nod. That's how I thought when it came to dance.

"Look, I'm not being an arrogant dick. I've practiced all my life to get there. I'm one of their top picks. I've already had recruiters contact me. This spring is a big year for me, and if I start talking like I might not make it, well then, the whole way I play changes. I lose confidence. I can't afford that."

"I get it. I don't think you're arrogant at all. I was nodding because...well...my attitude was pretty much the same before." I shake my head, not really wanting to go there. "But...so I understand. You're right. You can't get distracted."

My cup is empty, but I bring it to my lips anyway.

"No. You don't think I'm conceited?" He asks this, but I can tell he'd rather be asking about me. I slipped up by mentioning it.

"Of course not. You're far from it. You're dedicated. Committed. I admire that."

"Thank you."

He puts down his cup and I can tell it's empty.

"Wanna get going?" he asks.

"Sure."

In his car, he searches again for a music station. "I don't have any country CDs."

"I like One Republic. That's fine."

He's still searching the radio.

"But if you really want country, 96.1 should come in clear."

He tunes it to the station and it's right in the middle of "Who Says You Can't Go Home" by Bon Jovi.

"Bon Jovi? I thought this was a country station?"

Shaking my head, I laugh, saying, "But he sings this with the lead singer of Sugarland. A country band."

"Ah."

Several country songs and a buttload of commercials later, we're at my house, and Ben walks me to the door.

"Thank you for tonight, Ben. I had a really nice time."

Right away, my hands are in his. "I'm sorry I wasn't the best of company. I promise tomorrow I'll be happier."

It's funny how easily Ben promises things. Doesn't he realize that circumstances can make a promise a lie? "It's okay. Your friend is hurting. And if you're sad tomorrow, that's okay too."

"Thanks."

For a moment, we stare into each other's eyes. His are sad and it makes me feel bad. He's trying to read mine, questioning whether it's safe to kiss me? I'm not sure. I do want to kiss him. Taste him. See what it's like to be so close to him.

But before I get the image out of my head, the thought of his tongue out of my mouth, Ben leans into me, hugs me, and kisses me on the cheek.

"So breakfast. Ten o'clock."

"Yup. Breakfast is at ten."

"See you in the morning, half-pint," he jokes.

"See you in the morning."

***

After Ben leaves, I'm too wound up to sleep, and it's quite early anyway, so I open up my laptop and search 'disabled ballerinas.' Like I had found out in therapy when I was in the mental ward, there are plenty. And they seem to be doing well. But are they where they want to be? Were they better before and now have to *accept* their limitations? I don't want limitations. But I really want to dance again. I miss it. I want to get lost in the music while I'm on the dance floor, but with my leg tripping me up, it's just not going to happen.

Two hours of Googling later, I put on my dancing leg and tiptoe the best I can down to the basement again, making sure not to wake the now sleeping house.

I turn the stereo on low and start with the barre. I warm up, do my stretches, then try again to be as graceful as possible.

After an hour of stumbling and falling, instead of actually dancing, I've had enough. Not as quietly, I make it back to my room, and after practically ripping off the prosthetic, I go to bed, not bothering with my usual routine of brushing my teeth and caring for my leg.

Because I'm tossing and turning instead of sleeping, I hear my phone when it dings.

HOLLY: Hey. U up?

I sit up and text her back.

ME: Yup. What's up?

HOLLY: Come to Donny's tomorrow.

ME: Can't. Ben's coming up.

HOLLY: Bring him.

ME: I think I'll pass. Thanks tho. How r u?

HOLLY: Not good.

ME: WHY?! What happened?

HOLLY: I miss my BFF. :(

ME: Oh.

Not surprisingly, my phone rings.

"Yeah?" I say when I answer it.

"Oh? That's all you have to say?"

"What do you want me to say? I miss you too, but I don't want to go to the bar."

"You don't come out anymore, Rose."

"That's not true. I went out to dinner with Ben last night."

"That's good. But have you seen any of your old friends?"

"Holly. *You* are my old friends. Everyone else is just people I hung with with you."

"Yeah. And they miss you too."

I'm just too tired to respond anymore.

"What about next Friday night? I have off. Are you busy?"

"No. You wanna come up?" I ask, always happy to see Holly.

"Griffin's having a party." Dammit. "He hasn't had one in a while. Come with me. I'll ask Ben too. Not that he comes to parties, but with you there, he may," she rambles.

"Holly. No. I'm not up for a party."

"Come on, Rose. You can't stay up on your farm all the time."

"I like my farm, Holl."

"You know what I mean."

"I do. And you know why I don't want to come to the party. Just...have fun. Tell Griffin and Cali I said hi. I gotta go. I'm beat."

"This isn't over, Rose."

"I'm sure it's not. Good night, Holly."

"Night, Rose."

I do miss the gang at Hunter Hill, but the last thing I want to do is show up at a party with my fake leg and my scars. No, vanity is not pretty. But I feel as ugly as a hairless cat and I'm sure I'd arouse as many shock-filled gasps as one if I showed up.

***

Ben arrives twenty minutes before ten, holding a big white bakery box.

"You didn't have to bring anything."

"I wanted to. I stopped at the bakery on Belmont."

"Oh my God, I love that place. Crumb buns?"

"Yup. My favorite."

"Mine too."

We're smiling when we walk into the kitchen, so Mom says, "What are you two up to?"

"Morning, Mrs. Duncan."

"Morning, Ben."

"Mom, Ben brought crumb buns."

"Thank you, Ben. You didn't have to."

"I didn't mind," he says, placing the box down on the counter.

"Hey, Ben," Terri says from behind us.

I turn and plead silently, "Please don't," by mouthing the words. Ben made it clear he didn't like her, but I really like him, and I don't want her flirting with him and messing it up.

"Hi, Terri," he says with a benign smile.

She opens her mouth, but when her eyes meet mine, she snaps it shut and helps my mom at the counter.

Ben helps me grab the plates from the cupboard and we set the table. "You look pretty today," he whispers while placing napkins next to the plates I set down.

"Thank you," I whisper back as we make our way around the table. This morning, on top of my primer, concealer, and foundation, I brushed on some peach blush. Usually, before *and* after the accident, I'd stay away from colors - blush, eye shadow, eyeliner. Most times, I'd only fuss with styling my hair. Since Beth showed me how to apply the Spackle that covers my scar, I spend more time on *that* than my hair. Today, though, I did both, plus I added the blush and a little brown mascara. Ben noticed. Mission accomplished. I hate like heck to have to continue this routine, however. But I do feel prettier today than I did yesterday, and thus, less self-conscious.

Breakfast goes off without a hitch. Terri refrains from flirting, and conversation is pleasant and harmless. Amid the chatting, laughing, and eating, Ben keeps his left hand on my right knee the whole time. It benefits me that he's right handed and I try most times to sit to his left. It's a win-win for me.

My father chews off Ben's ear while my sisters and I help my mother clear the kitchen. The whole time, Ben is looking at me apologetically. I think he's learning that my father is the stereotypical man of the generation before him. My mother lets it be, explaining that he works very hard on the farm and it's her duty to take care of the house. It works for them. But my sisters and I learned early on that we'd much rather tend to the chickens than do "women's work" in the kitchen. My father, having no sons to help him on the farm, never objected to it.

Still, we don't like my mother to have to clean up after us, so we all pull our weight. Very *Little House on the Prairie* of us. I chuckle to myself, thinking how much Ben would enjoy that comparison.

"So, Rosebud, Ben tells me he's going to Florida over winter break," my dad says when I'm finished cleaning the breakfast dishes.

"I know. He gets to escape the cold," I say for lack of a better response.

"It's fun to travel with a team, isn't it, Ben?"

"Sure. We have a good time. Lots of work though," Ben answers, oblivious to the reason behind my father's question.

My dad looks pointedly at me. *Yes, Dad, I've done my share of traveling with my dance team. I'm acutely aware of that.*

"Wanna go watch a movie?" I ask Ben, ignoring my betraying father. The only one who hadn't been pestering me until now.

"Sure." His hand goes to the small of my back to lead me out of the room, even though it's my house.

We sit close to each other on the loveseat in the family room. Ben on my right. It's as if he already knows that's how I like it. While I flick through the On-Demand movies on the television, Ben's hand finds its way to my thigh again. His fingers make little circular motions and I end up not even reading the titles of the movies as I'm flicking.

"Holly called me this morning," he says quietly.

"Yeah?"

"She asked me to go to some college party Friday night."

Figures she'd call him. "Oh yeah?"

"At Griffin's."

"Hmmm." I do not want to encourage this conversation.

"She knows I don't do parties."

My eyes are still on the television. I don't want him to see how nervous I'm getting.

"I believe she thinks if I go, she has a better chance of getting you to go."

"Good. So you don't have to worry about going then.

'Cause I'm not."

"You don't do parties either?"

After a second's pause, "No."

"So can I just ask you something, then?"

I put down the remote and shift my eyes toward him, not looking completely at him.

"If it were *last* semester, would you be going?"

I pick up the remote and continue my movie search.

"You don't want to talk about it?"

I don't respond. He already knows the answer.

"It's fine," he says. "We don't have to talk about it. But one of these days, I'd like to find out more about you."

"I'm not that interesting," I say to the TV.

His fingers continue doing their thing on my good thigh. "I beg to differ. I find you *very* interesting. That's why I have this overwhelming desire to know more."

I barely shake my head. "How 'bout this?" I ask, pointing the remote at the screen. *Horrible Bosses* is highlighted in yellow.

"Sure. That's fine."

I look at him. "You saw this already?"

He uses his hand on my thigh to turn me toward him.

"I'm not here for the movie, Rose. I'm here to be with you."

I tuck my lips in at his admission.

"We can watch whatever you want or we can stare at a blank screen. I'm just so happy to be sitting here in the same room, on the same couch, in the same space as you. Breathing in your scent. Being able to touch you. This is all I want. You're happy with *Horrible Bosses* then I'm happy with *Horrible Bosses*."

His words make me want to cry. In fact, I'm finding it hard not to. It's crazy. Why do I want to cry so badly?

He takes his hand from my thigh, leaving a cold,

surprisingly absent feeling on my leg. But then he wraps his arm around my shoulder and tugs me closer. I close my eyes at the closeness and then his lips are pressed to the top of my head.

We sit there like that for I'm not sure how long. My eyes remain closed, his lips keep their contact. *Horrible Bosses* stays highlighted on the television. My eyes are still closed when I feel his touch on my face. When I open them, it's his thumb tracing my scar, up and down, up and down.

"You really are beautiful, you know?"

I shake my head.

"You are," he insists.

Again, I shake my head, but he stops me by spreading his fingers and cupping my face in his hand. Without thinking about it, I lean into it, taking a deep breath to appreciate the security of this moment. Even if it is only fleeting. My breathing picks up when his eyes pierce mine, and in the next second, he's leaning in closer. My eyes flutter when his lips touch mine. They're soft. Warm. And taste like bacon.

For several minutes, our lips are locked and our tongues are engaged. And my head and my heart are at conflict with one another.

This is nice. It feels right. But if we continue, where will it lead? Maybe not tonight. Maybe not next week. But if we take our friendship further, it's going to lead to sex. In clothes, we can pretend I look normal. Undressed, even in the dark, he's sure to see my mutilations.

But when he breaks our kiss, his hands on either side of my jaw, he gazes into my eyes again and all my worries fade into the background. His thumb grazes my scar again when he says, "I'm sorry you were hurt so badly."

I was not expecting that. I take a swallow, then hold my breath while he touches my scar with his lips. They first kiss the top of my scar where it begins at my temple. His lips then follow the scar down my cheek, pressing soft, short pecks as he travels lower until he reaches the part of my scar just below my neck. His lips feel so good on my mangled skin that I am once again conflicted. So badly I want to lean back and give him access to the rest of it.

But I can't.

I'm afraid he'll take one look at the whole thing and decide he can't handle the ugliness. The scar only gets worse as it travels down my body. My lower torso and what's left of my leg look like someone took a machete to it. Then there's the part where my leg went missing. If I didn't have scar tissue, I wouldn't have any skin covering the wound at all. *I* still can't look at myself in a full-length mirror. How could I expect the guy I like to look at me and not get grossed out?

When he kisses the last spot above my collarbone, he looks up at me and takes my cheek in his hand again. "I wish I could take your pain away."

My eyes sting from holding back tears that I'm not sure are trying to escape because of sadness or happiness. Ben's acknowledgement of my accident scares me. I don't want to talk about it. Or remember it.

But at the same time, it feels good that he's concerned. Then again, that's going to be bad for me. It means I have to talk about it. My mouth may be speaking words again, but it's not like I'm okay with talking about what happened. It just makes me depressed all over again. I try to forget. Which is ironic, because it's *all* I think about. My ugly leg. My *Skellington* face. My thwarted dreams.

But Ben's thumb running along my cheek distracts me again. "If you let me in, I might be able to do that."

"You trying to play counselor?" I joke, my quickening breaths making my words sound shaky.

"I'm trying to be your friend."

I smile.

"More than that if you'll let me."

"Thank you." How do I respond to that? *Okay, I'll let you*? But I keep the smile on my face to let him know I'm contemplating that idea.

He kisses me again on the lips and then says, "Okay. *Horrible Bosses.*"

I let out the most lame titter, because really, I'd much rather him be kissing me. But I don't let on. I can't.

We play the movie, but I hardly pay any attention. My mind and my heart are racing with each other to see which can move faster. The whole time, though, Ben's hand is back on my thigh and I'm leaning on him. It's nice. And it's over way too quickly. When he tells me he has to go, that his laundry's not going to jump into the machine by itself, I'm disappointed. But it's not like I didn't know he had laundry to do.

"Mind if I call you every day?" he asks at his car when I walk him out.

"No," I say, freakishly too coyly.

"Good. And then we can make plans for next weekend?"

"Sure. I'd like that."

***

As he promised, he stays true to his word and calls me every day. He texts too. But he says he wants to call so he can hear my voice each day. I want to hear his as well, but I don't tell him so.

The following Friday night, we finally go to the drive-in movies. It turns out they don't close the theater until after Christmas. People just stay in their cars to watch instead of sitting on lawn chairs outside of them.

It's a double feature. *Dumb and Dumber To* and *Horrible*

Bosses 2. Silly movies. My suggestion. I stay away from anything serious that may make me cry. At Ben's suggestion, we take my father's old truck. I tell him that means we'd have to park in the back, but he says he prefers that to sitting in the front and having a gearshift between us for four hours. When he puts it that way, I can't help but agree. He insists on driving.

For four hours, that pass by way too quickly, I sit right up against Ben, my hand on his thigh, his arm wrapped snug behind my shoulder, my head leaning on his. I laugh when I hear Ben laugh, but I'm barely paying attention to what's on the screen. Instead, I'm taking slow, deep breaths, concentrating on Ben's fresh, clean scent and the fact that I'm so comfortable in his arms. So much so that I stopped being conscious of being on his right side a few minutes after he had his arm around me. In between movies, we barely talked. We kissed instead. Again, Ben brushes kisses along the length of my scar that isn't hidden beneath my clothes. And again, I feel less and less self-conscious about it.

At the end of the second movie, rather than tear out of the parking space like every other car in a hurry to sit in line to exit the lot, we make out. This time, he doesn't kiss my scar at all. He keeps his lips on mine and his tongue in my mouth. He tastes like buttered popcorn, but I'm sure I taste the same.

We can feel the empty lot around us before we hear the rapping on the window. "Sir, you need to leave," the attendant says when Ben cranks down the window, "We're locking up."

"Sorry about that, we didn't realize."

"Obviously," he answers, but doesn't seem pissed.

***

211

"I had a nice time tonight," I say at my front door.

"Me too. And thank you for introducing me to drive-in movies."

I laugh. "Glad to oblige."

We kiss goodnight, long and French, and I hate to say goodbye. But Ben has practice in the morning, and kissing outside on the porch is safe.

When he finally lets me out of his arms, it's not just the brisk December night that makes me cold. It's the lack of his arms around me. He waits until I've shut the door before he gets back in the car, and from the window, it's actually painful to let him drive away. I did not want to feel this way with Ben. Soon he's going to be back in school and his life is going to get busy. He won't have time for me anymore. It'll be about baseball and homework. And I wonder, if like his high school girlfriend, I won't be able to handle it. As it is, I'm still so insecure, and I have so much free time that my mind will always be wondering where he is.

Now that I've gotten to know Ben a little better, I'm pretty sure I can trust him, but it doesn't change much. He'll still have a life that can't possibly include me.

Now that I've gone from excited to be out with Ben, to sad that he left, to uptight about where our relationship is going, I toss and turn all night. Finally, at 4:33 in the morning, I slip on my dancing leg and head back down to the basement, making sure to be really quiet. The last thing I want to do is wake anyone up.

My classical CD is already cued in the player. I don't bother trying out another one. There's no point. But I stand at the barre and do my warm-up and stretching bit, and then I practice balancing on my left leg. Progress is slow. I can stand without a problem now, but standing is not what I'm aiming to do. It's not even close to what I'm aiming to do.

26

BEN

As much as I've been looking forward to this trip, I'm going to miss Rose like crazy. I've come to enjoy our weekends together. I count on them. Every day, I'm anxious for the next day to come because it's one day closer to Friday. Talking on the phone with her each night and texting her throughout the day is nice, but it's no replacement for holding her in my arms and kissing her. There's nothing like it in the world. She's soft. She's sweet. And I'm not just talking about her personality. Her skin is softer than the lambskin leather jacket my Nona sent me from Italy, and she tastes as sweet as maple sugar - an actual staple in her family's kitchen.

Being away from Rose for the next three weeks is going to be harder than missing this last baseball season. And before Rose, there was *nothing* I'd ever miss more than I'd missed baseball. I'm almost tempted to have the doctor tell my coach I'm still not ready to return to the game.

But that would go against everything I've worked for. This morning is the last time I'll see Rose before I head home to Cherry Hill this afternoon. I finally made the appointment for the CAT Scan and the only time available is tomorrow morning at 8am. So after Sunday breakfast with the Duncans, I'll be taking off for home and preparing for Florida training.

***

"I'm going to miss you, Rose," I tell her after breakfast while we take a walk around the farm. Because of the cold, Rose is wearing mittens, so I don't have the benefit of touching her skin while I hold her hand. And I love touching her skin.

When we go into the barn to visit Cloud, I unzip my jacket and then unzip hers. My hands naturally go to her waist where I pull her against me and then wrap the two of us inside my coat. It's as close as we're going to get out here, and I'll take what I can get. "I really am going to miss you," I repeat.

"I'm gonna miss you too."

I rest my chin on her head and sigh. "I'm tempted to tell Coach my doctor won't let me go."

"What?" She pulls her head back to look at me. "Why?"

"Because the next three weeks are going to suck." *I can't believe I'm telling her this.*

"Ben. You were looking forward to this trip. Why's it gonna suck?" she asks, clueless.

"'Cause you won't be there."

She sighs and blushes at the same time. "Ben." That's all she says, but she looks sad too.

So I kiss her.

And I kiss her.

And I kiss her.

I could kiss her forever.

But then the alert I set on my phone goes off and she breaks the kiss.

"Ignore that," I say into her mouth, kissing her again. She lets my tongue swipe hers a couple of times before she breaks it off again. "Don't you have to get that?"

"It's my alarm. Don't worry about it." I kiss her again.

She breaks it again. "Alarm for what?"

With a moan, I say, "To let me know it's time to go."

She starts to pull away, but I hold her tighter. "No." I tuck her head beneath my chin and close my eyes. "I wish I could take you with me."

"Yeah. I'm sure your coach would love that," she says into my neck. "You'll be back soon. And then..." she sighs. "You're gonna be busier than ever with school and practice and games. You'll forget I even exist." She laughs, but it doesn't sound like she's joking.

Taking her face in my hands, I look directly into her green eyes. "I could *never* forget you exist. *Ever.*"

She smiles, but it doesn't reach her eyes.

"I'm serious, Rose. During these past two months, you've come to mean so much to me. Even before that. The first time I saw you, sitting in that wheelchair, as silent as—" I pause to find the perfect analogy "—the midnight sky in the dead of winter...I knew I needed to meet you. Know you."

Her smile is still so sad.

"Nothing was going to stop me from getting close to you, Rose..." I'm suddenly at a loss for words, so I kiss her. Again. I don't want to stop. And this time, she doesn't pull away. I do. Because my face is wet. And when I look at her, there are tears all over her face. "Rose. What's the matter?" She's crying so hard that I'm thinking, *Is she really gonna miss me that much?*

"Nothing, nothing it's just so cold out here. My eyes always tear so bad," she says it all in one breath.

"Oh." I wipe the tears with my thumbs, but her cheeks are so wet, I pull my sweater sleeve out from my jacket cuff and wipe her face with it. "Then let's get you inside."

She nods.

Back inside her house, I give her one last hug and one really long kiss goodbye. I can still taste the salt from her tears on my tongue. When we're finished, I don't say the words, I just let the kiss say goodbye for me.

The drive home is ridiculously solemn. I don't even turn on the radio.

***

After my CAT Scan on Monday, the first thing I do is call Rose. I want to Facetime her, but she won't have anything to do with that. I had asked her why once, but she said she doesn't like the camera and would rather stay away from it. She could have fooled me about the camera, considering her house is filled with photographs her mother took of her. Rose on the farm. Rose on her horse. Rose on the stage in her dance costumes.

But then again, they're all photos from *before*. And that makes me sad all over again.

As much as she's loosened up around me since my birthday, she's still struggling with the effects of her accident. She doesn't talk about it either. EVER. Even when I come right out and ask her about it. Eventually, I stop asking. I'm afraid I'll ask one too many times and she'll just stop talking again. I don't want that to happen. I always wondered how she could willingly stop talking in the first place. And why?

So I'm not going to ask any more questions. If she wants to talk about it when she's ready, she knows I'll listen.

***

I have to see Rose one last time before I leave for Florida. I can't help myself. So on Christmas Eve morning, I call her and ask if it's okay to come up.

"Of course it's okay," she says over the phone. "I'd love to see you. But you don't mind driving all that way? Isn't it, like, almost three hours away?"

"Not quite, but it doesn't matter. I'd really like to see you."

"Okay," she says, and I can hear the smile in her

voice.

"Good. I'm leaving in about five minutes. See you about twelve thirty?"

"Yup. See you then."

27

ROSE

He never showed up. Twelve thirty went by. One thirty. Two. By two thirty, I had a feeling it was more than traffic. Especially since he didn't respond to my text asking him if everything was all right. I don't know his home phone number. I don't even know his home address. Something had to have happened. He wouldn't just not show up. He's the one who asked *me* if he could come up.

I text him again.

ME: Ben. Just let me know you're okay. It doesn't matter you didn't come. Please. Thanks.

My stomach hurts. I can't settle down. I want to go downstairs to dance, but everyone's home. Even Terri. Dancing is how I relieve stress, and right now, I can't dance, and as awkward as I am now, I still need it as an outlet.

"Rosebud, what's going on? You've been jumping around like a bean all day."

"I don't jump, Daddy."

He's watching me from the kitchen table. Decorating cookies with my mom and Beth all day is usually one of my favorite things to do on Christmas Eve, but today...it's just not happening.

"You know what I mean, Bud. You're jittery."

"I'm fine," I snap at my father.

"What's going on?" Beth asks, more quietly than my father had.

"Nothing." I'd tell Beth, but my father's still watching and my mother hears everything. Not that it'd hurt anything for them to know I'm worried about Ben, but it'd be just one more thing they'd question me about relentlessly.

Beth nods. "Okay."

But later on in my room, I tell her why I'm nervous.

"Did you try calling him?"

"No. I texted him though. Twice."

"Can't hurt to try and call."

I guess it can't hurt, but I just shrug to Beth.

"He's a really nice guy, Rose. There's gotta be a reason he didn't show up."

I nod. She's right. I know she's right. And that's what has me so worried.

With Beth still in the room, I pick up my cell and call Ben. It goes directly to voice mail. "Hi. It's Rose. Just making sure you're okay. Let me know. Bye."

To Beth, I say, "Went straight to voice mail. Was that okay? I didn't sound desperate or anything, did I?"

"No. Not at all. Just concerned." She pats me on the knee. "Don't worry about it, Rose. I'm sure he's fine and there's a reasonable explanation."

I nod, but I don't agree with her. How many months did it take Holly to find out about *me*? All because my mother didn't have her phone number, nor did she even know much about my college friends to know *who* to call.

"Listen, Rose, it's Christmas. He's probably doing some family thing. He's Italian. Don't they do some big fish thing? His mother probably made him go. You know how parents are. His phone probably died and he didn't memorize your number to call."

"You got it all worked out, don't you?" I laugh, because she's probably right. It does sound feasible.

But in the morning, I still don't get a text or a call. So I spend Christmas day preoccupied with my own thoughts. It doesn't go unnoticed, I can tell by the looks I'm getting from everyone. Fortunately, after I ignore Terri's badgering, no one else bugs me with questions.

To stop myself from worrying if Ben was in a horrific accident like I was, I go through dance moves in my head - the last routine I did before being asked to perform on Broadway.

Later on that night, I hear my mother whispering to my father in the hallway. "She's gonna stop talking again. I know it. She was doing so well too."

"She was not doing well, Sam," my father says, his voice not so capable of whispering. "She's just going through the motions of living. She hasn't even mentioned going back to school. And...does she even use that leg you bought her?"

"The one for dancing?"

"Yeah."

"No."

"Dancing was her life, Samantha. Now she wants nothing to do with it?"

"It's hard for her." My mother chokes on her words. It sounds like she's crying.

"She can do it, Sam. She just doesn't want to try."

I am trying. They just don't know it.

"She doesn't want to do farm work the rest of her life. This life was never for her and you know it."

"She needs time, Bruce."

"She waits any longer, it's never gonna happen."

This is when I walk away. I can't listen to it anymore. If they saw me down in that studio, they wouldn't be urging me to get back to dancing. When I turn to go up the stairs, Patti is standing there.

"You know he's right."

Don't talk to me, Patti.

I don't say that to her though. I don't have the energy.

***

Christmas break goes by way too slowly - the days are long and the nights are unbearable. I don't spend any time in the studio, because Patti and Terri don't have school this week so they're up at all hours of the night watching movies or having friends over. I could go down there anyway, but then they would know, tell my mother, and she'd go and get her hopes up. I can't afford her to get her hopes up, because my dancing isn't getting any better. My moves are clumsy and jerky, and I'm embarrassed to even call it dancing. I'm never going to come close to where I was.

On New Year's Eve morning, tired of picking up shit and feeding chickens, I visit Cloud. "Hey, buddy, miss me?"

Cloud whinnies.

"I miss you too." I run my hands along his side and realize how much I've missed taking him out.

"Think you can be gentle?" I ask him.

Another whinny.

"Don't make promises you can't keep, boy."

I lift my saddle off its hook and grab Cloud's rump rug. I dress him up, take him outside, and lift myself up onto him from his right side.

"Be gentle, Cloud. Please, boy."

We start off slow, and once I get my bearings back, we pick up and settle into a fairly steady pace. It feels good to be back up on Cloud. I'm too uneasy to let my mind wander like I used to, but it's freeing just the same. The cold air on my face. The feeling that I'm flying. There's nothing like it. And for the first time since I hung up with Ben on Christmas Eve morning, I'm smiling.

28

BEN

Be careful what you wish for.
Isn't that how the saying goes?
Maybe it's because it gets the wish all fucking wrong.

I didn't go to Florida. But not because of Rose. I haven't even seen her this week. Or talked to her. She probably hates me now. Only assholes say they're going to be somewhere and then not show up. I've officially made it to asshole status.

But I can't make it up to her.
Not yet.
Hopefully someday.

29

ROSE

"Rosebud, I'm so happy you made this decision."

"Dad. It's only two classes."

"But it's a start. That's all that matters."

"I'm not promising anything, Dad. If people stare. If I feel uncomfortable. I'm gonna quit."

My father sighs, his face sinks and all. "Bud. You never cared about people staring. You got in front of hundreds of people at a time. You used to *love* the stares."

"Dad. They were watching, not staring. And it was because I was good. Now it'll be 'cause I'm a freak."

"You're not a freak, Rose," Holly says, grabbing my last suitcase. "You're a geek. Don't worry, Mr. Duncan, I'll make sure she doesn't quit."

"Thanks, Holly."

"And if people stare, it's only because she's so freaking beautiful."

"Oh shut up." I don't want to hear Holly's stupid praises. "I'll be all right, Dad. Don't worry."

"I love you, Rosebud." I give my father a big hug goodbye, then he hands me my cane. "Just in case you get tired walking."

"Thanks, Dad." They'll definitely stare if I use the cane. I'll have to make sure I don't get tired. With only two classes to get to, I'm sure I'll be fine.

After my father leaves, Holly gives me a hug. "Thank you, thank you for moving in with us."

"Yeah, well, thank you for talking me into it. I guess I am kind of looking forward to school again."

"You know it. You'll probably be kicking yourself for

not taking a full load."

"I doubt it, but yeah. So where's Griffin? I feel bad moving in when he's not here. You sure he's okay with this?"

"Of course he is. He's just as excited as I am. He's probably out with Cali. Sundays are their day together. They'll be back soon, I'm sure. But hey, so you're not alone, why don't you come to Donny's with me when I go into work?"

"I don't think so, Holl. I think I'll just unpack and get my room in order. I'll be fine. Really."

"If you're sure. Listen, I gotta take a shower, but let me get this in your room for you." She picks up the suitcase she set aside before.

"Holly. I can do it. Please. I can do everything you can do, really." Then I admit, "I just can't dance anymore."

"I don't believe that, but...one step at a time."

One step at a time. That's how Ben and I were supposed to take our relationship. Until he decided to take no steps at all. It still makes me sad to think about him, but he made the choice to disappear from my life. For whatever reason. I'll just have to respect that.

However...

Ben may have something to do with the reason I decided to come back to school. Maybe if I run into him, he'll tell me *why* he just stopped calling. I mean, after I checked online for any major accidents in the Cherry Hill area and, God forbid, the obituaries, I realized it most likely wasn't that. Then, I thought maybe it was another girl, but that would have meant he'd met her on the way up to visit me. But truthfully, as much as I worried about him being with another girl when I first started liking him, I got to know him enough to know that he'd be honest about it. I never met a more upstanding guy, so since Christmas Eve, I've had a sinking feeling in my stomach.

I don't have Johnny's phone number, and I don't even

know his last name, so I can't call him. But since Dad gave me his old truck to get me around down here, I'm thinking about stopping at his house to see him. Maybe he'll know something about Ben.

It takes me about two hours to set up my new room. I like it. It's bigger than my dorm room, and I don't have to share it. I'm just a little worried about the parties Griffin likes to throw. They're not particularly wild, Griffin doesn't run like that, but he does have quite a few friends, and it makes me nervous to think of so many people coming into the house. Since Halloween, I've only been around my parents, my sisters, Holly, and Ben. And Johnny that one time.

When I venture down into the kitchen, Griffin and Cali are at the counter.

"Rosalie." Griffin always liked my full name. "I wanted to come up and say hi, but I thought I'd give you time to get situated." He hugs me and kisses me on the left cheek. "How are you?" he asks happily.

"I'm good. Thank you so much for letting me stay here. You sure you don't want more than a hundred a month?"

"I'm sure. If the utilities go up, we'll talk about it then. No worries."

"Hi, Cali." I feel bad, I haven't even acknowledged her yet.

"Hi, Rose. It's good to see you. I'm glad you'll be living here."

"You don't mind?" She *is* Griffin's girlfriend. She might mind.

"Of course not. It'll be nice. I'm here whenever I'm not working or going to class, so it'll be fun hanging together."

"Yeah. I'm looking forward to it."

"Is that your Chevy C-10 out there?"

"Yeah. The ugly orange thing out there? Unfortunately, that's mine."

"Nothing unfortunate about it. It's a '65. It's a classic. I love classic cars and trucks."

"That's right. You have that little yellow thing, right?"

"Right. That little yellow BMW 2002."

"And that's *not* the year," Cali says.

I laugh. "That's right. It *is* a BMW, isn't it?"

"It's ugly, right?" Cali says.

Griffin shakes his head at our lack of reverence for classic cars.

"Rosalie?" Griffin asks. "Have you had time to check where everything is?"

"Not really. Just my room and the bathroom."

"Well feel free to open every cabinet, every drawer. What's yours is mine, and we split the grocery bill, so you can eat or drink anything in the house."

"Great. Thanks."

"Though you don't look like you eat very much. You lost a lot of weight."

"Not really. Lost more muscle than anything."

He just nods. "Hunter Hill has a gym. It's free."

"That's right. Maybe I'll use it." Last year when I was here, I never had time to use the gym. My dance schedule took up any free school time I had. I guess now I'll have the time.

"You want coffee, Rose?" Cali asks. "I'm getting one."

She gets up from her stool and goes to the coffee machine. "Griff's got all kinds of flavors."

"That's due to Holly," Griffin says. "She's girling up my house."

"Yeah, I think I will have a cup." I go by Cali and get a mug from the cabinet where Cali got one and fix myself a pumpkin spice coffee.

"We're staying in to watch a movie," Cali tells me. "Wanna watch with us?"

I don't want to be a third wheel, but I don't want to start off by turning anyone down. Before the accident, I would have taken them up on an offer like this, had I had time, so I say, "Sure."

And then I think about Ben and wonder if I'll see him on campus tomorrow. Even though I'm nervous as all heck, I sure hope so.

30

BEN

I'm back at school.

Not sure for how long, though.

I'm here because there's still a chance. And I need to know there's still a chance.

So I'm following protocol to stay on the team.

I'm staying a full-time student.

"Ben?"

I look up from my desk. "Holly."

"What's going on?" She sits at the desk next to me in Environmental Science on Monday morning.

"Rose is worried sick. She thinks something bad happened to you. What the fuck?"

"Holly. Not now."

"I thought you were one of the good guys. Man. The least you could have done was text her. Tell her you were okay."

"Holly. Please. I don't want to talk about this right now."

"You suck, Ben."

"Thanks for trusting me, Holl."

Despite the words, Holly stays seated next to me throughout the period and even walks out with me.

"So you gonna talk?" she starts as soon as we're outside.

"Yeah. Just not about what you wanna talk about."

She hikes her book bag's strap high on her shoulder in a move that tells me she's angry. "Again...you suck," she reminds me.

"I gotta go, Holly. I'll catch you later." I ignore her

angry commentary behind me as I walk away.

If I'm going to explain to anyone what's going on, it's not going to be to Holly. It's going to be to Rose. But I just can't burden her with this quite yet.

***

Three days later, I miss my first Musicology class. There's somewhere else I need to be.

And then I don't show up the following week either. For *any* of my classes. Because right now, I just can't deal with school, baseball, anyone. Even Rose. Especially Rose.

31

ROSE

"He wasn't in class again today, Rose."

"Holly. I don't care. Stop."

"Doesn't it bother you that he hasn't called you yet?"

"What bothers me is you reminding me all the time."

Holly sighs, shakes her head, and gets up to pour more coffee. She waited until Griffin left before she began her tortuous line of questioning.

"I just don't understand it. It's like he played me," she says. "Pretending he's all nice and shit."

"Played *you*? Holly. This isn't about you."

She puts her coffee down, laughs, and hugs me. "I didn't mean it like that, Rose. I'm sorry. I meant that usually I'm such a good judge of character and here, I misjudged him."

"I don't think you did. Just 'cause he didn't want to see me anymore doesn't mean he's a bad guy. We weren't official or anything."

"It doesn't bother you? Really?"

"No. It doesn't." Every single minute of every day it bothers me. But I'm not about to tell Holly that. Ben just got too busy for me. Whatever kept him from coming up Christmas Eve was most likely a good reason. I'm not going to stew about it.

I do wish things went differently. I liked him. A lot. But I always knew once he started school, it would end.

"Well, I don't believe you, but I won't bring it up again. I'm sorry if I upset you."

"You didn't upset me."

"Good. Because I never want to hurt you. Ever."

She hugs me again.

"Come to Donny's tonight. I gotta work, but you can sit at the bar and we can chat between customers."

"I don't know."

"Please. It's a Tuesday night. It'll be slow."

"I'll think about it. I have an appointment with my Musicology teacher at four. Maybe...*maybe*, I'll stop by after."

"Musicology? What the hell kinda class is that?"

"Music and the mind. I thought it'd be a neat class to take right now, since I have no idea what I'm gonna do for the rest of my life."

"Music and the mind. That sounds cool."

"You should take it. It's a psych class. I have it Thursdays and Fridays."

"Maybe next semester. So please try to come tonight. You sit at the bar. Talk to me. You won't have to talk to anyone else."

"I said maybe."

"Good. Now I need to get to class, and then I'm meeting Mick for lunch before I go to work." She squeezes me. "Love you, Rose."

"Love you too, Holl."

Considering I have no classes today, and I don't have to see the professor until four, I decide I'm finally going to visit Johnny today. I couldn't bring myself to do it last week, but now...I just feel I have to. Yes, part of the reason is selfish - I really do want to see if he knows anything about Ben. But I would also like to see how Johnny's holding up. He was so sad the last time I saw him, and I'm hoping that things are a little brighter for him now.

Because I take my showers at night here at Griffin's, it doesn't take me long to slip on yoga pants, a tank top, and a cardigan, and pull my hair back into a ponytail. And since I'm getting much quicker at the three-step process of concealing my scar, I'm ready in under thirty minutes. A record for me since losing my leg.

Before I head out the door, I grab my cane - it's easier getting in and out of my truck when I have it - and make sure I have my notebook and a granola bar in case I cut it close to four o'clock and have to head straight to school. I get in my truck, turn on the country station and sing out loud to Carrie Underwood's "Little Toy Guns" and whatever else comes on after that.

It takes about twenty minutes to get to Johnny's house once I remember he lives on Washington Place and then another five minutes circling the block, looking for his house. They all look the same. When I catch site of the ramp, I do a little jump for joy in my head, because I know I found the right place. I park my car, walk up the ramp, and ring the bell.

Isaiah opens the door.

"Hi," I say, and I'm more anxious than I thought I'd be.

"Hi. You're...Ben's friend."

"Yes. Rose."

"Rose. That's right," he says with a small smile.

"Honey, who is it?" Johnny's mother walks into the room, and her face drops when she sees me. "Oh. Ben's friend. Rose, right?"

"Yes." We stand there, awkwardly staring at each other. "I...I'm here to see Johnny...if he's not..." I stop talking, because Johnny's mother's hand flies to her mouth.

Isaiah takes her hand and says to me, "Johnny...Johnny died last week."

I suck in a bunch of air and stop breathing. I don't know how long I stand there not breathing, but it's long enough for Isaiah to say, "Rose," and put his arm around my waist. "Come in and sit. You look faint."

Placing my hand on Isaiah's arm, I say, "I'm oh...I'm okay. I, uh, better go." I move out from Isaiah's arms, begin to walk down the ramp, but turn to look at Johnny's mom. "I'm...I'm so sorry, Mrs...." and then I remember I don't know their last name. "I'm just...I'm sorry." Then I rush out, because I have so many thoughts and emotions running through my mind, and I can't escape quickly enough.

Once I'm in my truck, I drop my head to the wheel and continue crying in private. I hardly knew Johnny, so missing him is not exactly why I'm so sad. Besides the loss for his mother, I'm sad for how Johnny had to live the last of his days. A senior in high school should have been thinking of college and girls and prom and whatever else drives them to move forward into their college years and begin their adult lives. Instead, Johnny got a raw deal - and never got to realize any of his dreams.

Then I think about Ben. *Does he know? Is that why he hasn't called? How is he dealing with this?*

The first thing I do after I lift my head up is call Holly.

"Hi, Rose. I hope you're not canceling already."

"No."

"Rose, what's wrong?"

I'm still crying, so it's no surprise she knows something's the matter.

"I'll explain later. You don't happen to have Ben's address, do you?"

"Yeah. He lives in that huge house up on Alisa Road."

"But you said he hasn't been in class. Is he still in Haledon?"

"Oh. I have no idea. I haven't seen him since the first day of school. But, Rose, I don't have his Cherry Hill address, if that's what you're asking."

"Yeah. I guess it is, even though I knew you didn't

have it. Holly...is there any way you can find out if he's still in Haledon? I really need to talk to him, but I don't want to go visit a house full of baseball players."

"Did he contact you? Is that why you're crying?"

"No. Just...a friend of ours, from rehab, died, and I just want to...I need to talk to Ben."

"I'm so sorry, Rose."

"He was more Ben's friend than mine. That's why I'm worried."

"Okay. I'll see who knows anything about Ben. I'll call you back."

"Thanks."

There is no way I'm heading home. I'll go stir crazy. I need to dance. That's what I usually do when I'm upset. It's what I've always done. But I have no studio at Griffin's, and I didn't bring my dance leg with me anyway. So I drive. At first I don't know where I'm headed. I just make a left onto Union Boulevard and drive. I take an exit to a highway I've never been on, at least not while I'd been driving. As I go further down the highway, I realize I must have been on this road, because there are signs for the Lincoln Tunnel, and I've definitely gone through the Lincoln Tunnel. Before I get that far, though, I see an exit for the Garden State Parkway. Now I know that road leads to the shore points, so I take it. But about fifteen minutes later, there are signs for Orange. And impulsively, I decide to go back to the place I remember most vividly right after my life changed - a place where all my nightmares began. The one place I never wanted to see again.

I hated it there.

I hated even more the person I became while I was there.

But I need to find Ben, and I am almost positive he is not on campus. I need his Cherry Hill address, and I'm sure someone here will give it to me.

My whole body is shaking as I walk into the overwhelmingly large building, but I manage to limp inside, holding my head up high and keeping my body as steady as possible.

"Hi, may I help you?" There's a new woman at the reception desk.

"Yes, please. I'm here to see Lourdes—" God, I don't know her last name either. "Uh, Lourdes..."

"Lou?"

"Yes. Lou. I'm here to see Lou. Is she here?"

The woman picks up the phone and dials. "Who may I tell her is here to see her?"

"Rose Duncan."

She slides a sign-in sheet toward me and hands me a pen while she tells Lou I'm here to see her.

"Thank you."

I take a seat along the wall and tap my foot until she comes, the whole time looking down at my clasped hands.

"Rose Duncan, look at you." Lou's voice prompts me to lift my head.

Standing, I greet her with a loose hug. "Hi, Lou."

She holds me at arm's length. "Look at you. So beautiful."

"Thank you."

"And your voice is exactly how I expected it to be - soft and sweet," she says in her slight Portuguese accent.

"Sorry about that." The only time Lou ever heard my voice was when I was screaming incoherently.

"No apologies necessary. It was a traumatic time for you. But boy, look at you now. I'm so proud of you."

"Thank you." Her compliments make me cringe. I used to adore praise. Especially about my dancing. If it were about my appearance, I'd say a grateful thank you, and of course, I'd feel good about it. A boost to my confidence, I guess it was. But now when I receive them, I can't help but wonder if they're just showing a pitiful girl some mercy.

"So what are you doing here?" she asks, genuinely happy to see me.

"Um, I..."

"Is that Rose?" I hear from about ten feet away.

"Yes, Craig. Can you believe it?" Lou says to him as he approaches us.

"Hi," I say, not really remembering who this Craig is.

"Wow. Look at you. You look amazing, girl."

I blush, smile, and say, "Thank you."

Craig shakes his head and stands there, making me even more uncomfortable than I already am.

"So, Rose," Lou says. "What's going on? I imagine this is more than just a friendly visit."

I nod my head side to side. "Kinda."

She waits for me to speak again.

"I need Ben Falco's address."

"Oh, Rose, I'm sorry, but we can't do that. It's against policy," Lou tells me.

"Listen, Rose," Craig interrupts, "it was nice seeing you again. I gotta run."

I look at Craig. "Yes. Thanks." After he walks away, to Lou, I say, "I understand." Then I shrug.

"I'm really sorry, Rose."

"No. No. I'd never want you to do something that'd get you in trouble."

I receive one of those condolatory head-tilts from her.

"Thank you, Lou. I should..." I throw a thumb over my shoulder, "get going."

"It was nice to see you, Rose. You really do look great."

I smile and walk out the door. I don't feel like saying thank you again...not when it sounds like a lie.

I'm almost at my car when I hear my name being called behind me.

"Craig?" *That was his name, right?*

Still running up to me, he says, "Wait up," out of breath. I wait up, and when he reaches me, he hands me a slip of paper. "Ben's address. I heard about Johnny. Figured it had something to do with that."

"Yes, it does. Thank you so much."

"Tell Ben I said hi. He was my favorite patient." Craig's eyes crinkle with his admission.

I hold up the note. "Thanks for this."

"Anytime. Just...keep it between us."

"Definitely."

***

An hour and a half later, I pull up in front of Ben's house in Cherry Hill. My stomach is in dire straits, but I talk myself into getting out of the car and walking up to the front door. It takes me a few seconds once I'm there to ring the bell, but I do.

A short, stout Italian woman answers the door.

"Hi," I say first.

"Hello. Can I help you?" she asks in a strong Italian accent.

"Yes," I mutter, wiping my palms on the tops of my thighs. "I'm a friend of Ben's. Is he home?"

"Oh. No. Benito not home, but...you're Rose?"

I smile at the thought of Ben mentioning me to his mother. "Yes, I'm Rose. Do you know...is Ben up at school?"

"No. Benito took glove and baseballs...he probably at field down the street." She points to her right.

"Down this street?"

"Yes. At end of street, make left, then right. It's at

dead end."

I love her accent. "Oh. Okay. Thank you."

"Rose." She stops me from walking away. "My Benny...he talk about you all time. I think he in love."

I can't keep the smile from spreading across my whole face. I try to tamp it down, but I can't, so I bring my hand up to cover my mouth.

"Go. Go by Benny. He need you."

I nod and turn away. *He needs me?*

I'm back in my truck, but I don't go anywhere. I don't even start it. What am I going to say to Ben? I drove all this way, concerned with getting here but with no inkling what I would say when I got here. What if he doesn't want to talk to me? Maybe he needs to be alone. I've never had to deal with the grief of losing someone close to me. Would I want to mourn alone? Or would I need a shoulder to cry on?

When I was mourning the loss of my leg, however, I wanted no one. Is mourning a person the same thing?

I sit up straight, swallow some courage, and start the car. I don't second-guess myself again, and I just go.

It's February. No one is at the baseball field. Except for him. There's one of those padded walls behind home plate and Ben is on the pitcher's mound, a metal bucket of baseballs at his feet.

He doesn't see me, so I take advantage and watch him throw a few pitches. He's fast. And he throws hard. Through the padding, the wall vibrates, and a sound like thunder echoes through the empty field.

It's a frightening sound.

An angry sound.

And I'm suddenly afraid to approach him.

32

BEN

I've pitched the last of my balls.

It did *nothing* to release the anger boiling inside of me. It made it worse.

I yank up the bucket, nearly swinging it into my nose, when I see her red hair.

"Rose," I breathe through my lips.

She doesn't hear me, but she knows I see her. As soon as my eyes connect with hers, she looks away. She's scared. Why shouldn't she be? If she caught my pitches, there's no doubt in her mind she'd feel threatened.

There are so many things I want to say to her. So much I want to do to her. I want to run my hands through that hair and kiss those lips. I want to hold her. I want to feel her cheek against *my* cheek. Feel her skin against my skin. I want to do and say so much to her.

But I just stand there. My bucket hanging at my side. My gloved hand pressed against my chest. Her eyes finally meeting mine. But I can't move.

I can't move.

33

ROSE

Does he want me to go to him? Or should I wait for him to come to me?

I don't play games. Never did. So maybe I should go to him.

Again I muster up courage and take the first step. And I pray that my legs - the good one and the bad - don't fail me. I don't walk quickly. I probably couldn't if I wanted to. The space between us doesn't seem to shorten. With each step I take, I feel like he's farther away. He's not though. It's my breathing. And the pounding in my chest. And the fact that the faster I want to be somewhere, the longer it takes me to get there - at least in my mind, anyway.

I'm about fifteen feet away from him, and he's still standing in the same position. Still looking into my eyes. I can't break contact. I don't want to.

When I'm about ten feet away, he drops the bucket, lowers his other arm, and drops the glove. Then he rushes toward me in two long strides, lifting me up by the waist and pulling me into his chest. My good leg wraps around his waist, while the other one sort of dangles behind him. I haven't mastered movement of it yet.

He doesn't kiss me.

He just holds me.

His hug is as intense as the pitches he was throwing.

And it breaks my heart.

I let him hold me for as long as he needs to, because let's face it, I wouldn't want to be anywhere else right now anyway. When he finally does put me down, he keeps his arms around me and rests his chin on my head - something

I've missed since before Christmas.

Above my head, he says, "He died, Rose."

"I know."

His arms wrap a little tighter around me. "He gave up. He didn't want to try anymore."

I pull away just enough to look at him. "He...killed...himself?"

"No," he says quickly. "He just gave up fighting."

I'm still confused. I think Ben can tell.

"Pneumonia again. But...I think he lost the reason he was fighting in the first place."

I'm still looking at him when I ask, "What reason? What do you mean?"

"He told me once he *had* to get better because his mother needed him." Ben takes both my hands but continues to look at me. "At the funeral or wake, whatever the fuck's the difference, I noticed Johnny's nurse always standing at Mrs. Gleason's side. It took me a while, but...I realized...they must be a couple now. I think Johnny may have thought his mother didn't need him anymore."

"Ooh. That's...so sad."

Ben nods. "I know." He lets go of my left hand. "Let's sit."

He says nothing as we walk together to the dugout. When we sit, he lays both our hands on his lap then holds my hand in both of his. His thumb circles the spot just above my wrist. He keeps his eyes on our hands. "I'm sorry I haven't called."

"I figured you must have had a good reason."

He nods, but still keeps his gaze down, his thumb still circling my wrist. His breathing deepens. "I have cancer, Rose."

Cancer? "Oh my God."

"My knee." He says, opening his eyes and looking at

241

me. "It was the whole reason I fell in the first place."

I don't even know what fall he's talking about.

"When I tore my meniscus. I took a fall during a game that twisted my knee up." He looks down again. "It was the cancer that caused the fall...or however the cancer messed up my knee that caused it." He shrugs. "I thought it was a fluke thing...turns out...it wasn't."

"Oh my God, Ben, I'm so sorry. What...what do you have to do for it?"

He hesitates. "Chemo."

My shoulders sink.

"That's the *good* news."

"What?"

He shakes his head, and it looks like he's struggling to speak.

"Will you be okay?"

He shrugs, looks at me, and says, "I don't know."

"Ben. You're not gonna..." I can't finish the question. I can't say "die" out loud.

"Probably not."

"Ben?"

"They saw something on the MRI. So then they sent me for a CAT scan, and that resulted in a PET scan. Cute animal names for shitty cancer screenings. Anyway, I have Osteosarcoma. In my knee bone."

"Your knee?"

He nods.

"And chemo will help it?"

"The chemo's to keep it from coming back."

"Oh...so...what about...what about what's there now?"

He sighs. Shrugs. "That's...that's the kicker, because they didn't catch this earlier, I didn't have time for chemotherapy before, so...."

I wait.

He takes his left hand away and reaches over to place it on my left leg. Her runs his hand slowly up and down my thigh. "I have two options."

He stops talking again. His hand still grazes my leg while he looks at it.

I wait.

He kinda nods before he says, "I have to choose between an operation that will cause complications and infection the rest of my life..." His hand doesn't stop moving along my thigh, his gaze never leaves my leg. "Or...losing the whole thing," he whispers.

I think I hear what he's saying, but I ask, "The whole knee?"

He looks up at me and shakes his head. "The whole leg."

Oh. *What do I say to that?* I'm sorry doesn't seem enough. Because not only may he lose his leg, he's probably lost the chance to make the Majors. "Oh, Ben. I'm really sorry." Because though it's not the right thing to say, nothing else comes to mind.

He takes his hand from my leg, turns to face me, but keeps hold of my other hand. "Why'd you stop talking? In rehab. Why didn't you talk at first?"

I hesitate to answer, because it's hard for me to talk about. I haven't talked about the accident since the mental hospital.

"Rose...I just told you more today than you've told me ever. I've waited patiently for you to be ready to talk. But...I'm out of time. I don't know how to handle this. It would help if I could hear...well, your story."

I pull my hand out from his. "Why?"

"Why?" he asks, his forehead furrowed.

"Yeah. I don't..."

"I need to know. To help me. Is that an asshole thing

243

to ask? It looks like I've upset you."

I shrug. "I can't help you decide, Ben."

"Why'd you stop talking? Is it that hard? To deal with? I'm confused as hell these days. Did Johnny give up 'cause his dreams were shattered? Because the plans he made for the future ended up pointless?" Ben clasps his hands between his legs and leans on his elbows. He looks down at the ground. "Either decision I make, I'm done. There's no chance for me. My plans, all that time I spent practicing...hour after hour on the mound." He looks up at me, but his elbows are still resting on his thighs. "Pointless."

I close my eyes. I know exactly what he's talking about. "I don't know why Johnny gave up," I say after a long pause.

Ben sits up and looks at me for a long time. "I'm thinking of going with option one."

I have to replay our conversation to remember what option one was. "The surgery that will cause complications and infection?"

He nods. Doesn't take his eyes off me.

"Why?" His eyes bore into mine still. He wants my reaction? I'm not sure what he wants. "You don't want to lose your leg." It's not a question. I know he doesn't want to lose his leg. Who would?

"No."

That's when I figure out why he's staring into my eyes like that - he's afraid his decision would hurt my feelings. Well...it doesn't. At first. But as I sit there, looking at him, running our conversation through my head, I realize, maybe he really isn't okay with *my* missing leg. Maybe he does find it unappealing. Maybe...I was right all along and I can't have a relationship with Ben. He'd never see past it. "What are the complications with losing it?" I have to know what's driving his decision.

Both of our eyes are diverted now. His are cast down, mine are looking at all the baseballs gathered near home plate.

"Pretty much none, once the initial healing process is over."

Yes, I know this. Keeping my eyes on the balls, I say, "So you'd rather deal with a lifetime of problems than lose your leg."

He doesn't respond.

"So what do you *really* think about me, Ben?" I ask, this time looking directly at him.

He whips his head up. "I really like you, Rose. It has nothing to do with how I feel about you. This is totally separate. I just..."

"Don't want to be a gimp like me."

"No. You're not a gimp. Stop. This isn't about you. It's about me...and how *I'm* gonna deal with it."

"But it's about me sorta, because you asked why I stopped talking."

"So I could know what to expect, I guess. I don't know, Rose." He stands and paces. "You gotta admit, though, your life isn't the same anymore, is it?" He stops, looks at me, and waits for my response.

I don't give him one.

"You don't dance anymore."

"You said no matter what decision you make you can't make it to the Majors, so what's your point?"

"Holly said you're not the same. You lost confidence."

"I was in a major accident. It scarred my entire body. That's gonna take a knock on anyone's self-esteem."

"You won't even go back to school."

"I *am* back in school."

He sits back down next to me. "You are?"

"Yes."

"Oh."

245

We sit there quietly for a while. I want to walk away, but something's keeping me glued to the bench.

"Why don't you want to consider amputation?" I whisper. I really need to know.

After a minute or so, he answers me. "I'm afraid." He looks straight ahead, then at me. His knee is bouncing a mile a minute. "Making the decision to...cut it off...I can't. I almost wish they'd make the decision for me."

I nod. I get it.

"It doesn't mean I look at you any less than if you had two full legs. I promise."

"Don't. Promises. I don't believe them."

"What? You think I'd lie?"

"No. No. But...we were promised a future...it was taken away...from all of us. It's not fair."

"No." He shakes his head. "But...I wouldn't give up on promises. I would never break a promise to you."

"You didn't show up on Christmas Eve."

"That was not a promise, Rose. That's not fair," he tells me, sounding a little annoyed. "I never promised."

"I realize that...but my point is, something horrible came up...and you had to change your plans. I'm not sure what I can count on anymore. Not you, I'm not talking about that, just...you wanna know why I stopped talking?"

He quirks his lip and nods.

"Because once I uttered a word, it'd make it all real. If I didn't talk, I rationalized that it was all a dream...a nightmare. Most of the time I spent inside my own head...somewhere in the past. There were times I don't think I was even *in* the present. My mind blocked it all." I take a deep breath and exhale. "Until it couldn't anymore. I guess it was my version of denial - just ignore it and it'll go away. Only...it didn't. And I'm still living this nightmare." I stop to see if he needs to say anything.

He doesn't.

"Only now, I've accepted it."

"You have?"

"I've accepted that my life has changed. And I'll never dance again. I've accepted that I have to figure out something else to do. I've accepted to not even count on my new plans, because I can get hit by a truck all over again."

"That's a sad way to live, though, isn't it?"

"Yes. But I'm sad anyway, so what does it matter?"

"So...like Johnny, you're just gonna give up." He doesn't ask this, because he knows it's true. Kinda.

"I'm still here...so...I'm not giving up my existence...just...what I want to do with it."

"I can't live like that. I can't accept it."

"So what do you plan to do?" My leg's starting to hurt from sitting so long, so I stand. "God has the final say, so what's the point?"

"God? What's He have to do with this?"

"*Every*thing."

"So...you think no matter what you plan, it doesn't matter, because God will just stamp a null and void stamp across it and say, 'No, Rose, *this* is your fate.'"

"Pretty much."

"What if He's giving us these...challenges to overcome...to learn something from?"

"What am I learning? What did Johnny learn? That his life was supposed to be better spent in a wheelchair, unable to feed himself? I'm better off limping through life? For what reason?"

Ben stands and leans against the side wall while I walk off the pain in my knee. "I don't know. I'm not God. But I do know that I've worked too hard for it to be for nothing."

"Then why opt for option one? I would think a lifetime of complications wouldn't land you a spot in the

Majors...but maybe life with a prosthetic would."

"Yeah. Like it's allowed you to continue to dance?"

Now I'm mad. "You don't pitch with your freaking leg."

"And you don't know if you can't dance until you've tried."

I narrow my eyes at him. *Who the hell does he think he is?*

"Worry about your own problems, Ben, and I'll worry about mine."

I turn around and limp off the field.

He doesn't call for me to come back. And he doesn't follow me either. But I do feel his eyes on me as I walk away.

34

BEN

"What the fuck have I done?"

"Fuck. Fuck. Fuck." I kick the side wall of the dugout. "Fuck." I kick it again.

Then I sit down on the bench, rest my elbows on my legs, and cry.

I didn't cry when I found out I had cancer and that I may lose a leg.

I didn't cry when I found out that Johnny lost his will to live.

These things made me angry and sad, but I didn't cry.

Watching Rose walk off this field...

That makes me cry.

The whole reason I couldn't contact her in the first place was wondering what would happen when I did.

How could I bemoan the possible amputation of my leg to a girl who's already lost hers?

How do I tell her that I'd rather risk infection and a lifetime of surgeries than cut off my own leg?

I can't.

Because it would end in hurt feelings and heartache.

Hers *and* mine.

Just like it did today.

I don't continue to throw pitches. I pick up the balls, grab my glove, and walk home. Calling myself an asshole the whole way home.

"Benito," my mother calls from the kitchen. "That

you?"

"Yeah, Ma." I set my stuff in the back hall and climb up the steps to the kitchen.

"Did that pretty girl find you?"

"Yeah. Rose came to the field."

"You tell her?"

"Yeah."

My mother sets a cup of espresso in front of me. "Just made a pot."

"Thanks."

"Did you make decision?" My mother just wants this over with. Wants the cancer gone. I do too, but it's not as easy as that.

"No."

"Please don't take long to decide."

"Ma. I just can't just say...I can't. I'm going back to school tomorrow."

"What? Benny, no."

"Ma. Give me two weeks. Please. He said I have that long. Two more weeks."

"Okay, Benny. Two weeks."

"Thanks."

Going back to school is futile. I can't finish out the semester and I can't start the season, but I can't stay home. Since I haven't withdrawn yet, why not? I spend the rest of the night surfing the Net. Searching Osteosarcoma. Searching its risks. Searching Rose.

***

I skip Wednesday classes since I don't leave home until eleven, but I do go to practice. Coach knows what's going on with me, and I appreciate that he's promised not to say anything. I'm allowed to play until I can't anymore.

"Ben. What the fuck? Where you been?" Jax asked.

"Flu. All better." I hate lying, but I can't tell him.

"Cool. Now get your ass back on the mound. We need you. We're scrimmaging this weekend."

"I heard."

"Season starts in two weeks."

"Yup."

"Coach tell you a couple scouts are gonna be at the first game?"

"No. He didn't."

"Really?" Jax is surprised. "You'd think he'd tell his star player."

"You'd think." But I know the real reason he didn't tell me - because it doesn't matter anymore.

"Hmmm. He probably thinks there's no reason to worry with you. You're ready for the Majors *now*. You don't even need your senior year."

I ignore that and get on the mound. Jax jogs off to first base, and we throw the ball to each other until the rest of the team gets in place.

***

The next day in Musicology, before I even find a place to sit, I explain to the professor my absence from the first few sessions. She nods in understanding and as I go to take a seat, I nearly collide with Rose, whose eyes are on the floor.

"Rose."

"Ben." She draws out my name, a whisper on her lips.

We stare at each other a moment, but she breaks it first to find a seat. I sit down next to her.

"I'm sorry about the other day. I'd like to explain myself...if you'll let me."

She nods.

"Can I see you after class?"

"No. I have to meet with Professor Sherman."

"Oh."

I'll have to wait to talk with her, because class has started. Today's topic is music and the emotional voice - how psychologists are using music to elicit underlying emotions and help therapists unleash unconscious elements of human emotions. It's an interesting subject, one I'm sure will come in handy when I'm sitting across from some professional ball player who doesn't know why he's not playing at his full potential...or something like that, but I don't pay much attention. First of all, now that the possibility of never playing in the Majors has become more of a reality than ever, being a sports psychologist seems satirical. Second, all I can think about is the girl sitting next to me, and how I managed to hurt her, when she's the one person I never wanted to hurt.

After an hour and fifteen minutes of pretending to listen to the professor, I approach Rose at the end of class. I'd love to ask her why she decided to come back to school and what prompted her to take Musicology, but I have to clean up the mess I made first, so I beg for her forgiveness instead.

"I don't want to hold you up," I say while she slides her books into her bag, "but I really am sorry. I spoke wrong. How my words came out is not how I meant them. You have to forgive me. You just have to."

"Ben," she interrupts my third plea, "it's okay. I forgive you."

Whew. I feel myself starting to breathe easier. "Thank you. Then can we just...get back to where we were. There's so much to talk about."

"Ben." She shakes her head. "I don't want to get back to where we were. I'm sorry." She moves to head toward the front of the room.

"What? Wait. Please."

She turns toward me.

"Why?"

She shakes her head. "I just can't." I receive a sad smile before she walks away.

"Fuck," I whisper so she can't hear me.

***

I go to practice at three, but I suck. Every single pitch is angry and off mark. I throw my glove across the field and walk off. Twenty minutes into practice.

35

ROSE

"Come with us, Rose," Holly begs.

"Nah. You two go. I'll be fine."

"I'd love to get to know you, Rose," Mick says. "Holly talks about you all the time. I'd love to hang with my girlfriend's best friend."

I smile. "Thanks, Mick. Maybe another time. I'm not really up to it tonight. Thanks, though."

"You want me to stay home?" Holly asks.

"No. Go. Really. I have some research to do anyway."

"All right. Have it your way. I'll be home in the morning. I'm staying at Mick's tonight."

"Have fun."

Since no one is home tonight, I bring my laptop into the living room instead of staying in my room like I do most nights. Professor Sherman asked me to do a special assignment on *healing the mind through dance*. Her asking was not coincidental. Evidently, she'd heard of me and learned of my accident and has been asking my previous professors about me. Originally, I was disappointed that she'd gone through the trouble - it's just another form of staring if you ask me. But she said I'd get extra credit for the class, and she also hoped I'd get something out of it. Professor Sherman was a competitive dancer herself and had heard of me through the dance world. Since my accident, she'd researched dancers with disabilities to learn more. There are tons of us. It's not like I hadn't researched them myself, but it seems such a small percentage make it to competition level...or Broadway. In any event, I agreed to the assignment and thanked her for her concern. I still feel violated in a way, because why does every person who meets me think they can fix me? And why do they assume I need fixing at all?

All the while searching the Internet, my mind keeps returning to Ben. I feel bad that I told him I can't see him like we had been. He's sick right now. And he's struggling. Plus, he's mourning. He needs a friend. I want to be his friend, but I like him more than that, and though he may like me now, I know his real feelings toward someone with a prosthetic leg - he pities me. He may not have told me in so many words, but I read between the lines yesterday. I can't be with someone who pities me and finds me needy and unattractive.

I guess, though, I can put my issues aside for the time being, if only to comfort a friend. He is my friend after all. So I begin by researching Osteosarcoma...and its options.

***

I stop at the food store on my way to my Friday Musicology class. I have two classes: World Literature on Mondays and Wednesdays, and Musicology on Thursdays and Fridays. Not a real challenging schedule, but perfect for me right now.

When I walk into class, Ben is already sitting in the same seat as yesterday. The one next to it is empty, so I sit there again. We both nod to one another, but I can tell he's sad. In an effort to make him smile, I reach inside the small grocery bag I got at the food store, pull out the small container, and slide it across his desk.

Goosebumps run up my arms when a smile pulls on his face. "Chocolate pudding."

"Peace offering."

He laughs silently. "Thank you."

"Are you busy after class?"

His eyes pop. "No. Not at all. This is my only class

today. Except for practice at three. Can we go talk somewhere?"

"Sure."

Class starts, so I stop talking with Ben, but throughout class, I can't keep from glancing at him. Each time I do, he's looking at me too.

After class, while Ben waits for me to pack up my stuff, Professor Sherman calls me to see her before I leave.

"It'll probably just take a minute," I tell Ben.

"I'll wait for you in the hall."

Up at Professor Sherman's desk, she says, "Rose. I was talking to the fitness director yesterday. The group fitness room is open from ten to five if you're interested. It has a ballet barre and no one will bother you."

"What?"

She chuckles. "To practice."

"Oh. Thank you, but...I haven't...I don't."

"You should, Rose. They have prosthetic legs specifically for dance, but I'm sure with what you have, you can dance a bit."

I nod. "Yes. I have a dance prosthesis, but..."

"Rose. Then you must use the studio," she says excitedly. "I'd love to practice with you."

"Really? Why?"

"Because you're good. Even before your accident I'd heard of you. You're amazing."

"Thanks, but...I don't...you still compete?" I ask, to get her off the subject of me. Plus, I can't remember if she told me it was something she did now or in the past. She doesn't look too old to still be in competition.

"No. I stopped when I started studying for my PhD. Too much. But I'd love to put on my pointe shoes or tap."

I find myself smiling. I haven't put on a pair of tap shoes in so long.

256

"You like tap. I can tell by your smile. Dance with me, Rose."

"I don't have my shoes...or...or my leg." I say, embarrassed.

"Oh. Well, next time you go home..." She shrugs. "Maybe you can get them."

I feel bad, because she looks disappointed. "Thank you, Professor Sherman, I appreciate it."

"Please...call me Lindsay. I'm only twenty-six. I hate Professor Sherman. Or worse, Dr. Sherman. In class, I guess it's okay, but when we're not in class, please, call me Lindsay. And think about my offer. You'd be doing me a favor. I hardly dance anymore. And I'm not one of those dancers who enjoys solos. My adrenaline rushes when I dance with other dancers. Love it." She smiles, and I see the young girl she probably is when she's not teaching psych courses.

"Thanks, Lindsay. I'll think about it."

"Great."

Out in the hall, Ben is standing against the wall. "Everything okay?"

"Yeah. Fine. Thanks for waiting."

He holds up the container of chocolate pudding. "Thanks for this."

"Yeah, I guess you should eat it soon or...get it in a refrigerator."

"So...do you wanna go somewhere to sit?"

"Uh. Yeah. The courtyard?"

"Sure. Or I can buy you coffee?"

"Um, no. It'll...it'll be too busy. The courtyard's fine."

As we walk down the hall, from my peripheral vision, I see his hand reach out a little, but then he pulls it back and sticks it in the pocket of his leather coat.

"Are you sure you accepted my apology the other day?" he asks when we sit down. "Because it didn't seem like you did."

He holds up the pudding again. "Unless...this means you did."

"I did."

"Good. 'Cause I am sorry."

"You don't have to apologize. *I'm* sorry. You just found out bad news and I made it about me. That's what I do these days. I'm sorry."

"Shit. I get it. I'm always thinking about myself now too. Mostly pity parties." He shakes his head and turns so that he's fully facing me on the bench. He puts the pudding down in the triangular space between his legs. "I think you're great just the way you are. What I said the other day, that was because of *my* fears, Rose. But I can understand how you'd think if I didn't want this for me, I wouldn't like it for you. Which, well, I wish things were different for you, but it doesn't bother me either way. Geez, Rose, I'm rambling. No matter how I put it, it sounds wrong. I hope you..."

"Ben. It's okay. I understand."

He sighs. "So can we start again?"

After a moment's hesitation, I say, "Let's just deal with what's going on now. You have a lot in front of you. I'm here for you...like you are for me. Can that be enough for now?"

His smile is sad - his usual lately. "As much as I'd like to return to kissing you, I guess this is gonna have to be enough...you're right. I need the distraction though, Rose. You are the only good thing in my life right now." He takes me in both his arms and holds me, right here on the bench.

I feel like I should be holding him.

"Are you busy tomorrow?" he asks, still keeping his arms snug around me, the position of his legs making it awkward.

"Tomorrow?"

"Yes. It's Valentine's Day." He lets go and sits back.

"Oh."

"Rose Duncan, will you be my Valentine?"

"Uh. Well. Wouldn't that negate the whole let's-put-our-relationship-on-hold thing we *just* talked about?"

"*You* talked about?" He lifts his brow and smirks.

"*I* talked about. Okay. But..."

"Rose. What's *really* going on? It's not for my benefit that you're holding back. What is it?"

I slide a little away from him and sit back against the bench. "It's...I can't...it's hard for me to express it...I just...you...your decision not to lose your leg." I look at him. I want to see his reaction to what I'm saying. "It made me realize that you...may find me...needy or pathetic or...unattractive...*less* than normal, I guess."

"Oh, Rose. Rose." He reaches for my hands and turns toward me. "You are not less than *any*thing. You are more *every*thing than anyone I know. You gotta believe me." Ben runs his thumb up my wrist then slides his whole hand up and down my lower arm. "I told you...you missing a portion of your leg has no bearing on how I feel about you. The decision whether or not to have mine cut off in no way reflects how I feel about you." He nods and closes his eyes. "But it is a terribly difficult decision to make."

"I'm sure it is. I'm sorry. I don't think I could make that decision either...even knowing what was ahead for me if I didn't...have it amputated."

"Listen...let's forget it. Tomorrow...if you'll let me take you out...no talk of me...and the cancer. 'Kay? I don't want to think about it for a day. I have two weeks to decide. Tomorrow doesn't have to count." Both my hands are in his again. "So how 'bout it, Rose? Be my Valentine. Please?"

I smile.

I nod.

"Sure."

36

BEN

On Saturday morning, I show up for practice as usual. I'm not sure if it's psychosomatic or not, but my knee is hurting more today than it has since my surgery. It affects my pitching and the guys take notice.

"What's going on, Falco? You're playing like a girl," Brian says. They don't know I have cancer.

"I know some girls who play better than you, you fucking prick," Jax says to him in my defense.

Jax doesn't know, but I'm sure he figures something's up.

"You okay?" he asks after Brian shoots expletives back at him and walks away.

"Yeah. Doc says it's normal after surgery."

He nods, but he knows I'm lying.

I grin and bear the pain through the rest of practice, go home, and take a shower, then show up at Rose's door by one in the afternoon...holding a six-pack of refrigerated chocolate pudding in my hands.

"Hi," she says with a smile as bright as her green eyes.

"Hi." I hand her the pudding, which I'd attached a big red bow to before I got out of the car. "Happy Valentine's Day."

"Thank you. You're sweet. Happy Valentine's Day back."

I follow her into the kitchen so she can put the pudding in the fridge. "What would you like to do today? I know sometimes you're not up for going out, so...you can decide."

"Whatever you want. I'll go out today. I'm okay with

it."

"Really? Well...I know a cute place we can go for lunch if you want."

"Okay."

"C'mon. It's up north. I found it online when I found The Treemont."

We get in my car and head up Route 23. I put the country station on for her, but I keep it low enough so we can talk.

"Are we going toward my house?"

"Pretty much. Why?"

"Would you mind if after lunch we stop there? I'd like to pick up a couple things. We don't have to, though."

"No. It's fine. We can go before or after. Doesn't make a difference."

She runs her hands slowly up and down her thighs. "You must be starving from practice. Let's go to lunch first."

"Lunch first," I repeat. We drive a little while and then I say, "So I've been listening to your country music. It's not bad."

She chuckles. "I'm glad you approve."

"So where does your country music fit in with this musicology class? Or doesn't it?"

She chuckles again. "I like how you call it *my* country music. Like I'm the only one it belongs to."

I glance her way. She's both stunning and adorable when she's mid-laugh.

"As for the musicology thing, I think all music *fits in*, as you say. I think someone's mood lots of times determines what they'll listen to. Like, when I first came home, I don't think I wanted to listen to any music truthfully. The first time I listened to country music after the accident was that day in the car with you. I put on some classical music a couple times, but...that's what was already in my CD player."

"Classical?"

"I was dancing to it."

"Dancing? Was this...after?"

I don't hear her answer, but I quickly look her way and see she's nodding.

"I thought you haven't..." I don't finish the sentence. Don't know if I should go there.

"I've...been trying."

"Really. That's awesome."

"No. It's quite sad actually. I trip all over myself."

She's laughing, so I chuckle along. "At least you're trying."

She shrugs.

"So where does classical music fit in with the mind?" I ask just because.

"Everywhere, I'd imagine. It's so complex. It can be angry. It can be joyful. Sad. Classical music is amazing. That's why I dance to it. It moves me. When I was happy, I'd sometimes practice to "The Marriage of Figaro" by Mozart. When I was sad, I might have practiced to Petterson. He's pretty dark. Lately...I've just been practicing to whatever was in the CD from...before."

"Why?"

"Because I can't find my rhythm yet. And it really doesn't even matter anymore."

"So have you been practicing regularly?"

"No. Plus no one knows I've been, so please don't mention it to my family."

I turn to her again. "So I'm the only one who knows?"

"Yup." She smiles.

"Is it difficult?"

"What? Dancing? Now?"

"Yeah."

"Sorta."

I don't say anything, I just wait for her to explain if she wants to.

"I have a special leg. I guess I don't put it on enough and...maybe I'm not giving it a chance."

"Do you want to give it a chance?"

She doesn't respond immediately, but after some silence, she says, "I didn't want to. Not at first. Even after that."

"Sounds like a but's coming on."

"Yeah."

"But now you do? Wanna give it a chance, I mean."

"Maybe."

I nod. Maybe that's as far as the conversation should go today. "Now *this* sounds like a happy song," I say, referring to the wildly upbeat song playing on the radio.

"Ah. "Keep on the Sunny Side." That's Brad Paisley. It was written back before the 1900s. I looked it up once. Ironically...it was inspired by a boy in a wheelchair who always wanted to be pushed on the sunny side of the street. Kinda reminds me of Johnny."

"Mmm."

"I guess...how he used to be...before he...got sad."

"Yeah." Thinking about Johnny makes me sad. "Before he gave up?"

"Why are you so certain he gave up?"

"Why? You saw him. He was this tirelessly happy kid..."

"Maybe he got tired of pretending to be happy. It doesn't mean he gave up."

"Are you giving up, Rose?"

"Me? What's this got to do with me?"

I glance her way again. "It doesn't. I'm just wondering. This practicing you've been doing...does it mean you're gonna try dancing again or are you going to give it up?"

"Well, giving it up and giving up are two different things."

"Are they?"

"I don't know. You tell me. Is saving your leg but giving up your baseball career giving up?"

I realize when I see signs for Vernon that I passed our exit miles ago, so I continue heading to Rose's house instead. "That's not fair."

"How is it not fair? It's the same thing you're asking me."

"It isn't."

"It is, Ben. Saving your leg means a lifetime of complications, which you know means no Major League Baseball career. But losing your leg, and getting a new state-of-the-art prosthesis, and being back on the field within a few months, means you only put it on hold a year tops. I Googled it. Is your precious human leg that important to you?"

"Is yours? I haven't really seen you embracing the loss of yours."

From my side vision, I see her head dip.

"I'm sorry, Rose."

She just shakes her head.

"I didn't mean to get...fresh."

"I deserved it. I was fresh to you first."

"No, you weren't fresh. Just...honest."

"Yeah, well, call me pot, because I'm no better."

"Hi, Pot. I'm Kettle. Nice to meet you," I joke.

Thank God she laughs.

"How 'bout we make a deal," I suggest.

"No more talking about this? We weren't supposed to anyway, remember?"

"That's not what I was going to say. I was going to say, how 'bout if *you* put on that fancy dancing leg of yours,

I'll cut off my leg."

She snaps her head toward me. "Falco, you can't make this decision for *me*...or to get me to dance."

"Yeah, but, I really don't want you to quit dancing."

"Why? You've never even seen me dance. Why is it so important to you?"

"Because *you* are important to me. And I did some Googling myself. There are videos of you online."

"Oh geez."

"You were awesome. Remarkable actually. And you looked like you loved it."

"Probably as much as you love baseball, Falco. So what's your point?"

I have to pull over. I cannot continue to have this conversation while we're driving. So the first convenience store parking lot I see, I pull in. I slam the car in park and turn to face her. "The point is, Rose, I don't want you to fucking quit the one thing that makes your eyes light up. They were lit up so bright while you were dancing that I could see it on a fucking YouTube video. Your face was so radiant, and beaming, and...and all this time I've known you, I've *never* seen you that happy. You cannot give up that happiness, Rose. You just can't."

She closes her eyes. For quite a long time. And she breathes...slowly. She tucks in her lips and then she cries. Not a lot, but one tear follows another until her cheeks glisten. That's when she opens them.

"Then how can *you*?"

37

ROSE

He just stares at me.

"You can't answer that, can you?"

He looks at me some more, then he says, "Why do you keep throwing my questions back at me? Why can't you just answer them?"

"Why can't *you*?"

"Jesus Christ, Rose. Because I want what's best for you. Don't you get it? I love you. I care more about what the fuck happens to you than I do me. Now that I know how happy you once were, it kills me to see you like this...like some shell of who you used to be." He grabs my left thigh with both his hands and gently lifts it so he's touching right beneath my knee, where it sits inside the socket of my prosthesis. "This. You're letting *this* define you. This leg does not define you. It's a *part* of you. A special part. Just like your hair is the most beautiful color of red I've ever seen. Just like your skin is the color of the white sand on a Jamaican beach. Just like you smell like fucking maple sugar. It's a fuckin' part of who you are. And I fucking love every. Single. Part. I just want to reach in and shake your fears free, you goddamn stubborn woman. I love you."

I lick the tears that fall to my lips. Then I think before I speak. "I think that's why your decision bothers *me* so much."

He signs and closes his eyes.

"No. I mean..." It scares me to say this, because I've never said it before. "I love you too. And that's why your decision to save your leg scares *me*. I read about it. Those risks include more surgeries...and the infections...they can be fatal.

And definitely no baseball, and I know baseball makes *you* happy."

"Not as happy as you make me, Rose."

How can he say that? "How can you say that? It's all you've ever known."

"But now I know *you*." He sets down my leg but keeps his hand on my thigh.

"But that girl who broke up with you...because she couldn't allow baseball into your life..."

"She's not you, Rose. I didn't love her. You're more important to me than baseball...than...my education...than the goddamn air I breathe. Shit, Rose, to make you happy, I'll cut off my leg. To have you in my life forever, I'd..."

"Ben. The only reason getting your leg amputated would make me happy is because it would mean a possible career for you in the Majors. And...there are no real physical complications. I don't want you to have it *cut off*, as you say, just so I don't feel alone...or so you look like me. I hope you know that."

His hand reaches my face and he runs his fingertips down my scar. "Of course I know that." His fingertips glide down my arm until his hand reaches mine. He takes it in his and says, "After you came all the way down to Cherry Hill and showed up at the field that day...when I was so angry...I got to thinking. I did some research. I found out more about my options." He pauses. "You know, I never meant to make you feel bad about yourself that day."

"I know that. I was being...I was thinking about myself. I told you that. It's hard to look past...past my flaws. And I was thinking about you afterwards, and you're right. I'm sure it's easier having the decision made for you than having to make it yourself."

He smiles, and I just want to lean in to him.

"If I were conscious and they asked me to decide if I

wanted to keep my leg or risk...death. I have to be honest...I may have chosen death."

His face suddenly looks pained. "Then thank God you were unconscious."

"Small miracles, right?" I joke.

"It's a huge miracle, Rose. If you had died, I'd have never fallen in love."

Ben leans across the gearshift and kisses my lips. When we part, I can't help but say, "You make me happy to be alive."

And then he kisses me again. And for the first time since knowing Ben, I want to do more than just kiss him. I'm not sure how I'll feel about him seeing my body, but I know I feel less self-conscious around him. That thought makes me smile, and he's still kissing me.

"What?" he asks mid-kiss.

"What?"

"You're smiling. What's up?" His lips are still a breath away, but they're not on mine.

I want them on mine. "Nothing," I say, bringing my lips back to his.

After another few heated minutes, Ben breaks our kiss and says, "I'm sure we can find a more romantic place to do this." He pecks my lips one last time, then pulls out of the lot. While butterflies have a field day fluttering around in my stomach as if they were high on caffeine.

"So we missed the turn off to the restaurant a while back," Ben tells me once we're back on the road. "But we'll go to your house first and then get a late lunch...or early dinner."

I laugh. "Either's good."

The car ride up to my house goes fast, since the whole rest of the drive, I'm stuck in my head replaying our kiss. At one point, I stop just to thank God that He put Ben in my life. I hadn't *thanked* Him in a long time, but tonight, I feel like

He is finally on my side.

Hand in hand, we walk up to my house. I turn the doorknob, but it's locked. "Oh geez, I hope I have my key."

Ben just laughs.

I let go of his hand to check my purse, but it's the small bag that I throw across my shoulder and chest. I can't remember if I transferred my keys when I switched from my normal purse. "Oh thank goodness," I say, slipping my finger into the key ring.

Inside the house, all the lights are off, and only the afternoon sunlight is filtering in through the curtains.

"No one's home?" Ben asks.

"Guess not."

"Were they expecting you?"

"No, no. I wasn't planning on coming up until you said we were driving up 23."

"Oh."

"It's fine. It's better they're not home. My mom would ask all kinds of questions as to what I needed." I take off my thick cardigan and throw it over the banister. Ben does the same with his leather coat. Then I motion for him to follow me up the stairs. "If you want, or you can just stay down here, I'll be right back."

"You going to your room?"

"Yeah."

"I'll come," he says, smirking, trailing behind me up the stairs.

Luckily I'm in front of him, so he doesn't see me blushing.

I enter my room and go straight to my closet. I hear Ben plop down on my bed.

"Nice room. Coral's a pretty color."

I turn around to look at him.

"You look good in it."

I want to play it cool, but my flush face may give me away. I try anyway. "Falco, are you coming on to me?" I'm half joking. Of course he's coming on to me, but I'm nervous at the moment.

He stands from my bed, comes toward me, places his hands on my waist, and pulls me forward, where he sits on the edge of the bed again. Next thing I know, I'm sideways, sitting on his lap.

He says nothing when he slides one hand up my back and the other down to my right thigh, his eyes intent as they penetrate mine.

"I don't want to put our relationship on hold, Rose," he says after several moments of intense eye contact. "We got enough bad things to think about...You are the only good in my life right now. Ever since I found out about my cancer and then Johnny, I've been drowning...in the dark...and you...you're like the lighthouse shining on the shore. And I just need to get to shore. Don't let me drown, Rose." His eyes close. I think he's trying to keep from crying.

I bring my hand to his face and run a thumb across his cheek. "I won't let you drown, Ben."

His eyes squeeze tighter before he opens them. "So you'll be my girlfriend? Now? No waiting to get past all this?"

I shake my head. "No waiting. I want to go through this with you."

Both his arms wrap around me, and he squeezes me so hard it feels like all the butterflies in my stomach are going to pop right out and flutter around us.

"I love you, Rose Duncan," he says over my shoulder.

"I love you too, Falco," I say into his neck.

This time, I break the embrace first. And when I look at him, he's trying to blink away tears. "It's okay to cry, you know. Kids with cancer are allowed to cry."

He smiles despite the tears. "Who you calling a kid?

Just 'cause you're, what? A year, not even, older than me?"

"You're just a baby, Falco."

"I'll show you who's a baby, Duncan."

He flips me onto the bed and starts tickling me around my waist. On my stomach. Under the armpits. I'm thrashing so much that my legs and feet are flailing about, and without realizing, I kick Ben behind the leg with my prosthetic heel.

"Ow," he mutters unintentionally, and I know he didn't mean to utter it out loud. "I mean ooh, girl, you're..." He fails at finishing his sentence.

"I'm so sorry," I say, scooting out from underneath him.

"No, Rose, stop. It didn't hurt, I was just..."

"Was it your bad leg? I'm so sorry."

"No, no. It wasn't. It was the other one." He laughs. "Really. I was teasing." He drops the smile, sits up, and pulls me next to him. Then he lifts my bad leg and lays it over his lap. "Can I see it?"

I cringe.

His hand slides over my legging-covered artificial limb. "When you're ready."

"Promise you won't get grossed out?"

"You're asking for promises now? I thought you didn't believe in making promises." He's laughing, and I know he's joking, but he's right. Promises suck.

"I meant to say, *please* don't get grossed out."

"Sure, sure," he teases. "Seriously though, *nothing* that is a part of you could ever gross me out. But if you're not ready, I understand."

I don't know. Maybe I am ready. It would certainly be better for him to see me little bits at a time than all at once. So I slowly start rolling up the hem of my leggings.

As I do, his fingertips follow, lightly grazing the hard

plastic and stopping where my knee is inserted. "Does it still hurt?" he asks, circling my knee.

"Sometimes."

"Do you still get...phantom pain? I read about that."

"Yes, actually. Not as frequently as I did in the beginning, but...I don't let anyone know. I think they'd think I was crazy. After all these months, I still think my leg is there."

"That's not crazy at all. I read it's normal."

"After eight months?"

He shrugs. "I read it can last for some for years."

"God, I hope not."

"It's winter. Maybe the cold bothers it."

"Maybe. In the middle of the night or early in the morning, sometimes I feel like it's being crushed, but usually it's 'cause I'm dreaming about the accident all over again."

"So you remember the accident?"

I've never talked about this with anyone. Even in counseling. So I'm a little apprehensive now, but I think I want to talk about it with Ben.

"I'm sorry, Rose," he says, taking my silence for ignoring the question. "You don't have to answer."

"I don't remember anything. Except that I'd just left my friend Jordan and was going to..." My chest starts hurting and my breathing picks up.

Ben pulls me close and kisses my temple. "Rose, stop. You don't have to."

"I was going to practice. I was one of the background dancers for *Truckin*'...It was a new Broadway show."

"Broadway?" His eyebrows rise. He seems impressed.

I nod. "It was a summer gig."

"Wow."

"I was three weeks away from the opening show."

"Oh, Rose. I'm sorry."

"Wasn't meant to be, I guess." I plaster a smile on my

face. As much as I'm learning to trust in Ben, I'm still not ready to reveal how much it hurts to know my dreams have been crushed forever.

He brings his thumb to the corner of my lip. "Don't hide your feelings on my account, Rose."

My smile drops. I shake my head. "I'm not."

"You've never talked about this, have you?"

Again, I shake my head.

"You haven't really accepted it yet."

"No."

"I think I understand."

I look at Ben. Again I'm being selfish. "I'm sorry. We're talking about me, and you have this huge decision to make. Plus, you're facing chemo and all. I'm so sorry."

"No, Rose, don't be. I want to learn all about you. What scares you is part of that. You're my girlfriend now," he winks. "That means you *have* to tell me how you feel. Always."

"Well then the same goes for you, boyfriend."

He squeezes me again then cups his hand around my left knee. "I'm happy, Rose. Now that I have *you*, I can face this."

"You're not gonna give up the Majors, are you?"

"I don't know. It's gonna be even harder now. I mean, they're not easy to make to begin with."

"You never talked like that before. You were so sure of yourself."

"How can I be now?"

"It's not your pitching arm you're losing."

"No. But..."

"I've seen people run marathons with artificial legs. It's all over the Internet. Certainly you can run bases with one."

"But *you* can't dance?"

"Not gracefully."

"I guess that's a bit trickier."

"Do you want to know what I needed to get from here today?"

"Yeah."

I not-so-delicately get off Ben's lap and go back to my closet. Pulling out my box, I sit back down on the bed and open it. "My dancing leg."

He picks it up and turns it over in his hand. "It's sleeker. Robotic looking, though."

"Yeah, but the ankle rotates more effectively."

"Does this mean you're gonna start dancing again?"

I take the leg from Ben and place it in its box. "I don't know." I set the box beside me and stand up. "I need to get something else. Come."

"Yes, ma'am," he jokes.

Ben follows me to the basement.

"Wow," he says when we get there.

"My dad had this built for me."

"Your own dance studio? Wow. It's amazing."

"Thank you." I go to my shoe box and pull out my pointe shoes, my ballet shoes, my tap shoes, and my jazz shoes...just in case. I'm not sure I want to take up Professor Sherman on her offer, but I may as well be prepared.

"Are you gonna dance, Rose?"

Grabbing a dance bag from a hook on the wall, I answer Ben honestly. "I'm not sure. Professor Sherman told me I can use the fitness room if I wanted to practice."

"Professor Sherman? Musicology Professor Sherman?"

I laugh. "Yeah. Turns out she's a dancer too. She asked me to...to dance with her."

"Really?" He looks surprised. "You gonna take her up on that?"

I shrug. "I guess. I've been thinking about it."

"Well...one step at a time, half-pint. You got your shoes. Worry about the next step next time."

"Half-pint? Again?"

"We're at your farm, I couldn't resist."

"I am not like Laura Ingalls."

Ben walks up to me and takes my hair in two hands. "I don't know. Put this in a couple braids, put on one of those long granny dresses...I can see it."

I smack him in his stomach with the back of my hand, since my hands are full.

"I hear she's feisty too." He takes my bag, then pair by pair, puts my shoes in it.

"Thank you."

"Let's go get dinner, Ms. Duncan."

"Why thank you, Mr. Falco."

He puts my bag over his shoulder and holds my hand. "Not that it's even dinner time yet, but..."

"But you're starving."

"That's an understatement."

***

We're at the restaurant and seated in under an hour.

"Wow. Another cozy place, Ben. How do you find these places?"

"I type in 'cozy places.'"

"Really?"

He nods. "Cozy restaurants."

"It's nice here. I love the gingham tablecloths. My mom loves gingham."

"Is gingham a color?"

I start cracking up. "No. It's the little checkered squares."

"Ah. Very Ingalls-like."

"Yes. Very. You snot."

"So, Rose, what made you go back to school this semester? We never did talk about that."

"A couple reasons."

"Like?"

"Like...I was getting bored at home."

"Understandable. What is the other reason?"

"Well...my parents didn't really want me to take off another semester, and Holly begged me to live with her and Griffin. And Knox, when he's around."

"Knox?"

"He barely stays at the house anymore. Pretty much just when there's a party going on. He only lives in Teaneck, so I think he commutes most days. I've only seen him once since I've been living there."

"Ok. So...you're back at school 'cause you're bored and you want to please your parents and Holly."

"Pretty much." Do I tell him the real reason I forced myself to come back to school?

"Hmmm. Sounds legit. So why are you blushing?"

"I'm not blushing."

"You're blushing."

I bring my hand up to my face. "I am not."

"You are too."

I cover my mouth and say, "I was hoping to run into you."

"What was that? I couldn't hear you."

"You heard me."

He reaches over and lowers my hand from my mouth. "I'm glad you did."

"Well, I also need to continue my education." I backpedal. I don't want to seem too desperate.

He laughs. "You still going for education?"

"I really don't know. My intention was to dance for a

living and then teach it when I was older and exhausted from dance. I really didn't know about teaching in a real classroom." I shrug. "I guess I'll have to think about it."

"Me too."

"You're rethinking the psychology thing?"

"I don't know. I guess I want to get through this next phase in my life before deciding about the future again."

"One step at a time."

"You're learning, half-pint."

The rest of the night is fun and easy. We've gotten the dark subjects out of our system and are able to laugh the rest of the time. In the car ride back, Ben cranks up the country station and starts singing along to the chorus of some of the songs.

"So you *have* been listening to country," I shout over the music.

"You betcha, half-pint."

Because I'm high on Ben at the moment, I join him in belting out the words. For the first time in a mighty long time, I feel like myself again.

38

BEN

"So I'm kind of torn," I tell Rose, standing at her front door. "I want to be a gentleman and say goodnight at the door, but I *really* don't want to say goodnight yet." With the tips of my fingers, I make circles on the top of her hand. Then I bring my gaze back up to her face. "I can stare at your face all night."

Immediately, her hand flies to her scar.

"Rose." I lower her hand and replace it with mine. "You're beautiful with or without the scar. Don't ever cover it for me." I slide my finger down the length of it, like I've done before. "I know you cover it with makeup, but please know, in front of me, you don't have to."

She smiles and leans into my hand.

"You wear what's comfortable for you, but don't think you need to hide your real self for me. I *love* the real you."

She closes her eyes and inhales. "I don't want you to leave yet." She opens her eyes. "Wanna come in?"

"I'd love to."

"Hey, you two." We're greeted by Holly, Mick, Griffin, and Cali.

"Hey," Rose says quietly.

"Hey."

"Ben," Holly says, standing up from the couch.

"Holly," I say with a straight face, only pretending to be annoyed at how we left things the first day of school.

"Where've you been?" She comes up and hugs me.

"Home," I say, not leaning in to hug her back.

"Don't be mad at me, Ben. I was standing up for my

girl here," she says, hugging Rose. "So when did you come back?"

"Wednesday."

"Were you sick?" Holly continues with her questioning.

"Geez, Holl, cut the guy a break. Let him in the door first," Griffin teasingly scolds her.

Rose closes the door behind us and asks, "You want a drink, Ben?"

"Whatever you got. Soda Iced Tea?"

"I think we have cola."

"That's fine." I follow Rose into the kitchen.

"Sorry about the houseful, I didn't realize they'd be home on Valentine's night."

"I don't mind if you don't."

She shrugs.

"You're still not comfortable around them?" I ask quietly.

She pours the soda she got from the fridge into two ice-filled mugs. "Not really. Holly, yes, but...I know this is Griffin's house and all, but I don't know."

"You don't know him well yet?"

"Actually, I kinda do. I've known him as long as I've known Holly, it's just...I really don't know." She hands me the mug and sits at the island.

I pull out the stool next to where she's sitting and sit facing her. Then I turn her stool so she's facing me.

"I gotta get over myself, I think," she says, shaking her head. "Hey, want some chocolate pudding?"

"Sure. I'll get it. You sit." I get up, then ask, "That is, if you don't mind me going in your refrigerator."

"Don't be silly. Spoons are in the drawer next to the sink."

Back at the island, I open our pudding cups and give

one to Rose. "Cheers," I offer, holding up my cup. "To my new girlfriend."

She holds up her cup. "To my new boyfriend."

When I see her cheeks turn rosy peach, I can't even explain how it makes me feel right now. I'm her boyfriend. She's my girlfriend. And for the first time in forever, that means more to me than any other thing on Earth. I got Rose. And she loves me. Nothing else matters. Not baseball. Not the fucking cancer. Not losing my leg. I have the best girl in the world sitting in front of me. What more could I possibly want?

She's smirking. "What are you thinking? You have this funny look on your face."

"What am *I* thinking?" I ask her. "I'm thinking how I'm the luckiest guy in the world to have you as my girlfriend. God, I love you, half-pint."

She blushes again. "I love you too."

We've just scraped our pudding cups clean when Holly walks in. "We're just starting another movie. Wanna watch it with us?"

Rose and I look at each other.

"It's up to you, half-pint."

"Sure," she says, looking at Holly but grabbing my hand. Holly leaves, and with one hand, she scoops up the empty pudding cups and spoons. "Do you mind watching a movie?"

"Of course not." Of course, I'd rather be alone with her, but I have a feeling I know where that would lead, and I don't want our first time to be in a house filled with people.

"Really?" Mick says when the movie title pops on the screen. "*Valentine's Day?*"

"I don't know," Holly says. "What else we gonna watch? I think we've watched everything else on Netflix."

"How 'bout a horror flick?" Griffin suggests.

"Like what?" Holly asks, the remote pointed at the screen.

"How 'bout an old one?" Cali suggests. "*Carrie* or *Psycho*?"

"Oooh...*Psycho* sounds good," Mick says.

"Everybody? *Psycho*?"

"Sure."

"Yeah."

"Why not."

Since everyone is in agreement, though I don't really think Rose is, since I remember she doesn't like horror movies, Holly puts on *Psycho*, Griffin turns off the lights, and I don't give a shit what the others are doing, because Rose is cuddled close next to me, half on my lap, as we share the over-sized yet single recliner.

My left hand finds a comfortable spot right outside Rose's thigh, while my right arm holds her easily around her waist. I don't watch the movie much. Instead, I lean my head against hers and concentrate on the sweet scent of maple sugar as she breathes steadily so close to me. When *Psycho* finishes, Holly puts on *Carrie*, and by the end of it, Rose is asleep on my shoulder. The others quietly leave the room, and I hear their footsteps up the stairs. We're already reclined, but I push back on the chair until it's as far back as it can go, and I snuggle into Rose. There is no way I'm waking her up just to leave and go home. That'd be like leaving Heaven to go to Hell. I don't want to be alone, and I definitely don't want to unwrap my arms from the maple sugar angel they're holding right now.

Sometime during the night, I doze off along with Rose, and the next thing I know, soft gray light is peeking in through the blinds. Rose shifted slightly through the night, because her cheek is now resting against my chest, and the top of her head rests right beneath my chin. I'm glad this chair reclines back so far, because if it didn't, she may have woken up, and I would have had to leave. Instead, I got to spend the night holding the best thing that ever happened to me.

I try not to move to allow her to sleep some more, but I really have to take a piss, so it's hard to stay still. A few minutes later, I feel her breathing change anyway.

Her palm presses against my stomach, and she slowly lifts her head. "Oh my gosh, Ben." She looks toward the front windows then sits up straight, bringing the back of the recliner, and me, up with her. "Holy cow, did we sleep all night?"

"Yes we did, sweetheart," I say with a rasp.

"Oh my God, I'm so sorry." She sits up further. "You could have woken me up. I feel so bad you had to sleep in this chair all night." She's looking at me, waiting for my response.

I just stare at her. She's so goddamn beautiful.

"What? I am sorry."

"For what? There's no place else I would have rather spent the night." Even a bed wouldn't have been as perfect. One step at a time.

"Really?" She smiles, then shoots a hand to her mouth. "Oh my God, my breath."

I remove her hand. "Still as sweet as sugar, half-pint."

I'm treated to a light whack on the arm.

She wiggles out of the chair and rubs her leg. "You can go get a cup of coffee if you want, I have to go put cream on my leg and brush my teeth."

"Don't worry about your breath, Rose. But...should I have not let you sleep? Are you not supposed to have your prosthetic on all night?"

She shrugs one shoulder. "Not really. It'll be all right though. I'll be right back."

"Okay, but first, where's the bathroom?"

"Oh. Right off the kitchen, to the left."

I'm about three steps into the kitchen when I hear a yelp and two thuds. "Oh my God," I yell, running back toward the steps. "Holy shit. Rose."

She's lying on the floor at the bottom of the stairs.

39

ROSE

Really?

As if I'm not already mortified by my morning breath and the fact that I have to lubricate my...*knee* - I'm not yet ready to call it that ugly S word - but I have to go and fall backwards down the stairs and land on the floor. On my back. For Ben to find me. Oh my God. Why? Why can't I just live with a little dignity from time to time?

"Rose, are you okay?" He bends down to help me up.

Getting up onto my elbows as quickly as I can, I tell him, "I'm fine."

He scoops me up and I'm suddenly cradled in his arms like a baby.

"Really, Ben. I'm fine. You can put me down."

"Just tell me where to go." He begins carrying me up the stairs.

I feel so foolish. "Ben."

"Rose. Stop." At the top of the stairs, he whispers, "Where to?"

But it doesn't matter that he whispers, because Griffin and Cali just round the corner to see what the "Ruckus was," Griffin says.

Then Holly appears.

I bury my head in the crook of Ben's neck. And groan.

"Rose, what happened?" Holly exclaims.

"She took a tumble," Ben says, making no big deal, for my sake most likely.

"Oh, Rose." She rubs my shoulder. "You okay?"

"Ben, put me down, please," I murmur into his neck.

He does.

"I'm fine." I fake a smile and go to my room, third door to the left.

"I'm sorry if I embarrassed you," Ben says when we're alone.

"*You* didn't embarrass me. I embarrass myself." I carefully sit at the edge of the top of my bed where I keep all my lotions for my leg.

I take off my Converse hi-tops, cringe at the pain in my lower back, and begin rolling up my leggings in front of Ben...again. Only now, he's see my leg without the contraption. I stop for a moment and look at him.

"Would you like me to leave?"

I think about this for a second.

"I never did get to take a piss yet. How 'bout I do that...I'll be back."

He turns to leave. "Ben."

"Yeah?"

"There's a bathroom right here." I point to the door in front of me. "When you come out, I don't mind you seeing."

"Really?"

"Really."

"Be right back."

While he's in the bathroom, I unlatch my leg, take it out of the socket, pull off my sock, and massage it. It feels so good out in the open right now. I slide back against the headboard and pick up the tube of lotion. Then I grimace at the pain in my bottom from sitting this way.

Ben walks out as I'm about to squeeze the cream into my hand.

I hesitate just a second, but he sits down in front of me and holds out his hand. "May I?"

I look at him and he's staring into my eyes. I hand

him the tube without saying another word.

He squeezes the lotion into his hands and rubs them together. I watch as he continues looking at my face when his fingers first make contact with my skin. It's an odd sensation - his hand on my limb. The way he gently massages the cream into my skin almost feels sensual and not at all like the unpleasant sensation when I dutifully rub it on every night, trying my darndest not to look at the thing.

"Am I hurting you?" he asks quietly, looking up from my leg.

"No," I say, looking into his eyes.

"Is it feeling any better?"

I nod, still gazing into his brown eyes. "Much."

The cream is all rubbed in when he starts to massage my thigh. "You took some fall down there. Are you hurting from that?"

I know I'm turning red, because my cheeks feel warm and I'm suppressing a smile, but I tell him anyway. "My butt hurts quite a bit."

His lopsided grin and raised brow make my insides tingle. "I'll be happy to rub lotion there too."

I can't believe myself, but I want to say, "Please." Instead, I tell him, "I'll be fine."

"Seriously though, is there ice in the freezer? You should probably ice it."

I nod. "Yeah. You're right."

He rubs my limb again, then stands. "I'll be right back."

"No. Ben. It can wait."

"I'll be right back," he insists before walking out my bedroom door.

Resting back against the headboard, I close my eyes and think about Ben. I can't believe I've fallen so hard for him. Even more so, I can't believe how comfortable I feel with him. He saw my...thing...and he didn't cringe. Didn't even blink twice. And he wasn't too grossed out to touch it. Oh my God, at this moment, I don't think I could feel any happier.

Ben walks in with two mugs of coffee in his hands and an ice pack under his armpit. "Figured you'd want a cup," he says, sitting the mugs down on my nightstand. "Scooch up so I can put the ice on your back."

"Actually, I should probably go to the bathroom myself first."

He takes my hand and helps me stand. "You okay on your own, or does your back hurt too much?"

I like how he made it about my back and not that at the moment I'm one-legged. I reach for my crutches next to the nightstand - I still haven't perfected the hopping on one leg thing. Spinning yes. Hopping no. "I got these. I'm good."

He nods. "I'll be waiting."

After I pee, I finally brush my teeth and run a brush through my hair. Then I wash my face quickly, because it feels so scummy. But when I get a look at myself in the mirror, I see my scar. Do I cover it back up, or trust that Ben won't go running because he's seen too much of the real me today? It takes me a moment to think about it, but I decide that Ben meant what he'd said - I don't have to hide myself from him.

Slowly, I open the door. My chest is pounding a little harder, a little faster, and my stomach turns a bit. But one crutched step at a time, I walk out into my room.

The first thing I notice is Ben's eyes. They're smiling. "My God, Rose. You're beautiful."

Naturally, my hand flies to my cheek.

"Don't," he stands. "Don't cover it." He again removes my hand from my face. "I forgot you had freckles." He cups his right hand around my waist.

Freckles. All this worrying about my scar, I'd

forgotten to worry about my freckles. Not that I'd ever cared before, but since I started covering my scar and needed to wear foundation, I forgot that all this time my freckles were hidden too.

"I love them. They suit you." He takes the crutches and leans them against the nightstand, all the while keeping his hold on my waist. "Now you really look like half-pint," he says, lifting me up and laying me on the bed.

"That's not a compliment," I joke.

"Sure it is. You're way better looking than Laura Ingalls, but those freckles complement the whole pick-up-truck-driving, farm-girl package. I love it."

"Oh God." I blush.

"Now turn over, girl, and get on your stomach." He grabs the ice pack and a paper towel off the bed and holds it up. "We got some icing to do."

I turn on my stomach and he lifts my shirt. Expecting to feel the cold ice on my lower back, I'm more than pleasantly surprised. After he tugs down my waistband, his fingers sweep gently across my lower back. He doesn't press, he just lightly circles the entire area with his fingertips.

"Oh my," I end up muttering involuntarily.

That's when I feel him shift. My eyes are closed, but behind me, I feel him straddle my legs, and now both his hands are circling my lower back. This feels *much* better than an ice pack.

His fingers continue for several more minutes before he moves to my side and replaces them with the towel-covered ice.

"Ohhh," I groan, missing his touch already.

I feel him move again, so I open my eyes. He's lying next to me. "I had to stop, half-pint, before my hands went places they shouldn't."

Oh, they should. They should. But I don't say that out

loud. "Thank you," I whisper. "That felt so good."

He stares at me intently. "*You* feel so good." His fingers once again find my skin, but this time it's the ear he grazes when he tucks my hair behind it. "You are the prettiest girl I ever did see."

"Spoken like a true country boy."

"I'm trying, half-pint."

"Don't change for me. I don't care if you're a country boy or city boy...or suburban boy...as long as you're here next to me."

His middle finger traces the outline of the left side of my face, from my temple to my jaw. "Always." He moves closer until our foreheads and noses are touching each other. "I love you."

"I love you."

I don't know how long we remain in that position, but it's not long enough. Eventually, our stomachs gurgle and our hunger for food takes precedence. I change my clothes, put on my leg, and we go to Ben's so he can change. The rest of Sunday, we spend together...eating, laughing, and cuddling. And kissing. We definitely did some kissing.

Then Ben spends the night again. This time in my bed. "You sure, half-pint?"

"Yeah. I'm sure."

I stay in my flannels. I'd like to sleep in something sexier, but then he'd see more of my scar. What if it's a major turn-off?

He climbs into bed fully-clothed.

"You don't have to do that, you know. I'm sure it's uncomfortable sleeping in your jeans. For the second night in a row."

"You sure?"

"I'm sure."

He gets out of bed, slips out of his jeans, and pulls off

his tee, and I'm not surprised by my body's reaction to seeing his ripped abs and muscular legs. That's when I realize I better get over my body's flaws, because I'm not going to be able to keep it from Ben's for much longer.

When Ben gets back in bed, he stretches out his arm for me to curl into, and I rest my head between his shoulder and his neck. I wake up in the exact same position in the morning.

"Morning, sweetheart."

"Morning, Benito."

"Benito?" He rolls on top of me, tucking my arms to my sides. "Do not call me Benito. I hate that name."

I giggle. I never giggle. "Why?"

"Ugh. It makes me sound like some Italian greaser from the fifties. No. I'm not that guy."

"But your mother calls you that."

"Yeah. I hate it when she does. I've been trying to get her to call me Ben since I was five. The closest she gets is Benny."

"You're cute when you're embarrassed."

He kisses me then hops out of bed. "I better get going. I have class at nine. I'm not so sure it's so important to go, but I should at least tell the teacher what's going on." He says this all while getting his clothes back on.

I sit up in bed and watch him the whole time. He's god-awful handsome.

"What are your plans today?"

I shrug. "I may call Professor Sherman and take her up on her offer."

He sits on the bed. "You're gonna dance?"

"Should I not?"

"No, Rose, you should. Especially if that's what you want."

"Maybe."

Ben kisses me on the lips, then says, "Text me when you're done. I'll bring dinner."

"Okay."

***

I meet Professor Sherman, Lindsay, at the gym at eleven. My dancing leg feels lighter, but since the ankle is more flexible, walking in it for any length of time requires me to use my cane. At least until I get used to it. But it was so expensive for my parents to have made that I'm afraid of breaking it somehow, so I don't wear it for everyday use.

"Rose," Lindsay calls when she sees me. "I am so glad you decided to come," she says when she reaches me. She walks me into the studio and right away turns on the lights. Then she proceeds to put a CD in the stereo and turns it on.

"What shoes did you bring?" she asks.

"All four."

"Wanna start with tap? I love tap."

"Sure." I'm apprehensive no matter what type of dance we do, but I'm determined to move past my insecurities and do this.

We put on our taps and stand in the center of the room. "Follow what I do?" she asks. "I step. You follow. I step. You follow."

"Right. Like Simon Says," I joke.

"Right."

She shuffles. I shuffle.

She cross shuffles. I cross shuffle.

She side cross shuffles. I side cross shuffle.

Before we know it, we're doing the same moves at the same time and I'm beaming. Tap is not nearly as difficult with this leg as my ballet spins. Why on Earth I didn't start with tap when I first put this leg on escapes me. I may have grown in confidence and not beaten myself up for not doing a fouetté turn on my bad leg. One step at a time. That first step should have been something simpler. But hindsight is 20/20 and all that.

We continue tapping until Lindsay suggests jazz. Another *duh* moment for me before I say, "Of course." We spend the next hour dancing - tap and jazz. Something tells me Lindsay knows exactly what she's doing by not suggesting ballet and pointe. Then I remember, she's not just my musicology professor, she's a doctor of psychology.

Does God just put the right people in our paths at the right time for a reason?

Could it be that God really does know what He's doing?

I smile at that thought and continue dancing with Lindsay - my dancing angel sent to me by the Man Himself.

40

BEN

Two weeks go by way too quickly. The moment of truth, and change, is only a day away. I return home tomorrow, and as per the doctor's insistence, I go into surgery the following day.

Our first game of the season is about to begin. It's almost eight o'clock. A night game under the lights. I used to live for this not long ago. Though Coach still hasn't told me, and the team was expected to do the same, rumor has it Major League scouts are coming in to see me. Jax filled me in, because as he puts it, he thought it was right that I know.

"Coach told us, man," he said to me. "I'm really sorry to hear about your cancer. But who's Coach Rock to decide if the Majors matter anymore for you or not? Maybe by graduation, you'll be all cured and ready for them. Coach thinks he's protecting you, but I don't. You go out there and kick some fuckin' ass."

That was in the locker room this morning. Right now I'm in the bullpen, practicing my pitches, but all I can concentrate on is Rose sitting in the front row on the third base line between home and third. Probably not the best place to have her seated if I'm hoping to score the attention of a scout, but I don't care. If it weren't for her, I may have just passed on playing tonight altogether. Rose thought it'd be good to be conscious of the last game I play before my surgery, claiming that if she knew June 11th would have been her last time dancing, she would have taken the time to appreciate each dance step. So on her advice, I'm here. Even though as each day ends, I lose a little more hope that the Majors are in my future.

Before the game starts, I just need to see Rose one more time. I just need to hold her. And maybe kiss her. To get her out of my head for the game. If that's even possible anymore.

"Hey," I say to her from beneath the stands.

"Hey." She stands and leans over the rail to kiss me.

I wasn't planning to, but I grab her under the arms and lift her over the railing. She makes the cutest squeal when I do it. I set her down on her feet and take her in with my eyes. "God, you're gorgeous."

She gives me the sweetest smile.

She's wearing black today. She never wears black. But she wanted to wear a dress. And tights. Not leggings. Black tights like pantyhose. This is big for her, because she says it's more obvious that she has an artificial leg when she wears them. But Rose wants to show me that she is moving past her fears about her flaws - even though I don't think they're flaws at all - and accepting the new Rose.

"Aren't you cold?" I ask, rubbing her bare arms.

"I have my sweater." She motions to her seat. "I just got hot."

"Oh, you're hot, baby. No doubt."

I love it when she blushes.

"Tell me again why I'm here? 'Cause really, I just wanna be holding you in your bed tonight." I've been sleeping in her bed this last week, because it just makes sense, but we haven't made love yet. I'm not sure she's ready for me to see her, and I don't want to push her. She only recently started dancing again, I don't want her moving so quickly that she regresses. So we kiss. A lot. And fall asleep in each other's arms, her in her flannel pajamas, me in my boxers.

"You're here because *what if?* What if you never get to play again? What if you do, but you missed this chance for the scouts to see you? What if...I wanted to see you play at least once?"

I stare at her pretty, pleading face and smile. "Then tonight's for you, half-pint."

She smiles back at me, and then I kiss the shit outta her. "God, you taste delicious," I tell her when we're done. "And oh yeah, I love you."

"Ben...you take my breath away. Now go pitch the game of your life."

And that's exactly what I do. My pitches are perfect. No anger, just determination. In the end, I pitch a no-hitter and we win the game. I speak with a couple scouts afterward, explaining my situation to them and telling them I expect to return in the fall. I don't promise, because like Rose says, "Life has a way of breaking your promises." And I have no idea, really, what the near future holds for me. But I don't want to burn bridges, just in case. I have a good game and I'm reminded just how much I love playing, but I love Rose more. And anything I do from this day forward will be for her.

After the game, Rose and I celebrate alone. There is no way I'm going for pizza and beer with the team when I can feast on Rose's maple sugar lips.

"You're not hungry?" she asks on the way to Griffin's.

"Not as hungry as I am for you," I tease, but not really. I'm serious as hell.

She giggles. She's been doing that a lot lately, and I decide I've never heard a sweeter sound. "We have roast beef and ham if you want a sandwich."

"Seriously, Rose, I'm not hungry for food. Don't worry about it."

She smiles and her cheeks turn that wonderful shade of peach.

Inside the house, she goes right for the refrigerator and starts fumbling through the meat drawer. I walk up behind her, lift her hands from the drawer, and push it shut. Then I reach down beneath her knees and pick her up, cradling her in my arms as I close the refrigerator door with my foot. "This is my last night with you for God knows how long. I'm not gonna waste it by eating a sandwich." I carry her up the stairs and into her room, where I lay her on her bed, kick off my shoes, and lie down next to her. "All I want to do tonight is hold you. Can we do that?" I hate the sadness that suddenly creeps over me. I don't want to be sad. I just want to enjoy the scent and feel of Rose as I hold her until the sun comes up.

"We can do more than that if you want," she says quietly, circling her fingers over my t-shirt covered chest.

My mouth drops open as my heartbeat picks up. "What?" The word comes out more like an expression of air than an actual spoken word.

Her hand slips under my shirt. "We can do more than just...lie here." Again her voice is soft. Quiet.

I cup my hand behind her neck and bring her to me, where I then crush my lips to hers. "You wanna kiss me all night, half-pint? Is that it?" I say into her mouth.

She stops kissing me and places her hand on my face. "I want to do more than that."

I still at her words.

She nods.

I slowly turn her onto her back and run a finger down the side of her face. "We don't have to."

"I know," she says, looking directly into my eyes. "I want to."

"You sure?" I ask, my hand still on her freckled face.

"Yes."

I get up and kneel next to her, sitting on my heels. "I don't have a condom," I say with a shit-load of disappointment.

She sits up next to me. "I do," she whispers.

I widen my eyes.

She blushes. "I went to the store this morning when you were at practice," she says, looking embarrassed.

"Rose." I look at her in astonishment. "You really want this?"

"I really do."

Running my finger along her collar, I feel the zipper in the back. I stand on my knees and slowly unzip it. As I sit back down on my heels, I lower the dress down her shoulders. "You're positive? I'm really allowed to see all of you?" I ask, still not believing she really wants this.

"Yes." Her answer is more like a panting breath than a word, and it's one of many quickening breaths that cause her chest to rise more visibly.

I pull the dress down to her waist, then run my thumbs under her bra. "You are so amazingly beautiful, Rose."

She closes her eyes and inhales. With her exhale, she lets out a sated moan.

I grab hold of her dress again and slip it down further, lifting her ass to maneuver it past her hips. I bring it over her ankles and sit back on my heels again. In her black lace bra and panties, and her black stockings, complete with garter belt, she is a paradox. Wholesome yet absolutely sexy. "Holy shit," I say, tugging lightly on the garter belt, "I thought these were those full-length things. My God, you're sexy."

She blushes. And her smile, so innocent, makes me wonder if she's ever done this before.

"Rose," I say, sliding my palm up her right leg, but stopping at mid-thigh and lacing my fingers around the belt. "Have you ever done this before?"

She shakes her head, but keeps a small smile on her face. "No."

"You sure you want..."

She stops me. "One hundred and ten percent sure, Ben."

I start by unhooking the stocking on her right leg.

"Don't. Please. Keep them on."

She's biting her lip and looking nervous.

"At least this first time," she says quietly. "I don't want to be conscious of it. Not tonight."

"Of course," I say, looking directly into her eyes before hooking the stocking back to the belt. Then I appreciate the contours of her body with my hand, but bring my gaze back to her eyes. "If that's what makes you most comfortable. But please know...it will never bother me. Ever."

"I know that. But for tonight, I want to forget about it."

Running my other hand up her body, I gently lower her to her back and slowly peel off her bra and panties, taking my time to appreciate every inch of her perfect body with my eyes, my hands, my mouth. When there is not one part of her that's gone untouched, I slip on protection, and with all the tenderness and love I have for this flawless angel beneath me, I make love to her finally and completely.

41

ROSE

"You're sure I didn't hurt you?" Ben asks me for the third time since we made love an hour ago.

Extremely sated and very sleepily, I assure him he didn't hurt me. "You could never hurt me, Ben." I let out the yawn I stifled to answer him.

He squeezes me tighter and I snuggle closer into him, resting my head on his chest instead of his shoulder. Ben plays with my hair while I listen to the steady beat of his heart.

"Not that I want to leave this position, but aren't you supposed to take the prosthesis off?"

I sigh into his chest and then I groan. "Yeah, I guess I should."

"Can I do it for you?"

I lift my head to look at him. "You want to?"

He smiles. "I do."

His touch when slipping off my garter and stockings and unlatching my prosthesis is as tender and loving, and ironically, almost as erotic, as when his hands were exploring my body before he made love to me and gave me the most passionate experience of my life. At first it hurt...the moment he entered, but he was gentle and slow and made me feel like the most important person in the world. He even kept his eyes open to look at my face, so he could know for sure if he was causing me pain by my facial expressions. He wasn't. He felt so good. And I loved being connected to him that way.

"How'd I do?" he asks, and I'm so completely lost in the feel of his touch on my skin that I hadn't even paid attention to *what* he was doing.

"Oh." Now that I realize I'm completely naked - without anything covering me, not even the sock on my...residual limb - I am thoroughly and extremely self-conscious. Oh my God, my scar is out, and it ends so abruptly at the end of the limb.

I clutch the comforter on my bed and tug it up, but Ben is on it, and it doesn't cover anything but my foot and ankle of the good leg.

Ben gets off the bed and covers me with not only the comforter, but the sheets too. Then he climbs back in, slides under the covers with me, and holds me again. He doesn't say another word, and I silently thank him for that. Then I close my eyes and drift asleep in the crook of his arm.

I wake up before Ben, so I take the opportunity to rub my leg down and put the prosthetic back on. Then I go to my drawer and slip on my yoga pants and chartreuse cotton cami.

"That color green looks good on you."

I turn to find Ben sitting against the headboard, his arms crossed behind his head. "When did you get up?"

"Just when you were bending over to put on your pants."

"Oh," I say, realizing he probably got a full view of my butt up in the air.

"The sight of your rear end when I first wake up in the morning is a wonderful thing, half-pint," he says, grinning, confirming my thoughts.

He pats the bed next to him. "Come back to bed, Rose."

I do. I climb under the covers and sit next to him. He grips my waist and pulls me between his legs, then lets me rest my back against his chest, my head against his shoulder.

"Thank you for last night," he breathes into my ear.

"Thank *you*. Thank you for making me feel special."

301

"You *are* special, half-pint. Are you going somewhere?"

"No. Why?"

"Because you're dressed."

"Oh. Well." I don't know what to say.

"Did I tell you how beautiful you are, Rose?"

He must know why I'm dressed. "Thank you."

"And how absolutely heavenly you looked last night?"

My heart pounds at his words.

The backs of his fingers graze the spot just below my ear, and a wave of tingles crashes over my skin from the spot he touches all the way down to my toes. His fingers act like a drug on me. Especially after last night. I can't get enough. I lean my head to the side to give him better access to my neck. This accomplishes what I need him to do. His fingers travel beneath my jaw, down the front of my neck then one of them dips down the crevice between my breasts. It's amazing how his touch can transcend me beyond my fears. When he's touching me, I almost forget I'm not a whole person. It's when they stop touching me that I remember.

With both his hands, his fingers continue to journey the center of my body, under my shirt, under the band of my pants, when he says, "Every single inch of you is more beautiful than the last." Though his hands are beneath my clothes, he only encircles my stomach area, never dipping below my navel or up over my breasts. "Whatever sets *you* at ease, puts *me* at ease. You want to stay clothed, or covered, or anything, then that's what I want you to do too. But please know" –he talks into my ear, his fingers still navigating my belly— "that all I see is *you*. What you see as flaws, I see as something that makes you unique and extraordinary. Rare, Rose. Like a mint-condition 1955 Roberto Clemente rookie card..."

Turning to look at him, I interrupt his comparison.

"A baseball card?" I can't help but crack up. "You're comparing me to a baseball card?"

"A one-of-a-kind, Rose. Do you know how much it's worth?"

I shake my head in laughter.

"Seriously, Rose." He cups my chin in his hand. "You're a rarity. And you chose me. Do you know how much that means to me? One leg, two legs, shit, scars or no scars, all I see is perfection when I look at you, Rose."

Oh my God. Really? "Really?"

"Really. So if the next time we make love you want to stay covered or you don't, that's fine with me. But for the record...your naked body trumps your clothed body any day."

I close my eyes and let his words sink in. He wraps both his arms around my chest and pulls me back against him. I rest my head on his shoulder again.

"I love you so much, Rose."

"I love you too. Ben?"

"Yeah?"

"Are you scared?"

"Scared as shit, Rose."

"I wish I could make it all disappear for you. The cancer, I mean."

He doesn't respond right away. "Me too," he whispers.

"Can I come visit you?"

Again he takes his time answering. "I'd like you to, but I have no idea what state I'm gonna be in. Will you feel comfortable?"

"No. I'd be upset for you. Scared, kinda...but...I still want to be there. If you want me to."

His lips find my ear again. He kisses it, then whispers, "Then *please*." He drags out the word. "Be there. To wake up from surgery to your gorgeous face...it'd be like I'd died and gone to Heaven."

"Oh, please don't."

"Never. Not while you're in my life."

The two of us sit silently like this for a long while after we decide I would be there for his surgery tomorrow. Staying in bed seems to be our version of time standing still - we don't want today to end, so we sit rooted to this spot. On my bed. Ben's arms wrapped firmly around me. My body tucked neatly and comfortably within his.

42

BEN

I don't think I ever want to wake up without my arms around Rose again.

It's frightening.

For more than a week now, I've been waking up with Rose tucked safely in my arms.

Even this morning.

Last night, she followed me home to my house in Cherry Hill. I told her she could use my car while I'm laid up, but she insisted she's more comfortable in her big-ass old pick-up truck.

Though my mother wasn't so happy about Rose spending the night in my room, my father laughed at her and told her, in Italian, to open her eyes and get with the twenty-first century. This made Rose uncomfortable, but I explained how much I needed her to be there with me all night. She agreed and let me hold her in my arms, in my bed until early this morning.

But now, I'm lying in recovery where visitors are not allowed, and I've woken up without Rose anywhere to be found. This thought frightens me more than the operation they just performed on me.

I had a hard time deciding on which operation to have done, and I couldn't talk to Rose about it. As much as I love her and could probably talk to her about *any*thing else, I just could not bring myself to talk about *this* decision with her. Because, truthfully, I did not think I could deal without two-thirds of my leg. I never considered myself vain, but this...whole ordeal has made me think, *maybe I am*. I mean, I realize that there are prostheses out there that could help me walk and run, so why? Why has this decision been so difficult to make. Then I think about having sex with Rose. We've only made love once. How am I supposed to do that now? Is that vain? Or is that a legitimate worry? Will I be able to...get it up, or will I constantly have my missing leg on my mind? So how could I tell that to Rose? When she went so far as getting herself garter belts and stockings to cover hers up? How could I ever have told Rose my final decision?

I couldn't.

So I didn't.

Besides...she never asked.

I think something deep inside her didn't really want to know.

But I *need* her here. Now that it's all said and done, all I want is Rose. All I *care* about is Rose. And that same thought had crossed my mind early this morning. *All that matters to me is Rose.*

So at the last possible minute, I made the decision that would make Rose most comfortable. She'd never again have to worry that her missing limb was something I found unattractive, or something I thought made her less of a human being.

Because now...

I'll be missing part of my leg too.

And she can find comfort in knowing that I am no different than she is.

But she'll never know my reason for my final decision. That would just cause her pain.

***

When I'm finally rolled into my room, Rose is waiting in the hallway with my mother, my father, my sister, and my brother. They're told by the nurse that they can see me two at a time and for only five minutes each, but all I really want to see is Rose.

I catch her smile on my way into the room, but I know she won't be the first in to see me. My mother will want to be first.

"Oh, Benito, how you feel?" she asks when she walks in, her eyes already seeping tears.

"Eh." I'm quite groggy and can barely stay awake to speak.

"Oh," she cries and kisses me on the cheek.

"Domenica, basta, he doesn't need your crying right now," my father tells my mom.

"'Sokay, Dad," I manage to mumble. "I'm okay, Mom. Tired."

"Yes, yes...you sleep, Benito."

"Ma? Can you just send in Rose? Before I fall asleep?"

My father answers instead, "Si, certo. Let's go, Domenica. He want to see la sua ragazza. Benny," my dad says, "we be in the wait room."

"Grazie, Dad."

Rose steps in apprehensively, as if she's afraid to come in.

"Rose," I murmur when she approaches.

"How do you feel?" Her voice is soft. Unsure.

"Better now that you're here."

She blushes. "I'm supposed to be making *you* feel better, not the other way around."

"You are—" I reach for her hand "—just by being here."

She takes my hand, and I notice her eyes dart toward the bottom of my bed, but they're back on my face in an instant.

"They amputated it," I say in answer to her silent

307

question.

Her eyes close, her shoulders droop, and her whole body drops.

"Rose...Rose. Oh my God." I struggle to find the remote, then I press the nurse's call button. "Help," I screech out.

My brother comes running in. My parents and my sister follow. "What the hell?" one of them says at Rose's form sprawled out on the floor.

Her hand comes up. "I'm...I'm fine."

My brother is picking her up when the nurse comes in. "Oh goodness, put her here..." She instructs my brother to place her down on the empty bed next to mine.

"What happened?" the nurse asked.

"She...passed out, I think." I can barely talk I'm so groggy, but I'm worried about Rose.

"Really," I hear Rose say, "I'm fine."

I hear the nurse asking Rose questions, and I think I hear Rose answering, and I really *am* worried about her, but I'm fading quickly and everything's disappearing.

    ***

When I wake up next, it's sometime the next day. Rose is sleeping in the chair by the window, and it hits me that she literally felt like this...and a huge truck actually *did* run her over. She looks so uncomfortable the way she's sleeping, but I stare at her for a while and wonder if she slept here all night.

"I told her she could stay in the bed, but she wanted no part of it." The nurse comes in and starts fussing with the machines around me.

"Did she stay all night?"

"Yes. They wanted to admit her last night, but she

wouldn't let us. She's over eighteen, so we couldn't force her. She signed a release."

"Admit her? Why?"

"Because she passed out."

"What? When?"

"Yesterday. I was told she was talking with you, and then she just went down."

"I'm fine." I hear Rose's sweet voice to my right.

"Rose." She's standing next to my bed now and running her hand up and down my arm.

"How you feel?" she asks me.

"I'm good. A little pain right now. But...you passed out?"

She rolls her eyes. "I'm glad you don't remember."

"Remember?"

"Okay, son," the nurse interrupts, "I'll give you two some privacy. I'll be back." She leaves and closes the door.

"So, I was awake when you passed out?"

"Unfortunately."

"What happened?"

She lets go of my hand and pulls up her chair. "You...well...you told me you had...your...*it*...amputated."

"And that made you pass out?" I ask, not getting it.

She nods.

Then she cries.

"Rose?"

"I'm so sorry. I really am. You wanted to keep it and then I was saying all that stuff about infections, and I was selfish, and now you had it taken off, and I...Oh, Ben, I'm so sorry. I didn't mean for you...." She's rambling and sobbing at the same time. She only stops because her words get stuck in the tears in her throat.

"Rose. Rose." I place my hand on top of hers and squeeze as tightly as I can, considering I'm weak as hell right now. "Rose. It was *my* decision. Mine. I'm a big boy. No one makes me do anything I don't want to do. I swear to you. *My* choice."

She's still crying, but she seems to settle down a little. "Really?"

"Really. Did you pass out because you thought *you* made me do this?"

She's frowning and her eyes look so sad. "I don't know, Ben. I don't know why I passed out, but I remember feeling so sad that you...you lost your leg and...I know I made you feel bad about me and then I remembered how devastating it was when they told me they had to remove part of my leg and I thought, 'Oh my God, he's gonna be devastated too,' and...and the thoughts kept coming and I just couldn't get..."

"Rose." I squeeze her hand again. "Stop. You're gonna do this to yourself again. Just...it's okay. I'm okay. I really, really am. I had time to make this decision. You didn't. So there's a difference. I'm oh...kay. Please know that."

She nods, but still looks devastated.

"Please smile, half-pint. I need to see your smile."

She smiles. It doesn't reach her eyes, but it's a start.

"Now tell me...does this fuckin' pain go away any time soon?"

She shakes her head. "I don't think so, but I woke up almost two months *after* mine was amputated. I think you're probably gonna be in a lot more pain than I can remember." She still has tears running down her face.

"Please stop crying, Rose. Please. Seeing you sad makes me sad. I don't want to be sad right now...and I'm in so much fucking pain.
They have me so drugged up, but it still fucking hurts."

"Yeah...I can tell you're drugged up," she says, trying to rein in her tears and wiping her face with her sleeve. "You're kinda talking slow and slurring some words."

"Shit."

"It's okay. It sounds cute. But go to sleep, Ben. I'll be here. You need to sleep, I can tell. And I'm sorry I cried. I'm...I am."

"Half-pint, it's okay. Really. But don't stay. Go to school." I squeeze her hand, but my grip is quickly losing squeezing power. "I'm just gonna be sleeping or poked and prodded or whatever they have planned for me."

"I really want to stay."

"Dance, Rose. You just started dancing again. You got a routine going. Please, for me. You can come back on the weekend. Don't stop your life while I'm here. 'Kay? You'll go home and dance. For me?"

"I guess." She sighs and leans across my chest. "I'm so sorry," she cries.

"Rosie, stop. I'm fine." I rub my hand on her back, but then we're interrupted by the door opening.

Rose stands up, and I can't believe who just walked through my door.

"Hi, Ben. I hope this isn't too soon."

"You're the scout for the..."

"Yup. The New York..."

"Oh my God, why are you here?"

"We have an offer to make you."

43

ROSE

Forty-five minutes.

That's how long that New York team's scout has been in Ben's room.

I couldn't leave and go home; not before I knew whatever offer it was he was making Ben. So I've been sitting out here in the hall, waiting for him to walk out.

SO I CAN FIND OUT!

Another ten minutes later, the man walks out. Thank God.

I'm a little nervous going in, but I don't hesitate. "What was that all about?"

"You didn't go home?"

"How could I? That Major League scout comes in, says he wants to make you an offer, how could I leave? So, what kind of offer?"

"Oh my God, Rose, I had to force myself...to stay awake...but..."

His eyes keep closing.

"He wants..."

His eyes close again.

"Me..."

I touch my fingers to Ben's face, "Go to sleep, sweetheart."

"But I have to ask you what you think abo..."

"Ben, stop forcing yourself to stay awake. I'll wait."

"But..."

"I'll wait. Sleep." I lift his remote and lower his bed so it's more comfortable for him to sleep.

For the next two hours, I read *If I Stay* and try to

concentrate on the story. But mostly, I'm wondering what the heck a Major League scout would offer an undergraduate with cancer and a missing leg.

Drawing me from my thoughts, I hear, "You stayed."

With no hesitation, I stand and toss my book onto the seat. "Hey, sleepyhead. I told ya I'd stay."

"Thanks," he says smiling. "Kiss?"

I bend down to kiss him. "I love you."

"Love you too, babe...let me just..." He presses the button on his remote. "Adjust...there. Better."

"I lowered it before. Thought you'd be more comfortable."

Ben takes my hand and squeezes it, but he doesn't let go. "So," he starts, "what would you think if I quit college?"

"Quit? What? Why?"

"Well, the NCAA doesn't allow you to sign anything with a Major League team *and* play college ball. Plus, I'd be pretty busy playing for New York to attend class."

"What? I don't understand."

"They want to sign me, Rose."

"But...even though...your leg...and...the cancer?"

"If I sign with them, they give me enough money to pay for all my treatments. Rehabilitation too. I'd be ready for next season."

"But...they don't care about your leg?"

"Yeah...they do. They want to hook me up with some company that makes bionic prostheses."

"What? Like the six million dollar man?"

Ben laughs at me.

"Stop."

"You're cute. But no, not bionic like that. It's still a prosthetic that I'd take on and off. He showed me videos. It's got sensors or something. But it's a pretty good deal, Rose."

"Wow. The major leagues. That's...wow. Oh my

313

God."

"I'd have to quit college."

"Do you want to?"

"I think. I mean...my whole life, this was my goal. The psychologist thing was a back-up."

"And you can always go back," I add, "after...like when you're forty-six."

Ben chuckles. "Yup. If I'd want to play that long."

He pauses. Looks at me.

"Whaddya think, half-pint? Should I do it?"

"Ben. This is *your* decision. I can't..."

"Rose. I wanna spend the rest of my life with you. Any decisions I make have to include you, so I'm not gonna make them without your input."

Oh my God. *Oh my God.* "Really?"

"My goodness, Rose...you come first in my life. Everything else comes second."

"Thank you." Leaning in, I hug him, trying my best not to crush him because I'm so happy. "I love you."

"And I you, Rosie. So what do I do? I mean, it's New York, so I can stay in Jersey. Stay near you, but I will be traveling a lot. So there'd be times...that we wouldn't see each other."

"Ben. Do not worry about spending time apart from me. I'll be there when you get back."

"Really?"

"Really."

"So, I should accept the offer?"

"Would it make you happy to take it, Ben?"

"It would, Rose. Yeah. It would."

"Then do it, Ben. Do it. Accept the offer. And that bionic leg."

Both of us are smiling huge gigantic smiles. "Okay. Okay. I will."

44

BEN

A FIVE-YEAR CONTRACT WORTH NINE POINT NINE MILLION DOLLARS.
Plus the purchase of my bionic leg.
That's the offer I just accepted.
Now I just have to withdraw from school.

45

ROSE

The fitness room door slams open, and through the reflection in the mirror, I see Lindsay ungracefully running in, holding a piece of paper.

Spinning around to look at her directly, I stop her by the shoulders before she slips on her high heels. "What the heck, Lindsay?"

She pauses to take a breath.

"Holy cow, what's going on?"

"Sorry. I ran all the way here from class," she says, huffing. "Boy, it's not easy in these stiletto things. I thought dancing with you, I'd be in better shape."

"Lindsay. What? What's so important you had to run?"

"I didn't want to miss you. I know on Tuesdays you go right to Orange to see Ben after you're done here."

"Well, I do go home to shower after dancing for two hours, but what's your point?"

"Right." Her breathing seems back to normal. "Look," she says, handing me the paper in her hand.

"I take it from her and skim it. "A grant? A grant for what?" I look at her.

Her finger waves over the paper. "Keep reading. Come on."

Instead of skimming, I read the letter more carefully. When I'm finished, I look at her. "A grant for a dance team? What's this mean?"

"Rose, it means we got a grant to start a dance team at Hunter Hill. I didn't want to say anything until I knew for sure. I want you to run it!"

"Wait." I shake my head. "What?"

"I'll be the director, you know, oversee things, and I can be the *coach*," she says with air quotes, "so you can still be part of the team, but with my teaching schedule, and counseling, I don't have time to choreograph and teach new routines. And schedule rehearsals and eventually competitions. I want you to do that."

"Me? For Heaven's sake, why?"

"Because this university needs a dance team. Other colleges have one. Why can't we? And with all your experience, you're the perfect one to run this. Plus, didn't you say your goal was to one day teach dance? Well now...you can. You can be part of the team *and* teach it. Be the captain of it."

I can't keep from smiling, because...wow. But I still don't understand. "Lindsay, I got a bum leg, I can't teach *or* be on a competitive team. That wouldn't be fair to the team."

"Rose, even with your prosthetic leg, you're better than most. You're a superstar. And my vision for this team—" she pauses briefly "—accept anyone. Even those with bum legs or missing arms or wheelchairs. No discriminating based on physical limitations."

"Wow. Really?"

"Really. I've seen what you do out there on the floor. I *know* you can incorporate physically challenged dancers into your routines. You are amazing, Rose. And look how far you've come in just a few months. If you couldn't see it, no one would even know you were dancing with an artificial limb."

"Oh my God, Lindsay." I walk over to the bench, because I suddenly feel light-headed.

Lindsay follows me over and sits down. "So whattya say? Will you do this?"

"Oh my God. I want to."

"Then do it."

"But..."

"No buts. What else you gonna do? You said you didn't know what you wanted to major in, so do this while you decide. Dance, Rose."

"Yeah?" I look at her and I know I'm smiling huge, because my cheeks hurt.

"Yeah."

"Okay. I'll do it. Yeah." I stand up and scream, "Yeah. I'll do it. I'll do it. I'll do it, I'll do it." I run to the middle of the floor, get in position, and spin and spin and spin and spin. All on my bad leg.

"Oh my God, Rose. A fouetté turn? And so many! Look at you."

When I come to a stop, I say, "I've been practicing. A lot."

"Oh my God, Rose, you're awesome. See. You're gonna be the best one out there. Oh, and by the way, I'd like to pull this all together before the fall semester. Could you stay here for most of the summer?"

"Oh."

"If it's a problem, like finding a place to stay, you can move in with me. I kicked my boyfriend out, so I need a roommate anyway."

"Oh. Well. I think I'd be allowed to continue living where I'm living now, but I'd have to make sure my dad doesn't need me to help him on the farm." I think about this. "Yeah, I don't think he'd mind. Last summer I was allowed to live in Manhattan, so, yeah, I can probably stay."

"Ooh, yay." She claps her hands like a dork. "You want to move in with me?"

"Uh. Not that I wouldn't love to, but I'm pretty sure I can continue living at the house up the street." I'm really enjoying living with Griffin and Holly, I'd hate to give that up.

"Okay. No worries. If it doesn't work out, you got a place with me."

"Thanks, Lindsay. For everything."

"Oh, what are friends for?" She hugs me. "Now I better be going. Got my last class of the semester in ten minutes."

"Oh geez. Don't break a heel."

"Tell that boyfriend of yours I said hi," she yells as she sprints out the door.

***

After going home and showering, I am now en route to Orange Rehabilitation Center to see Ben. I've been making the forty-minute trip every Tuesday, Friday, and Saturday for the past two months. Ben was out of the hospital in three weeks and went straight to Orange. His recovery is going much quicker than mine did. I guess being cooperative is working to his benefit. But I won't knock myself for hindering my own recovery back then. I was scared. I thought my life was over. I thought I had nothing to look forward to, so I acted the only way I knew how to act last September.

Ben, however, has everything to look forward to. So that has *got* to be driving his swift improvement.

Rosie Girl, always a pleasure to see your shining face," Craig says when I walk into the rec room, greeting me like he does each time I visit Ben.

"Hi, Craig."

"You're boyfriend's takin' a piss." He points to the hallway. "As usual, he sped through morning therapy because you were coming."

"Yeah?"

"He always does. You know he's whipped, right?" Craig winks.

"Rose?" I hear Ben behind me.

"Ben," I cry, turning to greet him. When he walks toward me, I notice how gracefully he strides. "Oh my God, no limp?"

His arms spread out at his sides. "Nope," he says, smiling before he hugs me hello.

"Our boy's bionic now, Rose," Craig says.

"What? You got it?"

Ben nods. "Yup."

"Oh my God, can I see it?"

"Yeah." Ben leads me to a table to sit, then he rolls up his sweatpants and shows me his new bionic leg.

"Wow. It comes on and off like mine?"

"Yup. Only it has this wrap stuff." He points to the top of the leg where mesh-looking fabric wraps around the latches.

"And it's really bionic?"

"Yeah. It's got sensors and shit that actually calculate my next step, kinda like my brain would do."

"Wow, so it must move more fluidly than mine, obviously, since you don't even have a limp anymore."

He nods. "I guess. But then again, you have your own knee, so I don't think you'd need a leg this expensive."

"I still can't believe that scout paid for this. It's so much money."

"Yeah, well, he didn't, the team did, but that's not all though, Rose," Ben says.

"Hey, Ben, I'll see you at four," Craig says. "Rose, always a pleasure. Hope I'll see you again soon," he says, kissing me on the cheek.

"I'll see you Friday."

"Actually, you won't."

"What?"

"Ben'll tell you," Craig says before leaving the room.

I look back at Ben.

"I got another visit from Howey. The team's not only paying for this place, they're paying for extended therapy. In-home."

"Really?"

"Yup. Starting next Tuesday. So I'm leaving here Friday morning."

"So you'll be out for Memorial Day weekend?"

"Sure will, half-pint." Ben rolls down his pant leg, takes me by the hand, and sits me on his lap.

"Did you have to sign a different contract?"

"Nope. Still the same nine point nine million, five-year contract."

"Wow."

"Yeah. You know, I still can't believe I'm signed on to a Major League team, Rose. It's still so...surreal."

"You're *that* good, Ben. You know that."

"Yeah, but to take a chance on me now, and I'm not even done with chemo."

"You said the chemo was an extra precaution right? They found none of the cancer in the rest of the bone or the lymph nodes."

"Right. But to be safe, I just need the few sessions this summer."

"So why did they decide to pay for the extra therapy?"

"Howey said they're so happy to have me that they want to make things easy for me while I continue my chemo and they want to make sure I'm ready for them next season."

"So are you still getting sick?"

"It's not bad." Ben runs his hand up and down my arm while he talks. "Craig takes it easy on me when I'm not feeling great."

"That's good."

"So, Rose, when I leave here on Friday, I didn't

necessarily want to go home to Cherry Hill."

"No?"

"No. Are you moving back to Wantage this weekend?"

"No. I was gonna go back *next* weekend. You want to stay at Griffin's this weekend?"

"Yes. But I hate the thought of spending my whole summer so far away from you. Do you think Griffin would let me stay in *your* room while you're in Wantage? The house I'm staying in doesn't allow summer rentals. That's when they do repairs and stuff."

"I'm sure Griffin won't mind. But would you mind sharing the room with me?"

"Never, but what do you mean?"

"You're never gonna believe this, but Lindsay got a grant to start a dance team at Hunter. She wants *me* to head it up." I stop to appreciate the way Ben's eyes are bugging out of his head. With his recent lack of hair, his eyes look even bigger and browner.

"That's so cool, Rose."

"Yeah. She wants it ready for the fall semester, so I was hoping to stay this summer, too. After I go home for a bit and ask my parents."

"Oh, that is so awesome, sweetheart."

"So, if you want to share a room..."

He turns me to look at him, so I'm almost straddling him, and I'm suddenly embarrassed because there are other people in the room. "There's nothing I'd want more than to share a bed with you, sweetheart, but if we're going to *live together* like that, I'd want it to be in our own place."

"So, you *don't* want to share my room?"

He touches my face and moves his finger up and down my cheek. "That's not what I'm saying. I want to do things right, Rose. When we move in together, I want it to be the right way. Let's just...one step at a time. Is that okay, half-pint?"

"I guess."

" Let's talk to Griffin, maybe he's got room in that pool room of his."

All of a sudden I start cracking up.

"What's so funny, half-pint? You picturing me sleeping on the pool table?"

"No, although I believe Holly was going to be doing that when she first moved in, but that's not why I'm laughing."

"Then why?"

"You know how you always tell me to take *one step at a time*?"

"Yeah. I didn't realize that was material for side-aching laughter."

I nudge him in the stomach. "You do realize, don't you, that without our prosthetic legs, you and I can literally only take one step at a time. I know it's not really funny, but it just struck me that way just now." I can't stop laughing.

"Do you know that's the sweetest sound?"

"What is?"

"You laughing. I love it."

"You still gonna love me when you're a Major League ball player?"

"Now that's a silly question. I'm gonna love you forever, half-pint. You're never getting rid of me."

"Well that's good, because you're not getting rid of me either."

46
BEN

I'm finally leaving Orange today, but yesterday's chemo kicked my ass, so instead of staying with Rose at Griffin's, my father's picking me up and taking me home. There's no reason to have Rose see me like this yet. I'm going to miss her sweet smile, but I'll be seeing her next weekend. For now, I'm just going to sleep the Memorial Day weekend through.

47

ROSE

"Well, this is it, Rosebud," my father says, tossing the last of my things in the truck bed. When I came up on Saturday morning, I brought some of my clothes back so I could make room for my summer things. Plus my father bought me a bigger dresser and a new TV since Griffin's place will be my full-time home for a while.

"We're gonna miss you guys too," I tell him, talking to my mother, Beth, and Patti as well.

"I can't believe both you and Terri won't be home this summer," my mom says.

"Well, be thankful Terri found a boyfriend up at school," Beth says, "this way she'll leave Rose's alone."

Patti laughs, but Terri really pissed me off when she did that, so I just fake a smile.

"You know she only did that because of the situation, she was jealous of all the attention you were getting," Patti says. "She's over it."

"Yeah, well, Rose might not be," Beth says.

"I'm fine. So, you guys can come down anytime, you know. Griffin has lots of couches you can crash on if you just wanna hang or watch a movie."

"Or go to that bar y'all talk about," Patti says.

"Yup. That too, if you want."

"Rose, please come visit us too," Mom says.

"Of course. I'm only an hour away."

"I know. I just miss you when you're not here, but I'm glad you're happy again."

"And dancing," Dad chimes in.

"And dancing," Mom repeats.

"I love you, Rosebud."

"Love you too, Dad."

I say goodbye to everyone one more time and then get in my truck to head back to Haledon. Hopefully in time to help Ben move in.

***

Too late.

Griffin and Mick, in the kitchen having burgers, inform me that Ben's all moved in, but not feeling all that well.

"But he said as soon as you get here, to send you on up," Griffin tells me.

"Okay, thanks. And Griff, thanks so much for letting him move in. We really appreciate it."

"Hey, no problem. Worked out perfectly. Knox graduated, moved out, Ben moves in. Perfect."

"Yeah. Thanks." I smile. It did work out perfectly. I'd forgotten all about Knox being a senior, so Ben and I don't have to *move in* together, but we still get to live in the same house.

Ben's door is shut, so I knock.

"You can come in," Ben calls from the other side of the door.

"Half-pint," he says weakly when I come in.

"Were you sleeping?"

"No." He pats the spot next to him on the bed. "Just not feeling great. But I'm better now that you're here."

I kick off my shoes and climb into bed with him. "Chemo's kicking your butt?"

"Little bit, half-pint. But look, I wanna show you something." He takes his laptop off the nightstand and opens his email. "Isaiah sent me this this morning."

"Isaiah?"

"Johnny's nurse. His mother's new husband."

"She got married?"

Ben nods. "Yup. But that's not it. Johnny's mom got a call from one of those big gaming system companies. Apparently, Johnny was working on a program that would allow for voice-control gaming. I don't know the particulars, but evidently, he came up with a way to use voice codes to play actual games. He was using the technology they already have for quadriplegics, where they use their straws in some controller, but Johnny said they were too slow. So he came up with a voice code system."

"Wow."

"Yeah. Anyway, in his letter to the company, he said he'd love to work with them to bring this into fruition. They'd emailed him back, but they never heard back from him. They assumed he went with another company, but they called anyway. His mom told them he'd died. They offered her a substantial amount of money to use his system anyway. She accepted. One point five million."

"Holy crow."

"Best part is, Rose, he never gave up." Ben's eyes are tearing now. "He *did* fight until the end. This proves it." He taps on the screen. "Oh, half-pint." He closes the laptop and sets it aside. "You don't know how much it bothered me thinking he gave up. I know his life would have been difficult, but I hated to think he'd gotten so low he'd just waited to die." Ben wraps his arms around me and kisses me on the head. "He got what he wanted in the end. He's providing for his mom, and she's not alone."

"That's good news, Ben."

"Do you know when he submitted that email to the company?"

It's a rhetorical question, I know that, but I say, "No,"

anyway.

"The morning he died." Ben lets out a single silent chuckle. "At least God waited for him to hit send before He took him."

I think about this for a while and then I say, "Maybe that's the closest thing to a promise we're gonna get."

"What's that, half-pint?"

"We make our plans, do our best to get there, and hope God agrees with them, or trust Him to know better."

"Maybe." After a few moments of silence, Ben says, "So, half-pint, you know what'll make me feel better?"

"What's that, Benito?"

He shakes his head, then says, "Taking a nice hot bath together."

48

BEN

"What if Griffin and Mick hear us?"

"Who cares? Besides, it's a big house, half-pint, and I'm all the way on the third floor."

"But it's daytime."

"You've never taken a bath during the day?"

"Well, not recently, and when I take a shower during the day, I at least close the curtains and shut off...well, you have a skylight...and no curtain."

"No one'll see us from a passing plane flying by. Besides, it'll be nice and bright. The sun will keep us warm when the water cools."

"You're not going to take no for an answer, are you?"

"Nope. Water's already running, I'm already naked, my leg's off. It's your turn, Rosie."

She sighs, but it's accompanied by a smile and that sweet peach blush of her cheeks. So I sit down on the edge of the huge claw-foot tub and tug her toward me by the hem of her shirt. I lift it up over her head, then I tug down her pants and she steps out of them. While I unlatch her leg, she undoes her bra. Finally, I slide her panties down and can't help myself – I kiss her right in the center of all her red curls. "My God, you are beautiful, Rose."

Her hands are on my shoulders and though I'm tempted to have my way with her right here, I choose to be patient and make this night special. We've never been together naked without our legs, so this is huge. I want her to feel comfortable and ready. And there's no need to rush. We have the rest of our lives to make love, because there is no way I'm giving this woman up. EVER.

I stand up, sliding my hands up her body as I do, and

help her into the waiting tub. I climb in behind her, reach over to shut off the water, and hold Rose beneath the afternoon sun.

Epilogue

June 12th, 2015
ROSE

"Okay, before we go outside and you and your father get me up on one of those things, I have to give you this." Ben hands me a big shopping bag.

"What's this for?" I look inside the bag and see a bunch of different-colored tissue paper.

"Well, I know what today is and I wanted to give you a gift to acknowledge this past year. It wasn't your easiest year, but you came out of it stronger, braver, and more self-assured. I'm proud of you, Rose. A year ago, you thought your future held no value, and now look at you. You're captain of the college dance team and you didn't have to give up your education major at all. You are doing exactly what you always wanted to do, and you thought you'd never be able to do it. And well, I just wanted you to know how proud I am of you."

"Oh, Ben." I hug him. "This year ended up actually being the best year of my life. I met you. No matter how that had to happen, I wouldn't trade it for the world, because...what if I didn't get crushed by that truck a year ago today? I'd have never have met you."

"Well, you might have, since we both were going to the same college, but yeah, I get what you're saying."

I smack him in his side and break the hug. "Always a smart-ass."

"Always. Anyway, the other reason I got you this gift is because you were sneaky and didn't tell me your birthday was in March. I totally missed your twenty-third birthday."

"Well...you were kinda busy and all, what was the point?"

"The point is, I shouldn't have to find out when my girlfriend's birthday is from her best friend. That's the point."

"I'm sorry."

"It's okay. There'll be plenty more, old lady."

"Yeah, yeah. I'm only eleven months older than you."

"Whatever."

"Whatever."

"So open your gift."

I shake my head, but at the same time, I place the bag on the couch and take out all the tissue paper. At the bottom of the bag is a large box wrapped in gold wrapping paper with a red bow similar to the one he had stuck on top of my Valentine's Day pudding. "Let me guess, a whole bunch of chocolate pudding," I say while carefully unwrapping the present.

"Uh, no, but I can always get that for you."

I laugh. "No, just kidding." But I stop laughing when I see the name on the box. "You didn't?" I look at Ben before opening the box. "No."

"Just open it, half-pint."

"Oh my God." I lift the top off the Lucchese box. "Holy crap."

I pull them out and just stare at them in my hands.

"They're not for your hands, half-pint. They're for your feet."

My hands are shaking too much, so Ben takes them from me, takes off my sneakers, and slips on my present.

A pair of red Mad Dog goat-leather cowboy boots now adorn my two feet.

"I got an eight so they wouldn't be snug on your left foot." Ben says, his smile reaching both ears.

"These are Lucchese boots, Ben. They're like mad expensive."

"Yeah, but you're worth it. Besides, I can afford it

now."

"Still, I can't take these, Ben...they're..."

"Rose. Please. Since I've known you, what have I bought you? A six-pack of chocolate pudding, a trip to the movies, and a couple dinners? Between the two of us, this past year, we've spent more time in hospitals and rehabs than we did dating. Please let me give these to you."

I look at Ben and then I look down at my feet. "They *are* beautiful."

"Just like you." He takes my hand, and pulls me out of the living room. "Now come on, your parents are outside waiting for us. I got a horse to ride."

Outside, Daddy boosts me up onto a bareback Cloud and then helps Ben get up onto Sky, who's saddled. "Okay, Ben, I'm gonna go slow with you, so you don't have to worry 'bout nothin'. You're feeling well today, right? Because though my horses are gentle, it's still a bumpy ride."

"I'm feeling great. No chemo this week, so I'm good."

"Good. Now put that damn fancy new foot o' yours in the stirrup here, and do the same on the other side."

"I need a picture of them, Bruce," my mom says, standing in front of Cloud and me.

"Dang-it, Sam, I'm teachin' the boy here to ride."

"There's always time for a picture. Besides, I need a new one of Rosie." Mom looks at me and winks. My first picture since before the accident. "I want Ben in this picture too, so bring Sky to the right of Cloud. No to the left, my right. That's it," she says when my father reluctantly leads Ben and Sky toward my mom.

I reach over with my left hand to take Ben's.

"You sure I can let go of the horse?"

"Ben, you're worth millions, you think my girl there's gonna let you get hurt?"

"Daddy. That's not polite."

"It isn't, Bruce," my mom agrees.

"Well I'm sorry. I didn't think it was impolite."

"It's fine, Bruce. It's just money. *Your* girl here—" Ben looks at me, takes my outstretched hand, and smiles. "*My* girl. She's worth more than any amount of money I could ever make. Because she's absolutely priceless."

And that's when Mom snaps the picture.

The End

Acknowledgements

I'd like to start by thanking those of you who read my stories – you allow me to continue to write my daydreams down on paper. Thank you.

A big thank you goes out to my editor, Sue Toth, whose input and advice help to make my stories what they are. And a big thank you for knowing the NCAA rules, otherwise I would have been awfully embarrassed once someone caught on. Thank you so much.

And to the wonderful Murphy Rae – your attention to detail is out of this world. Thank you for your amazing eye, and I look forward to working with you again.

To the very talented Heather LaViola – thank you for spending hours taking photo after photo to get just the right one for my cover. And to Niina Cord, who did another awesome job making those photos into a fabulous cover. Isabella Freda and Joey Roccasanta – thank you, thank you, thank you for modeling for me. You two were so unbelievably patient.

As always, I'd like to thank Kathleen Ball, Amber Dane, and Stefan Ellery for their daily inspirations that help me get through the writing day.

To my brother Carmen – thank you for your baseball expertise. You were a wealth of information. Love you, baby brother.

And to my family – my children and my husband – thank you for your unending love and support. I love you guys with all my heart.